W9-ABV-268

THE LAST OF THE WHITFIELDS

ELISE SANGUINETTI

THE LAST OF THE WHITFIELDS

McGRAW-HILL BOOK COMPANY, INC.

NEW YORK   TORONTO   LONDON

THE LAST OF THE WHITFIELDS

Library of Congress Catalog Card Number: 61-18315

First Edition

54688

*To Alabama's Colonel
and Mrs. Harry Mell Ayers*

THE LAST OF THE WHITFIELDS

PART I

1

From the beginning you must know that the word "sorrow" is a word I'm very partial to. It gives you a good feeling inside, and besides, if I want to, I can sit all alone up in my room and think about Mother or Father or somebody dying and I can cry and cry all by myself. I know it sounds peculiar, but if I'm in the mood I can make myself cry any time I want to.

It's like my father's voice, the word sorrow, especially when we're at the farm. The farm is where he mostly likes to have his highball and talk about the soil. My father is quite well known for his unusual sense of the soil and he's exceedingly anxious that my brother Arthur and me learn to sense it, too. You see, Father is a banker, but he's also inclined to a number of spiritual ovulations. The Ashton Chamber of Commerce gave him an award for it two years ago. That's where we're from—Ashton. Ashton, Georgia.

My mother is originally from Charleston, South Carolina, but she's rather partial to Ashton anyway. The only thing about her is she's never been very fond of shirt sleeves. She's much more interested in the way the English do things, because they go on for centuries before ending up back in shirt sleeves. Charleston is a little that way, too, and Mother doesn't see why it can't be the same in Georgia.

Just frankly speaking, no one in our family has ever worn shirt sleeves—at least not for years, not even during carpetbagger days. Still, up until last year we were pretty frantic about ourselves. See, my brother Arthur is the last of the Whitfields. Of course, I'm one, too, but the girl—the last born—and only he can carry on the name. So it's all up to him now.

Arthur's two and one-half years older than me. (I'll be fourteen in exactly eighteen and one-half days. July 17.) Still, I just can't tell you how much we've worried over Arthur. With him being the last of the Whitfields—well, it's been ex-*as*-perating! We thought he would positively *never* reach the Age of Transgression.

When he was a mere child even, he came back from his first day at school with a drawing of a red and blue apple. On the red side he had written "blue" and on the blue side "red." I remember Mother sadly showing this to Father, and in that strange, far-sounding voice she gets sometimes, she said, "You know, Allison, 'as the twig is bent, so is the tree.' " She had looked at Arthur then and Arthur, a blond, frowning boy with glasses, looked up at her almost wonderingly. But she only shook her head and sighed a sigh that seemed to last through all those terrible years Arthur crept his way through the Ashton Grammar School. And then a kind of hope appeared. He matured.

All this just happened last year. Up in Connecticut. Suddenly one day we turned around and there was Arthur—matured. It was a great joy to us all, as you can imagine, and it pretty much changed our lives—especially *mine*. That's what I wish to tell about, but I fear, and selfishly, it's most about me since Arthur had to go and get sent away. It's quite pitiful.

My mother is of the opinion that Arthur has had the profoundest influence on my life of anybody. I heard her telling Mrs. Ewing. But I'm not really so sure. I mean, there's my cousin Winky over in Charleston. She's exceedingly inspirational even if she is going to have to marry a cheap-rich Northerner. It's torn my life asunder, Winky marrying someone like that. She'll lose

10

all her heritage and have to live up in the North somewhere. She's affected me profoundly, Winky has.

And there're others. People in Ashton. Mrs. Ewing. She's the richest person in Ashton. And quite a number of my friends. My father is of the opinion that we're nothing but just a mix-up of everybody we know. I share this belief also. There's this one girl in Ashton—she's got four telephones in her house—and she too has pretty much made me the way I am.

So, you see, it isn't just Arthur that's affected me, although I think it was him that first introduced me to the world of sorrow. His life, up until last year, was literally brimming with it. The main thing about him was he just *never* seemed to have any interests. When Mother was his age, she was interested in everything. But Arthur just seemed to want to stare and flip through worthless magazines all the time.

For a long time we thought he was the way he was because of his eyes. He's had to wear glasses ever since he was five even. At recess sometimes you could see him—always the last in line, looking as if he wanted to cry, and his glasses almost bigger than he was. Mother was always talking to the principal, Miss Weems, about it. Miss Weems, though, said she didn't think spectacles had anything to do with Arthur's troubles. "He dreams all the time," she said. "He just sits there and dreams."

Father said there wasn't a thing in this world wrong with Arthur. "He's just slow, that's all." Which is probably why those horrid boys were always teasing him. They would come running up behind him and pinch him, and then because they were quick and thin and could get away, Arthur never could catch them. The nicest thing about Arthur was he never complained and he never told on the boys. That is why we want something "grand" to happen to him. Mother's always going to church and praying something grand will happen to Arthur. I also.

The time I really prayed was after he appeared in that piano recital. This was way before he matured, but it was a special time because Mother believed at long last Arthur was getting an interest. He would come dragging home from school and the two of them, Arthur and Mother, would sit side by side on the piano bench before the piano and Mother would count out loud as Arthur, his chubby fingers spread out over the keys and his mouth twisted in darkest gloom, fumblingly and loudly would play "Three Little Indians." He liked the bass part, the part that sounded like a drum, and he always did this the loudest and best. But it was the top part that had nothing to do with Indians or drums that he never seemed to get somehow. Anyway, we all went to the basement of the Ashton Grammar School to hear Arthur, in recital, play "Three Little Indians" for the one-thousandth time. Even Father came, leaving his office in midafternoon. And the three of us sat together on the wooden folding chairs, anxiously waiting for Arthur's time to come.

When it was all over we rode home in silence—Mother, Father, and myself crowded together on the front seat, leaving Arthur, alone, in the back seat to think out his tragedy. He had failed again, *dreadfully* this time. Everyone else, the quicker and thinner students of Miss Ames, the music teacher, had triumphed greatly, hurrying to the piano and without a single wrong note just rippling through their pieces. But, as Mother said, it was "sooo embarrassing, Allison." Arthur hadn't even been able to play the bass part, the part about the drums. Instead, he just struck wildly at any chord and had to begin fifty thousand different times before he finally gave up, red faced and frowning, and left the stage. And there we were, sitting tall and proud for everyone to see.

It was some time after that that Mother started getting these brown envelopes in the mail. They were school catalogues, she said, and I would watch her as she looked through the folders and stared at the pictures of all those neatly dressed boys sitting around tables and reading books. They all looked as if they had interests, these boys, and I knew what a disappointment it was for her to look at them, other people's boys, and know what she knew about Arthur and twigs and things. Gradually, though, I learned what all the catalogues were for. I heard them talking, Mother and Father, and Mother was saying, "Something has *got* to be done about him, Allison." And Father said he guessed so, too, now.

12

Then she started talking about this one school up in Connecticut. It had self-help in it, she said. The boys had to wait on tables and wax floors and stuff. Father said he was *highly* partial to a place like that for Arthur. "The more work, the better."

I listened and, frankly, I was *horrified!* They were going to send Arthur away! Way up to *Connecticut!* My own parents. Just doing away with Arthur. I thought of David Copperfield and a huge sorrow came down. If only Arthur'd been able to play the top part of his piano piece or gotten better grades or an interest— just anything! Still, I must say and it's really the truth: I think I really sort of enjoyed some of Arthur's troubles. I can't exactly explain it, but when I was sitting around and Mother and Father were going over and over all of Arthur's handicaps, I just sat there feeling warm and safe inside. You see, I'm quite thin and exceedingly atriculated for my age. I have always enjoyed the pleasure of being the fastest runner in my entire grade. Some people might say I'm a selfish human being and I guess I am at times. But I'm also quite interested in the poor and downtrodden. And this makes up, I think, for my occasional days of selfishness. I think I'll get over it, though. It's much more spiritual if you do.

Anyway, it seemed a dreadful thing they were planning for Arthur. Way up to Connecticut! So one night after dinner I went up into his room and told him what they were going to do to him. He was sitting at his desk, tracing this picture off a magazine—a soldier with a bayonet in his hand.

"You're gonna get sent away, Arthur," I said. "To school. All the way up to Connecticut!"

He just looked at me, his spectacled eyes looking back at me, unblinking and round. "How do ya know?" he asked.

"We've been discussing it," I said. "For hours. You have to wait on tables and scrub floors and stuff."

He put down his pencil and didn't say anything.

"*Way* up to Connecticut," I said.

His eyes got rounder and I knew how afraid he was.

But the next day I discovered his drawing on his desk again and underneath the soldier was written: "ConnETicut. ConnetiCUT.

Dam! I hope—THEY *LIKE*—me!!! Dam! Dam! Arthur. AR-
THUR WHITFIELD. Georgia. I hope—" And below was a tiny
picture of a man with glasses on.

I just stared at it, then very quickly scrambled some papers
over it. I didn't want him to know I'd seen. It was just too vastly
pitiful.

Well, we had an exceedingly difficult time getting Arthur into
school. Mother and Father wrote literally everybody—thousands
of letters—and Arthur had to go all the way up to the high school
to take a test. We were extremely fearful about the test because
of Arthur's scholarship, but it came out rather interestingly, we
thought. It showed Arthur was quite inclined to vocabulary, but
that he was very inferior when it came to arithmetic. He must
have passed, though, because finally we got a letter from the
school.

The letter was from the Reverend John D. Sykes, and he said
that he was happy to inform us that Arthur had been accepted. He
said—and he was sure all the trusties agreed—that he had always
believed in geography and he felt a boy from our section of the
country would add great measures to the school.

Mother and Father were overjoyed. I might add, I also. It had
been very trying to get Arthur accepted. Also, the letter came on
Arthur's fourteenth birthday. It was his main birthday present.
But he wasn't very hilarious over it.

Anyway, the next task was getting Arthur ready for school. All
that late summer Mother was frantic getting him ready. Every
day they would go downtown—Mother walking with quick, busy
steps, and Arthur dragging along behind with his rimless glasses
and green baseball cap on. He wouldn't go out of the house without his cap and nobody knew why; he wasn't on a team or anything and he never talked about baseball; he just wore the cap.
They would go weaving in and out of stores, buying sweaters and
blankets and all that stuff. To look at Arthur you'd never guess it
was him that was getting sent away. He did want this one coat

14

though, one that had a hood on it, but Mother wouldn't have it. They also had an argument about name tapes. Arthur wanted the kind you glue on and Mother wouldn't have that either. She even made *me* stitch some of them on Arthur's socks. I hated it, because she was always making me rip them off if they weren't neat.

It was strange, but all the time we were doing this, Arthur never said one word about being sent away. The night before he left we had fried chicken and we were all trying to be very jolly. Father was talking about what an experience it would be for Arthur to be in the part of the country where history abounded, and Mother said Arthur would love the snow, that maybe they even had skiing at school. Arthur just sat there, frowning, and finally he said in this very deep voice he has—"I don't think I'll go."

Nobody said anything for a few minutes, then Mother said, "Why, *A*rthur! Why?"

"Just don't think I will, that's all."

"But your trunk and duffle bag are already gone!" I said. (This man with a black snake drawn on his arm had had a simply terrible time trying to get the trunk down from upstairs.)

"Yep," was all Arthur said, but you could tell by the way he said it he wasn't planning to go.

He went upstairs, and Mother and Father just sat there looking at each other. It was the most pitiful thing you ever saw, and I thought about going upstairs and trying to cry but I wasn't in too good a mood, so I just stayed on downstairs and stared for a few hours. Mother said it was best to leave Arthur alone. "He needs to think for a while."

The next morning, though, she came very cheerily into Arthur's room and clapping her hands said, "Only a little while before train time!"

Arthur's overnight suitcase was lying open on a chair by his bed. The only thing in it was his baseball cap.

"See, you haven't even finished packing," Mother said.

Arthur mumbled something and turned over.

"Up! Up!" Mother said. "Not much time."

15

Poor Arthur. It just wasn't the kind of day to be having to go up to Connecticut. It was warm and nice out and the sun was so bright it almost hurt your eyes to look at it.

Finally, Arthur came dragging down for breakfast and during the eggs Father told him he should start thinking about going away to school as a privilege, that boys all over the country would give anything to have the opportunity he was having. Arthur didn't say anything; he just mumbled something about wanting raisin-bread toast instead of just plain white.

Later, when he came back downstairs, he was dressed and wearing his old green baseball cap.

"You can't wear *that* on the train," Mother said.

"Why not?"

"It just isn't becoming for traveling," Mother said. "Now, here, take it off, Arthur."

Arthur shrugged his shoulders and stuffed it in his coat pocket.

"Put it in your suitcase," Father said.

"O—kay." Mother helped him fold it and put it in with his pitiful underwear.

All of us went to the train station. Even Velvet and Isaiah came. Velvet and Isaiah are colored and have worked for us forever. Velvet cooks and Isaiah does everything. What I mean is Isaiah's not a real butler or chauffeur or anything. He's only Velvet's son. We're not rich and all that. I guess you'd call us only the third nicest family in Ashton. As I told you, the Ewings are the richest. They even have a swimming pool! But, anyway, Velvet and Isaiah are very partial to Arthur and that's why they came to see him off also. Poor Arthur. There he was, all name-taped and dressed in his new brown suit. He sat in a green Pullman seat beside the window and I looked at him up there, bundled up in his suit and still chubby, and I thought how small he seemed and how tremendous the train was. Somehow I felt that Arthur, alone and unarmed, was going off to be killed. Then as his hand waved timidly good-bye and he tried to smile, the train began to move and I looked up at Mother; her eyes were filled with tears, but she was trying to smile anyway. I thought, "O Arthur, Arthur..."

16

and sadly watched the great black train until it rounded the bend, carrying Arthur away, I thought, forever.

But it wasn't forever! The very next night we were all jolted out of our beds by the ringing of the telephone. I lay in my bed and listened. I heard Father say, "Ohhhh, no." Then Mother said, "What, Allison? What is it?"

I crept to my door and looked out. Father was frowning and Mother was staring worriedly at the telephone. But then Father laughed a sort of soft laugh and said, "Well, thank you so much. We appreciate that. Yes. Yes. Tell him not to worry."

"What, Allison? What was it?" Mother asked when he put the receiver down.

"Arthur got lost," Father said and shook his head.

"Lost?" Mother said. "Where is he?"

"He's all right. He's at school now."

"What happened?" Mother and I asked together.

"He got lost in the station—in New York."

Arthur was supposed to change trains in New York, but somehow had got confused and wandered helplessly around in the station for hours. A policeman had found him sitting on a bench close to tears. The school had called to tell us Arthur had finally arrived.

"Oh, dear," Mother said. "Why didn't he ask someone where to go?"

"You know Arthur," Father said. "He'd probably forgotten where he was going himself."

"I guess we should have had someone meet him there. Sometimes I forget Arthur's still such a child."

"At *his* age?" I asked.

"You'd better go back to bed, Felicia," Mother said. "It's late."

I walked back to my room with my hip out of joint (a thing I learned at camp), but nobody noticed. I heard Mother say, "Well, thank goodness he's *there*."

"He's there. He's there," I said as I fell into bed. Then, staring at the ceiling I had a vision: I kept seeing Arthur lying on some pitiful iron cot in a high cement room with bars on the windows. Blizzards were raging outside and there were howling winds.

17

I couldn't sleep and I kept having that vision over and over. With all my heart I hoped they would like Arthur up there.

So finally, I got out of bed and went over to my desk. I decided I'd better write him a letter. I started off very cheerfully:

Hi, Arthur!

Nothing's going on here and we're literally bored out of our minds. I'm sorry about you getting lost in the train station. It must be huge. Mother and Father didn't mind at all.

I certainly do wish I was up in Connecticut. History must be abounding all over the place. I bet the snow is fun also. Isn't it? If they're mean to you, you can come home. Mother and Father won't mind at all. But it's pretty boring.

Miss White at school had to have a garter removed on her neck so we've got a substitute—Miss James. She's got this huge mole and sucks lemons in front of us all the time because she's horse.

I must return to my boring life again.

> With Kindest regards
> Your sister,
> *Felicia Carr Whitfield*

Very immature! But, of course, I was childish then. Only eleven. The thing was, I couldn't find a stamp so I never mailed it. I'm still quite careless like that.

2

I'm not going to tell you *all* the unfortunate things Arthur underwent his first months in Connecticut. We're pretty much a loyal family and don't particularly like exposing all our tragedies. Besides, I was only able to obtain a few of Arthur's letters because I didn't want anyone to know I was obtaining them. They're pretty important ones, but they don't explain some of the torture

18

we suffered on his behalf. *You* know. If you had a brother you wouldn't want to be going around telling everybody some of the things that, secretly, you'd feel like dying over. It's just something that's nicer to keep quiet.

Anyway, it was very peculiar not having Arthur in the house. To me it was as if somebody had died and there were pathetic reminders of the person everywhere—a shoe, Arthur's Cub Scout uniform, an old rope. Mother, I think, missed him more than anyone else. And after the third day she began waiting for the mailman to hear some word. But it wasn't until the end of the week that the word finally arrived. It was written in pencil and on slick theme paper, and since it was the first time Arthur had ever written a letter home, there was something sad to me about the "Dear Mother and Dad." But it was the rest of the letter that caused us worry. In a jerky scrawl he had written:

> . . . I got hear alright. Mr. Sykes said he called you all. That policeman was real nice and said he'd call too. Did he? I had five cheese sandwiches on the train.
>
> My roommate whets the bed every night. Hes name is Bob Leyden and he comes from a place called Marble Head, Massichusits. Mr. Woodford, he's my English teacher, comes in at nights and tries to wake up Bob, but he just goes on and whets anyway. It's real hard hear and we have to wash windows on Saturday—everybody does. Mr. Sykes said window washing can be fun, but it isn't. I've gotten to know a lot of the other boys but nobody likes my roomate. Wish I was home and there only 84 days until Christmas. Well, I gotta go.
>
> Sincerely,
Arthur
>
> P.S. They think I talk funny up hear.

It was the spelling of the word "whets," that seemed to excite Mother more than anything else. "Certainly, he knows better than that," she said. But the next morning I heard her telling Mrs. Johnston over the phone that she had heard from Arthur and that

19

it was too bad Arthur had to get a roommate who was suffering from—and she whispered the word, pronouncing each syllable, "en-u-re-sis." I supposed she was talking about wetting the bed, but I was too embarrassed to ask. That night, though, we all sat in the library because Mother said she wanted us to hear what she had written Arthur. And in the letter she told Arthur to be nice to his poor roommate, that he was probably just nervous being away from home for the first time and she was sure young Bob Leyden hated his difficulty just as much as anyone else and probably more.

The only thing about it was, everybody in town started asking me if we'd heard from Arthur. See, nobody else in Ashton hardly has ever gone up North to school before. We heard what Mrs. Findlay said. She said she thought it was terrible to send a boy that young to school and she wouldn't send a son of hers that far away from her for anything. Her son is Jack Findlay, and he's got the biggest Adams apple in Ashton. He got it two years ago when it just sort of came rising up. Anyway, I saw Jack going into the drugstore and he spoke. Usually he doesn't. "What's old Arthur doing up there?" he asked me, and I guess he thought I was insane because I started blushing and practically fell over the weighing scales trying to get away. I mean I didn't want to stand there and tell Jack Findlay about Arthur's letter and about that boy wetting the bed. Mother said for me just to say, "Why, yes, we had a lovely letter from Arthur and he's doing just fine." But people, especially boys, can read your mind sometimes, and I don't care whether Mother feels sorry for Arthur's roommate or not. I think he's HORRIBLE!

Then, to make things worse, we got another letter from Arthur —right away. It worried us no end and I didn't exactly understand all of it. Mother said she didn't either, but Father said he did and not to worry about it. It also was written in pencil and the envelope was dirty round the edges. It looked like one of those letters Velvet gets from her husband that's in jail. Mother started reading it out loud:

. . . Well, I guess you better send me the money to come home. There's one boy that's already left and his Mother came and got him. This is a terrible place and I hate, HATE my roomate. He says nobody in Georgia wears shoes and he bets all you all do is pick cotton all the time. I hate him and I have to keep the windows open all the time.

They put Saul and Peter in all the food and the spinach has got sand in it. Also they're making me take reading lessons in the afternoon because they say I never did learn to read properly. This one teacher said right out in front of everybody that hardly anybody in the South ever learns to read properly. I can pack up and be gone from here soon as the money comes.

I gotta go.

Sincerely,
Arthur

When Mother finished reading she looked up at us. Father was smiling with his horn-rimmed glasses on and he didn't look up. He just kept tapping his fingers on the arm of the red leather chair.

"Well, what do you think?" Mother asked.

"What's Saul and Peter?" I asked. "What's he talking about?" I really wanted to know.

Mother glanced at me. "I don't know. Allison, what *is* he talking about?"

"Oh, nothing," Father said. "Boys' talk." He still didn't look up.

But I kept looking at Father because even though he is fifty-two he happens to know a great deal about boys' talk. He went to Sewanee Military Academy and also the University of Virginia. He was a holy terror at the University of Virginia which, as you can imagine, is a thing we don't particularly like to speak of now.

"He does seem unhappy, Allison," Mother said.

Father looked up then. "Oh, he'll get over it."

21

"I don't blame him," I said. I looked down at my shoes. "They don't think we even wear shoes down here."

"I'll have to write him tonight," Mother said. "Of *course* he can't come home! How silly!"

"It's pitiful, I think," I said, but nobody heard me.

Mother should have written Arthur a nicer letter than she did. She wrote him to remember he was a Whitfield and that all Whitfields "stuck things out." She said as far back as she knew every member of the family—on both sides—had "stuck things out." She said for Arthur "to get some courage now" and say his prayers and study hard. "Whining is *never* attractive in a young man." She also said that Father had said to pay no attention whatsoever about what the boys said about Georgia. "It's a fine state and, of course, you know that as well as anyone." She said for Arthur also to eat what was before him as he had always been taught to do. At the end she was pretty nice. She said all three of us were counting on him and that it wouldn't be too long until Christmas.

But then this kindly tone from her didn't last very long. Arthur hadn't been in school more than a month when we started receiving sleek little envelopes from the headmaster, Mr. Sykes. Mr. Sykes never used the word, "I", but always "we." And it seemed every letter began either "we fear" or "we are sorry" or "we believe." Anyway, Mr. Sykes and "they" quite soon decided Arthur had to go back a grade. "Arthur just doesn't seem to have had the fundamental training some of the other boys have had," wrote Mr. Sykes. We were astonished and, naturally, this caused no end of talk. We were always having to sit down in the living room and discuss it. "He just can't keep up, that's all," Mother said. "He's just not trying. He never has tried." And she kept saying this over and over as other letters from the headmaster arrived those first few months Arthur was at school. Boring. Boring. That's all we ever talked about—Arthur and school. Arthur and school. Even so, I knew how exceedingly horrible it was for Arthur, being put back and being humiliated in front of all those Northerners. I decided I would never go to school in Connecticut, even if they beat me over the head and tried to drag me there.

22

Arthur, though, never wrote us about being put back a grade. He didn't write too much at all, and when he did it was mostly about his roommate. Bob Leyden's mother had been to school to visit and she was very rich and talked like an Englishman:

...I wanted to discuss with her about you know what. But she went poking around the room like I wasn't there. I just sat there on the bed and she never said one thing to me except "how-do-you-do." Then she and Bob kept talking about *his* bed, *his* desk and *his* clothes. She wanted to know if the other boys were still wearing his clothes. Nobody has ever worn anything of his except this one boy and you would've thought he'd killed somebody or something the way Bob kept shouting around about it.

Every afternoon we have to go down in the basement and sing "Yayzoo! Joy of Man's Desires." It's this very hard song by Bock and it's for the Christmas concert we're giving. People come from all over the north to here it. I nearly passed out because the music teacher made everyone of us sing something by ourselves to test us. He made me stand up and face the wall and sing Onward Christian Soldiers. I'm base.

I gotta go.

Sincerely,
Arthur

P.S. It snowed today. Algebra is terrible.

Mother felt quite pleased about this letter. "I think he's adjusting better now. Don't you Allison? It really makes me feel *so* much happier."

Father started to say something, but I said, "Let's not talk about it any more." Frankly, I was getting very bored talking about nothing but Arthur all the time. I mean I like Arthur, but I also had my own downtrodden life to think about, especially my relationships in connection with Mother and Father. This was an exceedingly trying period in my life. With Arthur gone, I was the only one left to be chastened. I hate times like that. There you are,

23

like some slave! And there they are, *two* of them! I think I'm adopted.

Well, practically the only thing I did in November was to sit around with Mother and Father and *their* friends all the time. Everybody at school had gotten up this new thing in which they were forced to go home as soon as school was over to get their homework done. It was also cold in Georgia, too. No snow, just sunny cold with all the branches bare. Very depressing. Thanksgiving came on and we didn't have anybody over to take Arthur's place. Boring. I threw up afterwards.

The only good thing that happened was Miss White, my teacher I wrote Arthur about, got through with her operation and made us write this theme. We had to write it in class and we could write it on anything we wanted to. I wrote it on Arthur's joint. You see, Arthur is inflicted with just one joint in his little finger. He inherited it from my Grandfather Whitfield. Father is the same way, too. Miss White said it was a fine example of inheritance and showed it to all these other teachers. It was very immature, but I received many compliments—not from anybody that mattered, only teachers. Miss White said maybe I was going to be a newspaperman like my uncle.

Mother was more interested in having these people out to the farm for a highball than she was in Arthur's joint. As I said, it was an exceedingly trying time. Mother and Father are always inviting people to come out to the farm and all I do is sit and pass the olives and nuts. I suppose I have turned out a tremendous disappointment to my father because I'm really not very partial to the farm. Even as a child I thought it was most boring just to stand there and stare at the cows. I don't think Father knows exactly how I feel and I wouldn't say it out loud for anything, because as I've told you Father has always enjoyed a love of the land. Also my Grandfather Whitfield—he's dead.

Really, I think Father is more pleased with being a farmer than he is a banker. He's president of the Ashton National Bank, but he doesn't own it or anything. The Ewings own it. They even own the Episcopal church. But all Father does is sit behind this desk that has nothing on it, and then at three o'clock he beats it out to the farm. They've started selling pine trees for lumber and rearing Black Angus cows. The main thing Father likes, though, is quail hunting. He goes tromping all over the place shooting up stuff. It's pitiful.

But the reason we're able to have the farm at all is, see, my Great-grandfather Whitfield, which is way back, used to have his plantation out there. The chimney from it is still there. The Northerners came down and pretty much raped it up during the War Between the States. They raped up the whole South, as you know. It was the tragic decade, and we aren't very partial to the North to this day. They didn't burn our house though, and the only reason they didn't was because my Great-grandmother Whitfield defied them. We get a great deal of our courage from Great-grandmother Whitfield. It was my *Grandmother* Whitfield that burned the house down. She and this colored boy were cleaning out the chimneys and the roof caught on fire. It was a tragedy, but that's how we got our house in town, thank goodness. After the plantation house burned, Grandmother and Grandfather moved into the house we're living in now. It's old, too, and this man from Charleston wrote it up in a book he wrote. We were exceedingly poor in those days. Carpetbaggers! And too the North wouldn't give us any money to recover. They still hate us, the North. I know.

Anyway, Mother and Father built this kind of cabin out on the farm, and they're always going out there and having people in for a highball. The only time I ever liked the farm was when Arthur and I used to play War Between the States with the Miller children. Mr. Miller oversees the farm and he has five children— Herman, Nadine, Bertha, Roy and Oscar. Everyone of them has white hair and white eyelashes.

If you knew the Millers you'd never feel as sorry for anyone in all your life. Velvet calls them "white trash." They live in this house with linoleum on the floor, and there's only one picture on the wall. It's of Nadine's and them's little brother that died. They

25

took a picture of him in the casket with all the flowers and that's the only picture they have on the wall. I guess it isn't very nice to stare at it, but the Millers never seem to mind too much.

One time when I was a child Nadine Miller asked me to come to their house for dinner. Only I was invited. Arthur was having difficulties learning his Cub Scout pledge and had to stay locked up in this room until he learned it. So just I was able to go. Velvet was out with us helping Mother and she got simply furious because I didn't want to wear shoes or a belt to the Millers' house. See, none of them ever wore shoes or belts and I didn't think it was very nice of me to go walking in with them on either, so I left them in my room.

I went walking out of the house and I hadn't gotten to the porch before Velvet started yelling. "Felicia! Where you thank you goin' without yo shoes?" She was very angry.

"I don't want to wear any," I told her.

"And yo belt! You looks worse'n them Miller trash!"

"They *aren't* trash, Velvet," I said.

"You go on and put yo clothes on," she told me. "If you don't I'm gwina tell yo mama!"

I went on back and put on my shoes and Velvet tied my belt so tight I thought she was trying to kill me!

"Don't see how come you mama letchu go down there no how."

"Because they want me to know all kinds of people," I said. I was mad at Velvet and what I said was true. My father is very partial to Arthur and I knowing all kinds of people. He said he didn't ever want us to grow up being hankty. Father knows all kinds of people and he's exceedingly nice to everyone, even white trash.

Anyway, I wore my shoes and belt until I got halfway down this red-clay road, and then I hid them on the edge of the cotton field. When I got to the Millers I was just like they were. My toenails were filthy with red clay, and I even put some dirt on my forehead. We went to the gasoline station and bought these huge, great bottles of orange and then we played SPIT.

What you do is, you sit up on this little hill on the highway and

26

try to spit on all the cars that pass by. The one that hits the most—wins. Herman always won. That was the most enjoyable thing almost I've ever done. But then later, we had an experience with some colored children. They kept calling Herman names. I don't know where they came from; they just sort of came out of the woods.

We went back and told Mrs. Miller about it. Mrs. Miller is this sandy-haired, tired-looking lady, and she asked Herman what the colored children had called him.

"White biscuit," Herman said.

Mrs. Miller, though, didn't seem to think it was so bad. "Whar your brains, Herman?" she asked him. "You know better'n to keep up fuss with niggers." That last word is a word my mother and father will not permit Arthur and I to say. The only reason I even put it in is to show you how the Millers talk. They say things like "whar" for "where," and they're always putting R's in words where there aren't supposed to be any. I don't know where they get that kind of talk.

Well, then this horrifyingly embarrassing thing happened. Mrs. Miller was just standing there on the porch with her arms crossed, and then without smiling or anything, she said, "Zip yerself up, Herman. Yer privates is showing!"

Nadine started giggling and I nearly dropped dead. Herman started getting red all over and then kind of turned and zipped. Mrs. Miller didn't say anything else. She just went on back in the house, and Herman went whistling off down the road somewhere.

For dinner we had turnip greens, side meat, and "chittlings." I'm not very partial to that kind of dinner, and I had hoped we were going to have a kind of picnic with sandwiches and everything. We didn't; we just sat at this table by the stove. Nadine told me that the green plates we were using came from the gasoline station. I said they certainly were pretty, and they were, in a way. Nadine was terribly proud of them.

But before we ate, Mr. Miller said we all had to thank the "Lard." Mr. Miller is this silent man most of the time, but I noticed he talked just like Mrs. Miller. I bowed my head and kind

27

of glanced once to see if anybody else was. They all were, except Mr. Miller. He just sat there with his eyes closed. He has a quite thin face and a very large nose that is red.

"Lard—" he said, "yer been good to us. You done put food in front of us agin. We ain't desarvin', Lard. Oscar here done broke a urange bottle on the highway and Nadine sassed her mama this mornin'. But, Lard, we're gonna try. We're gonna be better folks come dark. Thank ye, Lard. Amen."

I don't know why I thought that was kind of pitiful. The Millers are not Episcopalians. They go to a church down the road, but I thought there was something quite sorrowful about all of them sitting around thanking the Lord when they didn't even have everyday shoes to wear. I told Mother about it and she said she didn't think there was anything sorrowful about it at all. She said she thought it was "lovely and decent."

But, as I said, all this happened when I was a child. Now the Millers—I mean Nadine and Herman—won't hardly have a thing to do with me. Herman's Arthur's age and he helps his father out. They talk sometimes, but Nadine, who is my age, started getting this very bad skin and all she does is sit around and pout with lipstick on. I always wave to her, but she just flips her hand and goes on frowning. I think people are much more fun when they're children.

Anyway, I just put all that in to kind of show you what it's like at the farm. There's nothing much for me to do out there now except either go in the kitchen and talk to Velvet or sit around and watch Mother and them drink their highballs. She simply adores to have me there to pass the nuts. But I get bored to distraction, so that Saturday after Thanksgiving, when she said she was having the Ewings (richest people in town) and the Fosters out for drinks, we sort of had an argument. I said I had much rather stay in town with some of my friends. "I *never* have a good time," I said. "I'm always sitting around like an idiot listening to all *your* friends."

"That's all you ever do, is have a good time," she said. "Besides, you should learn to appreciate older people. It's developing being with older people."

I don't see why. All I can do is listen and, besides, I can't stand Mrs. Foster. Once she gets to the farm she starts acting like she'd flipped. She starts acting like she's this very young person that is madly in love with everyone on earth. She isn't, she really *hates* everybody! Also, I did the most immature thing you've ever heard of.

3

The main reason I want to tell you about the Fosters and the Ewings is because of something that happened later on. It concerns this Northern newspaperman that came down looking around after our race relations. It was simply a disgrace—what he wrote—and the maddest people of all were the Ewings and the Fosters. Mr. Ewing was exceedingly anxious that Father sue, but we just went on and turned the other cheek because of Arthur. He was home, too, and it affected him greatly. I declare, the North just beats all.

First, though, let me tell you about Mrs. Foster. Do you like women that go around talking to animals like they were people? I mean, asking them things and then standing there waiting for an answer? I think that's one of the most stupid things anybody can do. Well, that's what Mrs. Foster does. She talks baby talk to them and nobody else can say a word because she talks so loud all you can do is keep quiet and watch her carrying on like a large idiot. I don't think she cares a thing for cows and farms, not as much as I even.

One thing I know is that Mother and Father aren't particularly partial to Mrs. Foster. The only reason they have her is because she's always inviting them, and Mother says Ashton is too small a place to have hard feelings in. Sometimes I think Mother would like to move back to Charleston—with Father, of course. She never says anything about it, but there aren't too many congenial brains in Ashton. Father says practically nobody in Ashton ever reads a book. He doesn't just like people that read books, but of course older people, some of them, like to sit around talking about books. I guess when you get older there isn't much else to talk about except books, the price of cotton, and colored people. People in Georgia talk about colored people all the time.

Well, there we all were, sitting around this stone fireplace in the cabin. The Fosters hadn't come yet, but Mr. and Mrs. Ewing were there. As I told you, the Ewings are the richest people in Ashton. They're always going to New York, and in the summer they even go to Maine. The Ewings aren't like Mother and Father, though; they really *don't* have any friends in Ashton. And the reason they don't is because Mr. Ewing went to Harvard. He doesn't know what to do with himself when everybody starts talking about the University of Georgia football team. That's what most men in Ashton talk about—football and golf and how the Democratic party better get up on its haunches about the South.

Poor Mr. Ewing. Father says Bill Ewing isn't really conceited, he's just lonely. He gets all his clothes in New York, and he's the only one in the entire Episcopal church that looks like he comes from the North. I heard Mother say one time that when Bill Ewing goes North, he's a Southerner, but when he's home, in Ashton, he thinks he's from the East. She didn't mean to be ugly or anything. She likes Mr. Ewing, but somehow you get the feeling that Mr. and Mrs. Ewing are just visiting in Ashton.

The one thing about Mr. Ewing is he's the only Republican in town and he's always saying "damn." One time he called the Democrats a bunch of "damn rats." He really did, right in front of Mother and everybody. Nobody said anything, though, because he practically owns the town. He owns the bank, and the Ewing Textile Mills are known all over the world. I told you, didn't I, they have a swimming pool?

Mrs. Ewing is very nice. The only thing about her is she knits all the time. Even out at the farm she brings this long bag along and almost as soon as she gets there the needles start clicking. Mrs. Ewing isn't very pretty. Her face is awfully bony and she has this drab blonde hair that's got too much permanent in it. Sometimes you wonder why Mr. Ewing married her, because everybody thinks he's extremely handsome. I don't, because he has these tremendous shoulders and his black eyebrows go up in triangles so that you think he's laughing at everything.

What I like is a man that looks more like my father. But I never told you what Father looks like, or Mother either. The funny thing is they both sort of look alike. Father is very tall and thin and has this sandy hair with a lot of grey in it. A lot of people are scared when they first meet him because he never does say very much (except at home) and, too, because of his nose and eyes. He has these very piercing blue eyes and his nose has been broken twice—once when he was playing football at Sewanee and the next time when he was a holy terror at the University of Virginia. I suppose I shouldn't have put that in again about him being a holy terror, but he was. He was always riding around in these very fast cars and drinking whisky. He stopped, though, when Mother finally decided she would marry him. I mean he still has his highball and everything, but back when he was at the University he even drank white lightning. I heard him tell it once. It's amazing Mother ever did marry Father. She was getting ready to marry this other man, a man from Charleston, because her mother thought it was more suitable. My Charleston grandmother—she's dead too—was never very partial to people from Georgia. She liked South Carolina and Virginia better.

Mother and Father don't really look alike; there's just something about the look in their eyes or something. In the first place, Mother has this long, almost auburn hair and she can sit on it. She braids it and then pins the braids on the back of her head. Her eyes, though, are blue and they slant up. They *do*. Everybody in Ashton thinks Mother is beautiful. She is. Her nose has never been broken, and even at forty-two she's not fat or anything. As I told you, my father is quite elderly—fifty-two. That was another reason my grandmother in Charleston didn't want Mother to marry Father—because he was so much older and everything. Later, though, she got quite partial to him. Charleston is just a very peculiar place. Mother and I are always going there on trips and things.

Anyway, as I was saying, we were all sitting by the fire and as usual talking about the South! That's all anybody ever talks about nowadays. If they're not talking about colored people, they're talking about Southern potential and Northern potential and how the South's got more than the North. We are exceedingly anxious to have any industry that wants to to come and make their junk in the South. That's the sort of things they talk about. Mr. Ewing thinks the South would get somewhere quicker if we had two parties, the Democrats and the Republicans. But Father says we're not ready for that yet because we need Southern Democrats to stay in Washington to battle for us. We're in violent need for *somebody* to battle for us because the North does nothing but write about our bad points all the time. We're of the opinion that the South is going to be the hope of the nation some day.

Boring. I had to sit there on this wooden bench without a back and listen to all that. I kept watching Mrs. Ewing's knitting needles, and I watched them so hard I started getting dizzy and sort of sick in my stomach.

I went on back in the kitchen to talk to Velvet. Velvet doesn't much like to come out to the farm either. I don't blame her much. All she does is sit in there by the stove with her face in her hands and think about her high blood. I always try to cheer her up. She'd gotten another letter from her husband in jail. He's always writing Velvet to ask Father to get him off the road gang. He is more partial to working on the prison farm. I don't blame him because you have no idea how hot it gets working on a Georgia highway in summer. They also have these men with guns watching you and everything. But, see, the thing is Booker—that's Velvet's husband's name—killed a man. He killed Checkerboard Hudson because Checkerboard was all the time messing with Booker's money. I don't know everything about it and I don't think Velvet does either, but one day Booker just upped and shot Checker-

board dead. Velvet had prostrations, and Father g\
and everything to defend him. I'm overjoyed he d\
chair.

Velvet, though, says most menfolks are sorry. She\
wouldn't marry "no man again for nothin!" She says all m\
out of you anyway is a work horse. "Washin' and ironin\
cookin' all day, and in the end all they do is get up on their h\
and go off with some other woman."

That's what we started talking about in the kitchen. She needed
cheering up, and she simply adores to talk about what a mess it is
being married to somebody sorry. I asked her if she thought I
would ever marry and she started giggling all over the place. She
made me furious because she said if I ever did marry I'd probably
marry some "old man."

"Why?" I asked her.

She thought she'd said the funniest thing in the world. "Cause
you just puts me in mind of somebody old sometimes."

I frowned at her. "You mean *really* old, Velvet?"

"Sometimes you acts just like an old, old woman."

"I don't think I do."

"Sometimes you do."

"I can run faster than anybody at school," I said. "If you're
old, you can't do that. I'm going to marry somebody rich. You
just wait and see."

"I'm waitin'," she said, and started giggling again.

I started to say something else but then I heard Mrs. Foster.
At least I thought it was her because of the horn blowing. That's
the way she does. They have this station wagon and *she* always
drives. I don't know why because I'm always seeing Mr. Foster
driving around town. But you always know when she's driving
because she starts honking the horn about a mile away from the
cabin. That's the kind of person she is. Mother says that Mrs.
Foster used to be a real belle, that she was known all over the
South for being one. But she went on until she was twenty-seven
before she married and ended up with Harry Foster who sells insurance and is timid. Harry Foster's father died last year and now

33

ey have pretty much money. I guess the Foster boys—that's
their twin sons that are holy terrors in high school—will end up
in shirt sleeves, because Mrs. Foster is always spending all this
money on clothes. She even goes to Atlanta to buy.

I don't know why Mother wanted to have Mrs. Foster with Mr.
and Mrs. Ewing. They're not at all alike, except everybody likes
Mr. Foster because he's so timid and pitiful. He just sort of stands
there, but you know he's nice. I know I think he is because he's
the only one that says very much to me. Everybody else can be
talking away about the South and colored people and he'll always
come over and say something to me, right in the middle of it all.
Not many older people'll do that. I like Mr. Foster.

"Jeeeeee—zus," Velvet said, when Mrs. Foster kept honking.
"She gonna gimme the sick headache with all that fuss."

I just sighed and took my nut plate and went on back into the
living room. I wanted to be there when Mrs. Foster started
springing around the way she does. She's exceedingly agrarian.

4

Mrs. Foster is very large at the top. She can't help it or anything,
but there's no one else in Ashton like her. Mother told Father one
time that she didn't think sweaters were very becoming to Mrs.
Foster, but Father said he was rather partial to her in sweaters,
and they had an argument. The thing is my father doesn't have
much taste about women's clothes. I guess I don't either because,
even though I literally loathe mentioning it, I think Mrs. Foster
has beautiful clothes. When she came in she made Mother and
Mrs. Ewing look actually pathetic. Both of them had on these
old beat-up-looking tweed suits, but Mrs. Foster had on this white
wool dress with a gold belt and shoes that matched! She really is
pretty. Her hair is short and she turned grey even when she was
twenty-five. Then, too, she has these wide, brown eyes and ex-

ceedingly white teeth. The only thing about her is she wears too much perfume. It comes sort of floating into the room and before long you're practically gasping for breath. She also dangles with bracelets.

I don't know why it is but Mrs. Foster always makes me feel pathetic. Never in my entire life have I ever had any clothes I like. I like pink and blue dresses, and all I ever get are these sad-looking plaids and dark blues. Even in the summertime, nothing but checks and plaids, and they have to be made! I've never had a bought dress in my life.

She came into the room just like I knew she would, all breathy as if she'd been running or something, and then she started trotting around the room kissing everybody. I despise beginnings with people. I mean people you know very well but haven't seen for a while. You're supposed to act like you're overwhelmed to meet them and you have to hug and kiss and faint all over the place.

"Aaaaallison, you cutie pie," she said to Father and pecked him on the cheek.

Father pretended he was overjoyed, but I knew he wasn't because right away he started asking her what she wanted to drink. But she didn't say anything, she just kept on her rounds and poor Mr. Ewing had to stand up.

"You deserve one too, Bill," she said and *smack!* I thought I was going to throw up.

Mrs. Ewing just glanced up from her knitting needles and didn't say anything, but Mr. Ewing was overjoyed and suddenly became this very gay person. He never carries on like that with just Mother and Father.

"Now that's the kind of greeting I like," he said and started jerking his shoulders up and down. Why is it some older people are always acting so stupid? It's embarrassing even to watch. Mother and Father never act that way.

Poor Mr. Foster was just standing there, trying to smile. It's very peculiar about him, but he doesn't look like someone who would be timid. He's short, but he has this close-cropped hair and thousands of muscles. He looks like he could have been a cheer-

35

leader or something, but you know he never was because he would have died of embarrassment.

Mother shook hands with him and then, I knew it, Mrs. Foster got around to me. I got up from the bench and stretched out my pathetic hand and started to curtsy, but she didn't take my hand—she started patting me on top of the head.

"Ohhhh, Sarah!" she said to Mother. "How pretty this child is getting!"

Lies! Nothing but lies! I'm not pretty. I wish I were, but I'm not.

"Her hair! Such a pretty blonde!" She brushed my bangs back further. "I love the way she wears it—just straight! Don't ever give her a permanent!"

See. See what I mean? What she meant was that Mother ought to do something about my hair. What she was really thinking was that I *should* have a permanent. I wish I could have one, but I can't. Mother won't let me have one, so I go around with this sad straight hair and my plaid dresses. For one million years practically I even had to wear high socks. Nobody else in Ashton did— nobody but me!

"Such a pretty forehead," she said. I guess that was the only thing she could think of to say that was pretty. But who wants a pretty forehead! I just smiled at her and looked at Mother. Everybody was staring. The whole room was staring.

"I think Felicia's going to be all right some day," was all Mother said, and she didn't smile or anything.

I was never so glad in all my life when Father handed Mrs. Foster her highball. I decided I'd give her time enough for two sips, then I'd go on my rounds with the nuts again.

Mrs. Foster flopped down on the sofa and held her feet up so everybody could see her shoes. "Ahhhh," she said, "I love this place!"

Mrs. Ewing glanced up from her knitting again and Mrs. Foster saw her.

"How was New York, Margaret?" she asked Mrs. Ewing. You could tell she was sort of afraid of Mrs. Ewing, because every

36

time she said anything to her she used a different voice, lower and not nearly as loud. Mrs. Ewing has a way of scaring a lot of people. I think it's because she's so rich and knits and, too, she sort of goes around looking bored all the time and you feel as if you've got to make her unbored.

"We weren't in New York long," Mrs. Ewing said. "Bill had some business there, that's all." Mr. Ewing is the only man in Ashton that's ever had any business in New York, but also you could tell Mrs. Ewing was mad about the question because the Ewings don't ever like for anybody to know what they're doing. Even if they go to Europe they don't want anybody to know beforehand. They just sort of pop up there, rich as ever.

There wasn't much else for Mrs. Foster to say, but she doesn't ever like to be quiet for long. "Allison!" she said. "You promised me. You pro-mised me." She started wagging her finger at Father. Her fingernail was violently red.

"What's that, Elaine?" Father said. He had just put another log on the fire and was rubbing his hands.

"You promised to show me around. You promised to show me everything!"

"I'm afraid you'll ruin your shoes, Elaine," Mother said. "It's rather damp out."

Mrs. Foster never even looked at Mother. "You promised me, Allison," she said, and began pouting in this babyish way.

"Show the lady around, Allison," Mr. Ewing said, and he was just sitting there, grinning and staring at Mrs. Foster's top. I don't think anybody else noticed, but I did. He was sitting beside her and I could see. I don't know why it is that men that are married and all, even older ones, do that.

"I want to see the spring you've been telling me about," she said, "and the barn and the bittie chicks."

I told you! I told you! Mrs. Foster is the worst person in Ashton. Even Mother despises women that go around talking baby talk and Mother really doesn't despise anybody. But if you think about it, maybe that's why Mrs. Foster was so popular when she was young. There's this girl, Virgie Harris, in Ashton, and she goes around talking baby talk all the time. She's exceedingly popular with boys, but I don't think I could do it if it killed me. People would think I was insane.

Poor Father, he had to get up and go out in the cold and show Mrs. Foster around the farm. He started putting on this ancient jacket he has. "How about you, Harry?" he said to Mr. Foster. "Would you like the tour, too?"

"Well, yes. Yes, I would. Thanks, Allison," he said in this very pathetic voice. Mr. Foster is always going around thanking people.

Actually, though, I really don't think Father minded too much, I mean showing them around and everything. Even in November, Father is partial to the earth. He tries so hard to give Arthur and me an appreciation of it. He thinks even a blade of grass is beautiful. One time he picked this blade and told Arthur and I, "Now *this* was a living thing. Life—a great, moving, stirring thing." I could have cried. I don't know why. His voice was so filled with sorrow.

It's tragic, but I don't think even Arthur cares much about the farm. The only thing he likes is the peach orchard and that's because he likes to eat them. Arthur and I both are completely lacking in any spiritual sense, and it's very peculiar because all our family, on both sides, have always enjoyed one. Even our connections in Charleston are fond of flowers. Of course I like flowers, but I can't gasp and scream around about them like a lot of women do. I just don't understand how anybody could, but I don't understand a lot of things about a lot of people.

When Father and them had gone, Mr. Ewing leaned back on the sofa and said, "Astonishing. Astonishing girl!" He was talking about Mrs. Foster, but I don't know why he called her a girl. She's Mother's age.

"She's so very pretty," Mother said. Mother had just sat down on this straight-backed chair, and I thought she was pretty, too, much prettier than Mrs. Foster really. The glow of the fire was in her hair and I like the hollows in her cheeks. Mrs. Foster doesn't have hollows. Her face is like a valentine box. Mother also sits very daintily. She never lounges around like I do.

38

Anyway—and I knew they would—they started talking about the Episcopal church, Mr. and Mrs. Ewing and Mother. Mr. Ewing is the Senior Warden and, as I've told you before, he owns the church. Mother started it, that about the Episcopal church. And you could tell Mrs. Ewing was interested because she stopped knitting. They were talking about firing the rector—poor, pitiful Reverend Agee. They fired him because he read his pitiful sermons and his wife didn't have any graces.

"Does he know, Bill?" Mother asked. She was talking about the Reverend Agee.

"Yes," Mrs. Ewing said, answering for Mr. Ewing. "The Bishop came over and had a little talk with him. It was *so* hard on Bill. Bill had to chat with him afterwards himself—tell him what the vestry's reasons were."

"Oh dear," Mother said. "It's just such a sensitive thing. I really hope he isn't hurt."

Mr. Ewing started lighting his pipe. "Well," he said, cupping his hand around the bowl and lighting it, "I don't think he's very upset. He just never was the one for St. Peter's and I think he knew it."

"No, he wasn't the one for St. Peter's," Mrs. Ewing said. "He had absolutely no idea about finances either. He just went wild when it came to money." She looked over at her knitting bag. "Frankly, I'm very pleased he's leaving."

"He was good with the young people, though," Mother said. "Arthur seemed to like him and all the young boys. He was very good with the Sunday school."

"Perhaps," Mr. Ewing said. "But they were a peculiar couple."

"Imagine her, refusing the Ashton Study Club!" Mrs. Ewing said.

"Perhaps she just wasn't interested in it," Mother said.

I got up and passed the nuts around again, but nobody took one. I didn't want to sit there and listen about the Ashton Study Club. It's this small group of women that sit around and some speaker comes in and reads a play or reviews a book or something. Afterwards they go and stand around the dining-room table and eat everything in sight. They're always blackballing everybody, and if you do get in it's practically the greatest thing in the world.

They didn't talk about it though, thank goodness. They talked about who they were going to get to take the Reverend Agee's place. Mr. and Mrs. Ewing said they wanted someone that had sympathy with the South—about colored people and all—and someone with background that would fit in with the families at St. Peter's. Mr. Ewing said he was extremely partial to this man in Virginia that went around fox hunting all the time, but he didn't know whether he could get him to come to Ashton.

"Well, I want someone I wouldn't mind having bury me," Mother said, and both Mr. and Mrs. Ewing laughed. I didn't think it was very funny. I don't much like to talk about dying. Mother simply adores to. She says there's no sense in being silly about it, that it's only practical to discuss it. Mother can be exceedingly morbid sometimes.

They didn't get to finish about who was going to take the Reverend Agee's place because Father and the Fosters came bouncing back into the room. The Fosters are Methodists and I guess the Ewings didn't want them to hear. So—they started talking about Arthur! Mrs. Foster started it, by asking about him. Mother said they were exceedingly happy with the school so far and she thought it was just "grand" for a young boy to get a change of atmosphere. I guess she shouldn't have said that because the Foster twins aren't getting a change of atmosphere. They're just right here in Ashton, running around in the same old atmosphere. But I guess Mrs. Foster didn't mind too much.

"That cutie pie," she said. She was talking about Arthur. "He's so terribly serious about everything. I used to see him walking home from school and he looked like he had the weight of the world on his shoulders. He's absolutely precious with his little glasses and everything."

See! That's exactly like Mrs. Foster. She doesn't think Arthur's precious at all. Her twin sons don't wear glasses and they're supposed to be marvelously handsome with their black eyes and all.

"Well, Arthur's going to be an interesting man," Mrs. Ewing

40

said. "I gave him a ride home once, and he kept me perfectly fascinated talking about catsup."

"About catsup!" Mother said.

"Yes, he went into considerable detail about how bad it was for you."

I laughed, too. I knew where Arthur got that. Velvet used to tell this story about a boy she knew that kept eating catsup, and one by one his legs and arms kept falling off and then finally his head! Arthur and I used to be terrified the boy's head would come floating into our rooms at night.

"Children pick up the strangest things," Mrs. Ewing said.

They all had another highball and I thought they'd never leave. Father and Mr. Ewing started talking about colored people again. Mr. Ewing was in a pretty bad mood about colored people, because he'd had to pay nine hundred dollars to save his cook's house. She'd forgotten to make payments on it, and the loan company was going to put it up for sale.

"They'd just bought a four-hundred-dollar television set and a car," he said.

Father just shook his head. "I know," he said. And he does too. Father's always having to help out Isaiah and people. He sipped his drink and kind of leaned forward. "Had a letter yesterday—from a newspaperman in New York. Seems he wants to come down and write something about this situation."

Mr. Ewing frowned. "Well, for Godsake tell him not to come! We've got enough trouble without those birds stirring up any more."

"I don't think he's that sort," Father said. "He said he was a friend of one of Sarah's cousins. Newspaperman, too."

"Yes, well, they're all alike. There hasn't been a decent word written about the South in ten years—not a word in *one* of those damn Yankee newspapers."

Father kind of laughed. "They don't seem to understand us. Do they?"

Mr. Ewing leaned back. "Hell, no. I wish some of those left-wing liberals would come down here and pay that last bill I paid."

41

I was violently interested in this—not about colored people but about that newspaperman. I know I shouldn't have interrupted or anything but I just wanted to know. I asked Father just right out—"Will that man stay with us? In our house and everything?"

Father winked at me and put his finger to his lips. "I haven't told your mother yet."

I knew what he meant. Father's always asking people to come and visit us and Mother has to do all the junk about them. Father just doesn't understand how much work it is having people all the time. Still, we never have had anything like that in our house—I mean somebody like a Northern newspaperman!

I wanted to hear more about it, but Mrs. Foster butted in. "Aaaaaallison," she said, "I want you to get Harry and me a little farm. I want one just like this—with some little calves and eeeeverything."

Throw up! I got up with my nuts again. Mr. Foster took one and asked me how school was. That's about all he ever asks, but at least he asks. I said, "Fine."

But, frankly, I was exasperated out of my mind. So what I did was I went on back to the kitchen. Right away I saw this glass on the sink and it had a lot of highball still left in it. I guess it was Mother's, because she really isn't wild about drinking very much.

"Hey, Velvet," I said, but she just kind of made a noise in her throat and didn't take her hands down from her face.

"Well, I do declare," I said, and took a huge swallow out of the glass. It tasted just lovely, so I took another one.

"Feeeee-licia!" Velvet said.

"I'm drunk! I'm drunk! I'm drunk!" I said, and started weaving around in the kitchen. "I'm the biggest drunkard in town!"

"Now you stop that!" Velvet said. "You oughtta be shamed."

"I'ze so drunk I can't even sheeee." I started slurping around all over the place.

Velvet took the glass from my hand.

"Give it to me," I said. "I've gotta have my booze. Gotta have it." I got the glass back and some of it slopped on the floor.

"You ain't funny."

"Wheeeee," I said. "I'm drunk...I'm drunk...." And started staggering over toward the stove.

But then I heard Velvet. She was out in the living room!

"Miz Sarah, you better come 'ere. Feeeelicia been dranking whisky agin."

I put the glass down. They were all laughing. Velvet! I could have killed her. In front of the Ewings and everybody. Telling on me, in front of everybody. She hates me. Everybody hates me. They worship Arthur, but they hate me—Velvet, Mother—Father—all of them. They despise me! I went on back by the refrigerator on the back porch and waited for Velvet and Mother to start shouting at me. But then I heard Mr. Foster's voice—loud—from the living room.

He let out a kind of yell. "The South's gonna RIIISE agin!"

I nearly dropped dead. Pitiful Mr. Foster must have got drunk.

5

Velvet and I sat in the back seat on the way home and didn't say one word to each other. Both of us just sat there with our mouths clamped shut and Mother kept talking about Christmas, how much she had to do, but it was all worth it, she guessed, because Arthur would be coming home.

We didn't hear too much from Arthur after Thanksgiving. He did write that they had had a blizzard up in Connecticut and we read something in the paper about it, too. Arthur said he nearly froze to death, and his algebra teacher got mad with him because all he did was sit in class and stare at the snow.

He also wrote about their Christmas concert. He said it was a tremendous success except one of the Wise Men let out this tremendous burp right in the middle of "Silent Night" and the whole audience got hysterical. Mother said she thought that was very

43

crude of Arthur to write that and she hoped he wasn't losing his "fine feeling for things." You see, another odd thing about Arthur is he really seems to like music, not just jazz and stuff like that. He likes deep music, too. That's why Mother let him take music lessons.

Anyway, Mother had started having prostrations over Christmas. I can't understand why she does that. When it comes, she loves Christmas, but for weeks beforehand she's mad at everybody and says not one soul will help her and that she's tired of always being the one that has to create the spirit in the house.

I try to help with decorating the tree and things like that, but it's all the other junk that makes her so furious. For days before Arthur actually got home, she was busy "getting things ready" for him. She decorated the silver epergne and chandelier in the dining room with holly, and when she asked me how I thought Arthur would like it, I said I thought he would, but I knew he probably wouldn't even notice it. Then we had to weave smilax all the way up the stairway, even to the third floor where Arthur's room is. Mother got furious with Isaiah and I because she said we had stuffed the railing instead of weaving it gracefully. Mother is very partial to graceful things. On our door we have a boxwood wreath she makes herself instead of just a bought one.

Well, it was just too bad Arthur's report card had to arrive the day before he did. It came winging in with all the Christmas cards, and at first I thought it was a bill. But then I saw the postmark. Arthur had made all C's and D's, even though he had been put back a grade. I kept looking at the card and thinking how beautifully someone up there had written the letter D.

But even without the report card I didn't think Arthur had changed very much. He got off the train, wrinkled and grinning, and I thought his hair had grown a lot and his socks were very wide and stretched at the top. Other than that, I couldn't see any real difference.

He did seem to have more energy though. I did notice that and I heard Mother say, "He does seem to be more alert, don't you

44

think, Allison?" But that was about all, except for this one very horrifying thing he started doing.

Arthur got home on Saturday, and on Sunday, Mother and Arthur and I went to church. The Reverend Agee had already left and they were having supply rectors until Mr. Ewing could go up to Virginia and persuade the fox-hunting rector to come to Ashton. Mother said we had to be loyal to the church and support the supply rectors. Father usually goes but he said he thought he was getting flu and believed he would stay home this time. It was a good thing he did, too, because if he had gone he would have died of horror over Arthur.

See, our church is very small and low because we're Episcopalians. Just about everybody else in Ashton are Baptists or Methodists, and we don't have any high Episcopalians because the South doesn't much like them. I used to be very ashamed of being Episcopalian because we have to kneel and Baptists and Methodists don't. I never used to kneel if I saw a Baptist in the church, but I got over it last year. Anyway, Mother always walks down the aisle first and then I and Arthur. That was what was so terrible. As soon as Arthur got inside the church he started curtsying!

It was terrible. Crossing himself and curtsying! He did it again when we got to our pew, and Mother saw him this time. She just glanced at him and went right on singing "Stand Up, Stand Up For Jesus."

I punched Arthur and whispered, "What're you doing *that* for?" I could feel the red all over my face and even on my neck.

Arthur didn't say anything. He just looked at me like I was an idiot. Then when the cross came by—down he went again and nearly knocked his kneecap off on the pew in front of him. It made this loud noise and I could have killed him.

Afterward, Mother asked him where he had learned to do that. And Arthur said "at school." Boys genuflected all over the place at school, he said. But Mother said she didn't believe it was a good idea to do that at home because no one else seemed to be

45

doing it. She thought it was a good idea to follow the service just as we always had. Arthur said well maybe, but he was rubbing his knee.

We had roast beef for Sunday dinner and Arthur started talking about school again. He had been talking about it all the night before and I thought we'd heard enough by that time. Frankly, I don't think I was terribly happy with the sort of atmosphere Arthur's return had caused in the house. No one could have cared less, even if I'd dropped dead right in the middle of the roast beef.

"They certainly do write pretty D's up there, Arthur," I said. But Mother said since it was Sunday we shouldn't talk about that now and she smiled at Arthur.

"How are you getting along with your roommate now, Arthur?" she asked. "You haven't said a word about him."

Arthur frowned. "Horrible! He's the worst old bastard I ever saw. Everybody calls him 'Mr. Peabody!'"

Father's fork came down on the table and Mother said, "Arthur!"

"Huh?" Arthur said, looking from Mother to Father.

"We don't speak that way in this house," Father said.

"Well, that's what they call him."

Most of the time Mother and Father are extremely partial to Arthur. Grade time and when he does all those stupid things is the time they hate him.

Two days after Christmas he lost the new topcoat he'd gotten. I heard Mother out in the hall, "You're the most careless child I've ever known! Well, you'll just have to freeze to death!"

Poor Arthur. He can't ever seem to do anything right. The atmosphere in the house was pretty bad after that. Arthur started his old sitting around and staring again. One afternoon I went into the library and there he was, rared back in Father's red leather chair by the Christmas tree. He was flipping through an old copy of the *Saturday Evening Post*. I was bored. I'd called up everybody in town and they all were doing something, at least nobody answered the phone.

46

"Have you ever been so bored you thought you'd scream?" I asked him.

"Uh uh," he said, which is his way of saying he doesn't want to talk. He kept right on flipping. He was all stretched out in the chair with his feet on the footstool. He had on this T-shirt and khaki pants and I got to thinking it was strange that Arthur was so chubby round the waist. Everybody else in the family is so thin. I wish it had been me that was chubby instead of him. It's pretty good to be chubby if you're a girl.

"Is everybody rich up there, Arthur?" I asked him in this very mild voice. I wanted him to talk. "Up there in Connecticut? Really rich?"

"Pretty," he said. Flip. Flip.

"Are they all rich?"

He looked at me then and started getting interested, because he stretched and the magazine fell on the floor.

"There's this one boy's father—he's from Pittsburgh and he owns the United States Steel Company and also Gulf Oil Company." He started striking this match on his shoe.

"Is he nice?" I asked and laid down on my stomach on the sofa.

"He's not bad." He blew out the match. "You oughtta see when his mother and father come to school. They come up in this tremendous Cadillac and everybody starts flying around all over the place. They're gonna give a building or something."

"Gosh," I said. "I don't think I'd like it up there." I was wondering if anybody would fly around when Mother and Father came. I guess not. "Isn't everybody different and all?"

"Pretty. There's not another Southerner but me and they're always laughing at everything I do. They even laugh because the name of the train I come up on is named The Southerner."

"What's so funny about that?"

"I dunno. They just go around knocking themselves out over anything. Always talking about 'cotton-pickin' something or other.' They hate Georgia."

Poor Arthur. It isn't so good being the poor one when everybody else is so rich. I was wondering if that was why everybody laughed at him—because he was poorer than everybody and not just because he was a Southerner.

"Do you guess we'll ever be rich?" I asked.

"Nawww. Not a chance."

"Why?"

"Cause, shoot, you've got to live in the North."

"I don't see why. There're people in Atlanta that're rich. And the Ewings are."

"The Ewings aren't anything. Nobody's like they are up there. They've got the whole thing sewed up. Up there, there're people that own their own jets and stuff."

"Really?" I was wondering what it would be like to be that rich. "Would you want to live up there, Arthur? I mean if you could? Forever?"

"Nawwww."

"Why not?"

"They're just no good, that's all."

"Why?"

He started screwing up his mouth like he does sometimes when he's really thinking. "There's some pretty good folks up there, I guess, but most of them think they're pretty hot stuff."

"Snobs, you mean."

"Yeah."

"I wouldn't be a snob for anything. Would you?"

"Naw."

A red Christmas ball fell off the tree and crashed to the floor. I looked at it splattered on the floor, the silver insides. In a week it would be New Year's, and we'd have to start taking the decorations down. After that Arthur'd be leaving again. "Do you want to go back?" I asked.

"Oh, it'll do," he said and gave out this huge yawn. "When you get to be a senior you can smoke and stuff."

"Not 'til then?"

"A pipe, that's all. You gotta go in this one room to do it."

48

"Gosh, you've got almost five more years before you can do that. I mean, being put back a grade and everything."

"Yeah, I guess so." He looked exceedingly tragic.

Then I asked him, and I don't know why I did, but I did. I said—"You've never really ever had a very good time, have you, Arthur? I mean a really good time?"

He looked up at the ceiling and his eyes behind his glasses looked wide. "I guess I have," he said. "I've had *some* pretty good times."

I wanted to cry, really this time. He literally hadn't ever had a good time, and I knew he didn't like it up in Connecticut either. He was just saying so. I guess he didn't want us to have to suffer for him.

"I think you're going to be rich some day, Arthur," I said.

"Me? Why?"

"I just do, that's all. You just sort of look rich."

"How does somebody look like that, for hellsake?"

Arthur had started cursing all the time. I told him so.

He picked up another match on Father's table and struck it. "Shoot, you oughtta hear what they say at school! Even the masters. Mother'd have one million fits."

"Even the masters?"

"Yep."

I sat up. "What'd they say? What do they say, Arthur?"

"Aw, they're always calling everybody bastards and stuff like that. Even worse."

"The masters?"

Out went the match. "Yeah, old Jimerson—he teaches history— one day the chalk broke off and he said 'goddamn bastard'—right in front of everybody, and then he tried to cover it up. Everybody cusses in the North. It's not so bad when you think about it."

"I guess you have to, if everybody else does."

"Yep," he said. And I guess he was bored because he picked up the magazine and started looking through it again. I went on outside and decided I was going to start calling everybody bastard. Everybody at school would die.

49

That night at dinner we all had an unpleasantness. Father started it by talking about Mother's renegade cousin, Hugo, up in New York, and Mother wanted to know why Father had to bring him up at the table.

"Because we've got a guest coming," Father said.

"Coming here?" Mother said. "Now, at *this* time?"

Then Father told her about that Northern newspaperman.

"Did Hugo tell him about us?" She was using a very annoyed tone of voice because Hugo is a disgrace. He works in New York on this news magazine that's always laughing about the South.

"I guess so," Father said. "He wants to come down for the weekend. Hugo told him we were typical Southerners or something like that. I guess he wants our reactions."

"You mean about—?" Mother pointed at the kitchen which meant Velvet and Isaiah.

"I suppose." Father looked tired.

"You mean he's coming from town?" Arthur asked.

"What town?" I said.

"New Yo*rrrrr*k! What else?"

"Yes," Father said, "He works there. Seems he also writes novels."

Arthur's eyes started getting very wide. I guess he was scared of meeting somebody that famous, too.

Mother plumped her coffee cup down on the saucer. "Do we have to have him here?" she asked. "Right after Christmas. I think that's rather nervy."

"He's on his way to Florida," Father said.

"Well, do we have to have him in the house?" I knew Mother would be mad.

"Where else?" Father asked.

"Oh, Allison! Now, I'm just not prepared to have another guest. Especially now when Arthur's home."

"I don't care," Arthur said. "This English teacher of mine—he used to be a newspaperman up there. Man, he worships Negroes. I know all about stuff like that."

Mother let out her exasperated sigh. "Oh, dear."

50

But I was out of my mind with glee. "You mean we're going to be written up?" I asked.

Mother's eyes got very blue. "Heavens, Allison! I hope not! Well, I just won't stand for it."

"Why?" Father asked. "Have you got something to hide?"

"Of course not. But I just don't like things like that! You know that." She really doesn't either. In Charleston it isn't good manners to be written up in newspapers—just when you're married and dead. Then it's all right. Other times it's common, as you know.

Father folded his napkin and pushed back the chair. "Why, you'll be famous, Sarah. Don't you want to be famous?"

"No!"

They both left, and Arthur and I just stayed on at the table.

"*Us* written up!" I said.

"He doesn't want to write us up," Arthur said.

"What's he coming for then?"

"Just to look at us. People up there think we're peculiar or something."

"Why?" I asked. "I don't think we are."

"Well, *they* do."

I got to thinking about that. I knew a Northern girl once. She came to Ashton visiting. She talked very fast and I couldn't hardly understand a word she said, except that she said her father hadn't wanted her to come down here because everybody had worms. I told her nobody had worms, but she said all Southerners did but didn't know it. I asked Mother and she said "no." I thought that girl was very peculiar herself. She had a white nurse.

"I'll betcha he wants to write us up," I said. "Just think. Us!"

"That's nothing," Arthur said. "There's this one boy at school and his father owns the *Times,* you know, and practically every other paper in town, and he's written up practically every day."

Arthur had certainly met a lot of great people. It made you feel pretty pathetic. "Yeah, but us," I said. "Everybody in the North'll see it. Even in Connecticut."

Arthur kind of looked up at the ceiling and tried not to smile.

51

I knew how thrilled he was. The people up there'd think we weren't so bad after all. I couldn't wait to tell Velvet and Isaiah. They'd die.

I went on back to the kitchen. Velvet was washing dishes and Isaiah was sitting on this small stepladder we've got in the pantry.

"Guess what?" I said.

"Whut?" Velvet was in a very bored mood. Isaiah didn't say anything. He was in a bored mood, too.

"We're all going to be written up—you and me and Isaiah and everybody."

Velvet glanced around at me. "Whatchu talkin' 'bout?"

"This newspaperman from New York is coming—" I could scarcely get it out—"and he's going to write us all up!"

"Whut for?" Velvet asked. She turned her mouth down and frowned at me in that way she has when she thinks I'm telling a story. (I have a faculty sometimes of being untruthful.)

I looked at Isaiah. His neck was getting awfully long. "Because we're all Southerners and because Father's president of the bank, I guess. He'll probably have to take our picture, too."

"Ain't nobody gonna take Velvet's picture." She turned back to the sink.

"Aw, Velvet, just because you haven't had your open-faced crowns fixed yet." Velvet's gold crowns are always coming off her two front teeth and she despises her dentist. "Don't you think it's thrilling, Isaiah?"

Isaiah giggled. "Sho *is*." I knew he'd be glad.

Velvet took off her apron and took down her black hat.

"Get your crowns fixed *tonight*, Velvet! You'll look really pretty."

"That black dentist ain't doin' nothin' but robbin' me blind." She put on her hat and opened the kitchen door. "Come on, Isaiah."

"See you tomorrow," I called after them.

"O—kay," Velvet said.

I stayed on in the kitchen for a while, but it was boring with everybody gone. I decided I'd go right on upstairs and brush my hair one thousand times. If they took our picture I certainly didn't want to look poor and hicky. I vowed I wasn't going to look that way if it killed me! I wanted Arthur's friends up in Connecticut to think we were nice.

6

Ohhhhhh me. You don't know what it's like around our house when we're getting ready to have guests. We're positively the most peculiar family you ever saw. Velvet's in a bad mood, Mother's in a bad mood, and I just try to stay out of the way. Velvet doesn't like to have guests because of all the extra work and Mother thinks everything ought to be decent. Everything in the guest room has to be cleaned, and she even puts flowers by the bedside. It was camellia time, so who do you guess had to go out and pick one million camellias? Me! Mother told me to be sure and get the stems long enough because she likes to put them in my grandmother's old crystal bowl.

Arthur wasn't doing one thing but fixing himself a Coca-Cola. "*You* oughtta be doing this," I said, as I came into the kitchen.

"Do what? Fix flow-ers?"

"Yes, it's developing. You oughtta know how in case you ever get a home of your own."

"When I get one I'm not gonna have any flowers. To me, they're revolting." He started rattling the ice in his glass.

I jerked off one of the leaves. "Arthur, you have absolutely no spiritual sense. None a-tall."

"Stop trying to talk like Mother," he said. "You're always trying to talk like her and it sounds stupid."

"No, I'm not." Arthur's always saying that, which is the most insane thing in the world.

He went on back into the living room to finish his Coca-Cola and, I guess, to stare. Finally, I got the flowers fixed and went dragging on upstairs with them. The guest room looked all right

53

when Mother and Velvet got through. The curtains were fluffy and white, and Velvet had just got through washing the canopies on the beds. If you ask me, I think camellias and canopy beds look silly for a man, especially a Northern newspaperman that writes novels. I told Mother so, but she said for me just to "run along now."

There wasn't much of any place for me to run to though. Isaiah was in the kitchen polishing all the silver, and with the place smelling like polish and the quails unfreezing and junk all over the place, it was the most depressing place you ever saw. Isaiah never has a clean white coat and that always brings up another fuss. Mother has told him time and time again he ought to have one in readiness, but he doesn't wear one much, just when he's waiting on the table at night and most of the time his sleeves are too short. Velvet had to stop what she was doing and wash Isaiah a coat and let the sleeves down. Mother started walking around clicking garden scissors and giving out orders. Sometimes, especially guest time, Mother can be almost like an officer in the army.

About an hour before the person gets there though, she's all dressed and calmed down and talking cheerily about how really, actually good it is to have guests because you get so much general cleaning done. You never have seen anybody that has as much energy as my mother. By the end of the day we're all dragging around—Velvet, Isaiah, Arthur and me—but she's all ready to go and is delighted someone is coming.

"What's the man's name?" I asked her.

"Mr. Hopper," she said. "Mr. Hopper. Felicia, don't put your feet on the coffee table that way. Go get dressed. You look like a ragamuffin."

"He's not coming 'til five-thirty."

"Well, it's four-thirty now. Up!" She started clapping her hands. "Where's Arthur?"

"Upstairs, in his room. He hasn't done one thing all day."

"Well, he's got to look decent now." She started out the room but glanced around. "Up now!"

I was exhausted and started staring with my eyes bulged open.

54

"Stop being silly!" Mother said.

My eyes finally banged shut. "Ohhhhh me." I dragged myself off the sofa and went up and put on my black and white plaid dress. It's the only one that makes me look fatter because it has a pretty wide skirt. I also brushed my poor sad hair again and stared at myself in the mirror for about a half hour. I do that a lot—when nobody's looking. When somebody's looking I hardly even glance. Mother says just very selfish people stare at themselves in the mirror. As I told you, I'm rather selfish at times, but I speak to everybody.

When I went back downstairs I heard Mother tell Isaiah to go to the bus station now and pick up Mr. Hopper.

"To de *bus* station?" Isaiah asked. "He must be mighty po."

"Why?" Mother asked him.

"No rich folks ever rides on de bus."

Mother smiled. "He probably couldn't get connections—train connections," was all she said.

"He's famous, Isaiah," I said. "He writes books and everything."

Isaiah's eyes started getting very wide. I knew he was scared to death because I knew I was. I've never met any really famous people. We tried to find Mr. Hopper's novels at the library so we could mention them to him, but Miss Cramer, the librarian, said she didn't buy just every bit of trash that came out. Miss Cramer thinks most new books are trash, but she has gall-bladder trouble.

After Isaiah had gone, Mother said, "I wonder how long he plans to stay?"

"I don't know. Velvet wanted to know, too."

"People should let you know how long they plan to stay," she said. "Now, Felicia, you remember that. If you ever visit anybody, let them know exactly when you're arriving and exactly when you're leaving. It's thoughtless not to."

"I probably won't ever visit anybody," I said, "except Winky or somebody in Charleston."

"Well, you might some day. Someone might ask you."

"I doubt it," I said, and started thinking about my tragic life ahead. I have this feeling my life is going to be terribly tragic.

I'll probably die writhing in a gutter somewhere. Somebody'll find me and they'll say, "Why, it's Felicia Whitfield. What a pity!"

I plopped down in a chair.

"Why do you have to sit like that, Felicia—with your legs all sprawled that way?"

"I don't know. It's uncomfortable to sit all straight all the time."

"Well, don't do that when the guest comes. Some day we'll have to practice sitting."

I straightened up. "How are you supposed to sit?"

She sat down. "Like this," she said. "Slightly forward in the chair—shoulders straight—and your ankles crossed."

She looked very pretty. She had on a grey tweed dress and the color made her eyes seem sort of grey, too.

"Not like this," she said, and she started imitating me, slinking down in the chair with her legs stretched out in front of her.

I died laughing and so did she. Mother and I have worlds of fun sometimes. A lot of the time she's like an army officer, but sometimes she's more fun than anybody I know. She has a tremendous sense of humor when she wants to.

But then we heard the car coming down the driveway in front. Mother stood up. "Well, here he is."

I got up, too. Frankly, my heart was pounding away inside. "Arthur's not down yet!" I said.

She must not have heard me, because she went on out onto the veranda. Mother always does that and I think it's nice because she really welcomes people. Besides, it's stupid, I think, just to wait in the living room and pretend you're lazily sitting around when everybody knows you're not.

I didn't go out with her, but the door was open so I could see. Gosh, I was scared! I thought my heart was going to pop right out of me. Never in our entire existence have we ever had somebody like a Northern newspaperman visiting in our house.

Well, I nearly dropped dead when the man got out of the car. He had this iron-grey hair and it was crew cut! Also he was wearing tennis shoes! Really, he was. He had on this ancient green

56

jacket and a camera hanging off his shoulder. I guess maybe he'd worn all that, just because he was riding on the bus.

Right away he started looking up at the house, and then when he saw Mother he sort of waved and came galloping up the steps to her.

"Mrs. *Whit*-full?" he said, grabbing Mother's hand and then he let out this kind of scratching laugh. "Heavens," he said, looking down at his jacket, "I'm a wreck! A complete wreck. Pardon the way I look. I didn't have a second to change."

"I think you look very comfortable," Mother said.

"The bus was a nightmare! A complete nightmare! Women with sacks of food, crying babies"—he glanced back at the car where Isaiah was—"and the Neeeeegroes jammed in the back."

"Well, come in and relax," Mother said. "Maybe an Old Fashioned will bring you back again."

"You're a darling," he said, "a complete darling!"

Nobody's ever called Mother a "darling" before. I don't think even Father has.

But then there *I* was, standing in the hall, grinning. I hate times like that. You never know what to do until you're introduced. Mother says if I'm not introduced I'm supposed to go up to the person, curtsy, and say "I'm the daughter of the house." I've only done it once, and I think the person thought I was insane. I could have killed Arthur for not being down. I always have to do everything first.

"And who may I ask is this?" he said, smiling down at me. He had the reddest face I'd ever seen—sort of purple. But he was still kind of handsome, I thought. His nose wasn't broken or anything.

"I'm—" I started to say, and I was wondering if he thought I would take a pretty good picture.

"This is Felicia," Mother said, "our daughter."

Down I went, but I just kind of jerked a curtsy and stretched out my hand. I was really beaming though.

"Charming," he said. "Absolutely charming." His hand was pretty wet. He wanted to know if I was the only one, but Mother said, no, we had a son and he'd be down in a few minutes.

57

That was the end of me. Right away Mr. Hopper started looking around the hall. We still had our Christmas decorations up. We never take them down until the day before New Year's. The smilax going up the stairway was sort of dry.

"Lovely. Perfectly lovely home," Mr. Hopper said, and he kind of bent backward and glanced into the living room. "And that," he said, pointing, "just a-bout *there* is a Sully. Lovely. Ab-so-lute-ly lovely. I knew Sully did mostly Southerners."

"Then you're interested in art, Mr. Hopper?" Mother asked.

"Bob," he said. "Please, just Bob." He let out his scratching laugh. "Yes, actually I am. Especially the old. The contemporary unglues me." Scratch. Scratch.

I decided I was going to remember that—"unglues me." I was going to say it Monday at school.

"Well, come now," Mother said. "Isaiah—" Isaiah was coming through the door, struggling with Mr. Hopper's luggage. "Isaiah, would you bring us two Old Fashioneds, please?"

Mr. Hopper just stood there, smiling at Isaiah and all his struggling. "Isaiah was lovely to meet me at the bus. We had a very nice chat coming to the house. Didn't we, Isaiah?"

Isaiah came through the door. "Yes *sir,*" he said, but then on his way up the stairs he turned and glanced at Mr. Hopper with these tremendous white eyes. I guess Isaiah'd never seen anybody like Mr. Hopper before either.

Mr. Hopper took off his camera. "Goodness," he said, looking down at his jacket again. "I am a wreck. It's been hectic, absolutely hectic."

"Well, come in and be seated, Bob," Mother said. It sounded funny, her calling him Bob. "Or would you rather go up and freshen up a bit?"

"No, I'm all right, really." Scratch. Scratch. I guess he was sort of embarrassed, Mother's mentioning going upstairs to freshen up, because *you* know what that means!

We went on into the living room. "White walls," he said. "High ceilings and—and—the molding! Charming! I adore these old Georgian homes."

"The house is quite old," Mother said. "It has quite a history. If you're interested, I'm sure Mr. Whitfield would like to tell you about it."

"My grandmother burned our other house down," I said.

Both of them looked at me. I guess I shouldn't have said that. It does sound kind of strange if you don't explain.

Mr. Hopper didn't say anything, but I saw this twinkle in Mother's eye. I kept wondering where in the world Arthur was.

"Beauti-ful rugs," Mr. Hopper said. "Old, worn Persians."

I thought that was kind of rude of him, saying our rugs were worn.

"Yes, the older Persians are nice, aren't they?" was all Mother said.

"Bless you," Mr. Hopper said, almost touching Mother's shoulder with his open palm. "Bless you for not having wall-to-wall. I *loathe* wall-to-wall."

Mother just smiled at him. Mr. Hopper wasn't conceited at all, being from New York and everything.

Then he started weaving around looking at everything—the portraits, tables, silver, chairs. I think Mother sort of enjoyed it though. She's mad about all the junk in our house. A lot of the stuff is from her family in Charleston and the rest is Whitfield. Some of the things, though, aren't so hot. I mean there's one table she had this man out in the country make and Mr. Hopper started yelling around about it. I guess he thought that was a "gem," too. Everything else was a gem, he said. He thought our whole house was a gem. That's the way famous novelists and people talk. They kind of scare you because every time they look at you, you think they're thinking about how to write you up.

Anyway, I thought Mr. Hopper was very nice saying such lovely things about our house. I wondered if he really meant it, because you know up in New York where everybody's so rich their things are one million times better than our old stuff. We can't afford to even build a new bathroom.

When we sat down Mother said, "Well, now, tell me *how* is Hugo?" She had her hands pressed together as if she really wanted to know, but I knew she didn't care much because she definitely is not very partial to our Cousin Hugo. He's from South Carolina, too, but he had to go up to New York before he could get a job on a magazine. He wrote one write-up about Georgia that was simply terrible. It was when all those people started throwing rocks at the University of Georgia. Of course, it was terrible to throw rocks, but that didn't mean the whole state of Georgia and everybody in it was terrible. Hugo even made fun of the way we talk in the South and Mother says Hugo used to talk exactly the same way. Everybody that knows him calls him a renegade, even in Charleston. He ought to be ashamed, but he isn't. Father says he's trying to win a prize because the only way you can win a prize nowadays is by having courage and telling how glorious Negroes are and how horrible Southern white people are—even nice ones. I was wondering if Mr. Hopper was trying to win a prize, too.

He leaned back in the winged-back chair. "Hugo is fine!" he said. "Doing a remarkable job. Really remarkable. You know he's going to Africa on this Congo thing."

"I don't particularly envy him that," Mother said. "Such a *frightful* situation."

"Yesssssss," said Mr. Hopper. He suddenly looked one million years older. All these lines round his mouth and eyes started popping out. He surely did sit funny, too. But I guess it was because of the tennis shoes. When you wear tennis shoes you do all sorts of strange things you don't do when you have on just plain shoes.

"Which paper are you with, Bob?" Mother asked.

"No paper. I free-lance. The piece I'm doing now is for the *News Review.*"

"Oh, fine," Mother said. "We take the magazine. We'll look forward to your article."

"Yes, well, these pieces keep me in money so I can write books."

"Do you feel as if you've been successful—so far?"

Mr. Hopper hit his head with his palm. "Lordy, yes! The South is absolutely exploding! Had an hour's talk with Ralph McGill on the *Constitution.* Fascinating. McGill's in an enviable position. Also talked to Luther King. Clear as a bell and"—he sat up straighter, practically knocking himself out with delight over what he was going to say next—"and this adorable old Neeeeegress. Her father had been a slave! Imagine. She must have been ninety, at least. *She* told me some things—" he frowned and shook his head. "It shouldn't be, Mrs. Whit-full. Negroes are human beings, too. It shouldn't be. No."

Boy, I'll bet Mother was mad about that. That's one expression that can really make her mad—people that try to tell her colored people are human beings, as if she doesn't know it. She didn't show she was mad though.

"Do call me Sarah," Mother said. She took a handkerchief from her pocket. "Tell me—what can we do for you here in Ashton?"

Mr. Hopper crossed one leg over the other. "Ohhhhh, I don't know really. Atmosphere more than anything else, I guess. You see, I haven't had a chance to talk to—" he smiled—"someone in your, well, someone who enjoys the social advantages you do."

"Social?" Mother said and she gave a short laugh. "We're the last people on earth who are social."

"Well, class then. Let me put it that way." Scratch. Scratch. "I was thrilled when Hugo suggested I might come here. You see, Hugo and I were in Italy together. He was writing a piece on Russia—" he looked around as if somebody was lurking in a corner trying to hear him. "Don't tell him, but the bird never left his hotel room in Rome. I don't think he even *saw* Russia." Mr. Hopper thought that was hilariously funny. "Damn guy nearly won a prize for it, too."

"I remember the article," Mother said.

"Yessssss," Mr. Hopper said, still grinning over cousin Hugo.

Then this great huge silence came down. It was embarrassing and we were all straining our brains, trying to think of something else to say.

"Are you going to write *us* up?" I asked. It just came out and I don't know how I got up the nerve to just come right out and ask it.

61

Mr. Hopper looked at me as if I'd just popped into the room, then he looked right away at Mother again. "I do hope—"

But then Isaiah came in with the Old Fashioneds. Right away I saw my old kitchen glass standing up there on the tray by a coke bottle. The old coke bottle looked stupid on a silver tray. I'm going to die of joy when I can start drinking Old Fashioneds. To me, they're the best drinks in the world. I've tasted them thousands of times.

"Lovely," said Mr. Hopper as he took his glass. "Just what I've been waiting for." Scratch. Scratch.

Mother took hers and told Isaiah to bring us some napkins. Isaiah never remembers napkins.

"But back to your question," Mr. Hopper said, stirring the drink with one of the tiny silver spoons Mother always uses. He looked at her as if it had been her that had asked the question. "But let me ask you first—*would* you mind if I referred to you as a family—*you* know—typical Southern family, good connections, that sort of thing?" He looked older again.

Mother sat up straighter. I couldn't wait to hear what she had to say.

"I don't think so, Mr. Hopper." She didn't call him Bob. "You see, some of us here in the South are very conservative people. We really don't like publicity."

Mr. Hopper started getting all nervous. "Of course. Of course," he said. "You wouldn't believe it, but I'm a pretty conservative bird myself. I certainly understand your fears."

"There aren't any fears actually."

"Well, I know—" he was smiling at Mother as if she had said something extremely pathetic. "Mr. Whitfull, a banker—bad for business—things like that. I understand some Southerners have been almost ruined by some of their views."

"No, it isn't that at all," Mother said. "Whatever we believe we don't mind saying. We're just not partial to publicity of any sort, that's all." She touched the handkerchief to her nose again.

I wish Mother hadn't said that! It sounded kind of rude to me. Besides, I knew Mr. Hopper was sitting there thinking we were hicks. I was glad Mother was having the Ewings and them over after dinner. The Ewings know how things are up in New York.

"I like Negroes," I said. But both Mother and Mr. Hopper laughed.

"Heh, heh, heh," laughed Mr. Hopper in this new laugh. Heh, heh, heh, I thought. He doesn't know, but I think I know some things he doesn't know. Velvet's told me more things than she'd ever tell Mother and Father.

"Fascinating. Ab-so-lute-ly...." But then I nearly passed out through the sofa. Arthur came into the room! He had a pencil stuck behind his ear and he was wearing tennis shoes! White ones! They looked tremendous!

I just stared at him and Mr. Hopper got up from his chair.

"This is our son, Bob," Mother said in this very pale voice. "Arthur—Mr. Hopper."

Arthur kind of stood up very straight and lunged his hand into Mr. Hopper's. "Hopper! How ya, man?"

Horrible! I have never, never, in all my entire life seen Arthur act or talk like that.

Mr. Hopper started rubbing his hand.

"Arthur's home for the holidays," Mother said. "He's at a little school in Connecticut this year."

"Is that soooo?" Mr. Hopper said, looking very curiously at Arthur. "Do you like Connecticut, Arthur?"

"I like being in town better," Arthur said.

"In town?"

"Yep!"

"Oh, in New York! Well, that's fine."

"Come and sit with us, Arthur," Mother said. "We were just telling Mr. Hopper something about Ashton."

"Yeh?" Arthur said, and kind of touched his pencil behind his ear. "It's kind of a hick town, this town."

I could have killed Arthur for saying that. I knew exactly what he was doing. He was trying to make Mr. Hopper think he was this ancient somebody that knew all about New York and all

63

that. What he'd done, I bet, was look out the upstairs window when Mr. Hopper came in. That's the only time he could have seen the tennis shoes. I knew Mother was about to die.

Mr. Hopper sat back down and Arthur kind of swaggered over to the sofa where I was. When he sat down he threw one leg over the other like Mr. Ewing does sometimes.

Mr. Hopper sipped his drink again, then looked at Mother. "Yes, well, as I was saying, I *would* like to include some of your views in this piece. I want to be as fair as possible, get both sides. Of course I wouldn't use your name."

"Why don't you ask Allison about that," Mother said, and she smiled very prettily.

"You want to know about colored people and stuff?" Arthur asked.

I didn't even look at him. Arthur knows as well as I do that it's terrible to butt in.

"That's the general idea, Arthur." But then Mr. Hopper looked at me. "Felicia," he said in this extremely childish voice, "would *you* mind going to school with little Neeeeegro children?" He asked it as if I were this dumb idiot that didn't know about things.

"I dunno," I said, jerking my shoulders up and down. "I haven't thought much about it," which was a lie! Just the other day I was thinking that it might be kind of fun, marching into school with a bayonet in my back and soldiers and tanks wandering all over the place. I had this image of myself on *Life* magazine with this helmeted soldier pointing his bayonet at me. All these big city newspapermen and everybody would be hanging around watching, and Mother and Velvet would be dying because they'd be afraid I'd get hurt, and Arthur up in Connecticut would see my picture on *Life* and show it to everybody.

"I'm gonna have to go to school with 'em," Arthur said.

Mother looked at him sharply. "Why, Arthur, what are you talking about?"

"Yeah, really," Arthur said, grinning this tremendous grin. "Mr. Sykes—" he looked at Mr. Hopper—"he's the headmaster at this

64

school I go to. He can't wait to get a whole bunch of colored boys in. I may turn out rooming with one."

Mr. Hopper kind of nodded his head. "I understand that's so. A great many of the Eastern prep schools are admitting Neeeeegroes now."

"Yeh," Arthur said. "We haven't gotten one yet, but old Sykes, he's thinking about bringing a whole tribe over from Africa."

"Now, Arthur, stop exaggerating," Mother said. "Mr. Hopper is very serious about all this."

Arthur popped his eyes open at Mother. "So am I; I'm not kidding. Really. Old Jimerson—he teaches history—and he told me at dinner before I left they were going to bring all these Africans over. He said the school had to on account of the world seeing how bad the South treats 'em and everything. Everybody up there— Mr. Sykes and all of 'em—*hate* the South."

"Well, I think you're just a bit confused," Mother said.

Mr. Hopper let out his laugh again. "It all seems so impossible, sitting here," he said. "All the things you know that really exist, the underlying treachery in these sleepy old Southern towns."

Mother laughed her forced laugh. "I don't seem to see the treachery," she said. "There have been incidents, of course, but I imagine these are everywhere. Where is *your* home, Bob? I mean, originally."

"Plainfield. New Jersey." He flicked a large speck off his trouser leg. "Yessir, I'm a New Jersey boy."

"Plainfield must be a lovely town," Mother said. "I've never been there."

"It's all right, I guess. Nothing much to do. Industrial people mostly. I got out quite young." He lit this long cigarette and blew the smoke straight up in the air. "But what do you find to do *here?*"

I told you. I knew he thought we were hicks. I was so embarrassed I could have thrown up.

"Oh, I'm frightfully busy," Mother said. "I do a great deal of church work and entertaining is mostly in the home, you know. Of course I like to garden and there's the children."

65

They both looked at Arthur and I. I felt like a great, huge white rabbit sitting there.

"You're not married, Mr. Hopper?" Mother asked.

"I was." He started moving around in his chair. "Divorced."

Pitiful. I knew he didn't want to tell us that. "My uncle's divorced, too," I said in this loud voice. I wanted him to feel better.

"Yes, well," Mother said and glanced at me. I guess she was furious I'd said that. It's Father's brother that's divorced and he's the biggest scandal in the whole family.

Mr. Hopper was smirking and he took another long drag on his cigarette and started rattling the ice in his glass. "Well," he said finally, "I guess I'm just going to have to come right out and ask you." He was smiling at Mother. "Let me ask you. *Are* you opposed to integration of the races?" He leaned forward and looked like he was studying Mother's face. "I mean truthfully, just for my own curiosity. Are you?"

The way he asked it scared me to death. It was like a dare.

But then the back door slammed. Father had come home.

We had wine for dinner! And I got some. Mr. Hopper talked them into giving it to me.

"Well, all right then," Mother said. "Isaiah, bring Felicia a glass."

"Gooo-ud night!" Arthur said. He shouldn't have been so surprised. It was the first time he'd had any either. Isaiah, though, nearly died, but he brought me a glass anyway and Father got up and poured me some—just this little, but not near as much as Arthur's.

It was a very sour wine and I thought it was charming. Father has bottles and bottles of wine down in the basement, but he keeps the room locked up because Isaiah has tendencies toward drunkenness and we're trying to protect him from it.

I thought it was exceedingly nice of Mr. Hopper to see that I had some wine, too. I really slurped it up. And it was a good dinner, too. We had quails and brown rice and these very long asparagus tips that Velvet and Mother are very partial to. Mother had fixed the epergne with white camellias, and there was a breeze coming in through the French windows which made the candles keep flickering. Mr. Hopper ate four of the little graham biscuits. Mother said, "Now butter them while they're hot!" and the next time Isaiah came around he had some more!

Mr. Hopper looked much better than he did when he first came. He had on a dark suit and real shoes. Also, Arthur. Before dinner Mother insisted that Arthur go back upstairs and put on his other shoes. She said the others just weren't becoming for evening. I guess he was glad he did when he saw Mr. Hopper had changed, too.

Another thing Mr. Hopper liked was the quails. He was entranced with Father because he goes shooting around the farm all the time. He said he was going to remember us next year and try to come down and do some hunting with Father. I guess he thought Georgia was a pretty good place after all.

"We'd like to have you," Father said. But Mother got this funny expression in her eyes which I knew meant she wasn't very overjoyed with having Mr. Hopper come again.

I think Mr. Hopper sort of liked Father. He kept listening to all his talk about cattle and how they were developing into quite an industry in Georgia. I don't know why Mr. Hopper was so interested in that. I would much rather have heard him talk about New York and stuff. During desserttime, which was fruit and cheese (I hate it!), he said Georgia seemed almost like a foreign country.

"And that's exactly how we've been treated for too long," Father said, and he rared back in his chair at the head of the table.

Scratch! Scratch! But it was Arthur that let out the laugh—

67

exactly like Mr. Hopper's. We all just stared at him and he stared right back. I don't know what had come over Arthur. Usually when we have a guest he doesn't say hardly a thing. In some ways Connecticut had made Arthur quite peculiar.

"Yes," Father said, pretending like he didn't notice Arthur, "the South has become the nation's whipping boy again."

"Why do you say that?" Mr. Hopper asked.

Father started folding his napkin. "It's become popular to damn the South—especially in print. This sort of careless editorializing is hurting us—industrially as well as spiritually."

"But wouldn't you say you've deserved it? Criticism, that is?"

Father leaned forward and looked at Mr. Hopper. His eyes were bluer than I've ever seen them. "No, sir," he said very softly.

"That's interesting," Mr. Hopper said.

Father was still looking at him. "We need help down here, Hopper, the right kind. Of course, we have evils here! There are evil people. But I dare say there are in other parts of the country too—yours as well as ours." He leaned back. "*Your* press and *your* commentators do not help us with pious moralizing. It agitates us, hurts us, and we do not appreciate it!"

I wanted to cry. I've never heard Father talk like that and he had made Mr. Hopper feel horrible. He was just sitting there looking down at his napkin. I thought it was terrible for us to all be four and him only one. Father ought not to have talked to such a famous man that way.

But then Mr. Hopper looked up. "I certainly understand your loyalty," he said. "I *do*. But how can you live with people who throw stones and women who scream in the streets at innocent children? How can you? I just can't understand it." He frowned. "And the view it gives the rest of the world—"

"I guess we can live with it just as you in the North apparently live with rioting, prejudice, delinquency, and out-and-out gangsterism." Father picked up his napkin and put it down again. "We don't all throw stones in the South, you know, and our ladies don't all scream at Negro children."

I was terrified Father was going to get really mad, and I think Mother was, too, because she said, "Well, we can talk about this later, gentlemen. Let's have coffee in the other room."

"Yes," Father said, and he smiled at Mr. Hopper. "I'm afraid Sarah's invited some more Rebels for you to meet."

"Good!" Mr. Hopper said, and kind of sprung up from the chair.

Scratch! Scratch! Arthur laughed again. I punched him violently in the ribs and he just frowned at me. Arthur was being the rudest person I'd ever seen.

"Arthur," Mother said. "I'd like to speak with you for a second."

They went into the breakfast room and in a few minutes I kind of sauntered in, too (with my hip out of joint, but nobody was looking).

"But *I* wasn't doing anything," Arthur was saying.

"Well, let's try and be our normal way," Mother said.

"Gooo-ud night, you can't even laugh around this house. Can't even open your mouth without somebody jumping in it."

"That's enough, Arthur," Mother said.

"Well, you can't even—"

Isaiah came in the room with the tray full of coffee cups.

"Bring some ice too please, Isaiah," Mother said. "Some of the others might want something to drink."

"Who all's coming?" I asked.

"The Ewings and the Fosters, and Miss Esther said she'd run over for a minute."

"Miss Esther?" I asked.

"Gooooo-ud night," Arthur said. (He'd started saying that all the time.) "What'ya wanta have *her* for?"

"Because I think Mr. Hopper would like to meet her." Mother was counting the coffee cups on the tray.

"I don't think he would," I kind of mumbled.

"Well, *I* do," Mother said. She gets pretty mad if she thinks somebody's saying something ugly about Miss Esther. Mother simply adores her, but I don't. She never speaks. She's always sending Mother violets and stuff like that. Mother says Esther Stein "is one of the finest people I've ever known." See, she's poor. A long time ago the Steins were very rich. Her father was this famous lawyer that was known all over Georgia, and Miss Esther even studied violin in Germany. But now everybody but Miss Esther is dead and she had to go to work at the water company. She reads books, and everybody in Ashton says she's the most intellectual person in town. She's never hardly ever spoken to me. If you meet her downtown or something she just might—might— say, "Good afternoon, Felicia," but that's all. All the older people worship her, but I don't see why. Frankly, she kind of scares me. She has this black cape she wears all the time.

"Here, Arthur," Mother said. "You take the coffee tray in the living room while Isaiah gets the ice."

"Can I go in for a while, too?" I asked.

"If you want to," Mother said. "But you'd better get to bed soon."

I was delighted. I just hoped Mr. Hopper wouldn't think all our friends were bad. If he was going to write us up and everything, I certainly wanted it to sound nice. Too, I hoped to heaven Mr. Ewing wouldn't get mad at him. I remembered what he'd said out at the farm about Northern newspapermen and things.

When I went in, Mr. Hopper and Arthur were standing up in the middle of the room. Arthur had dumped the tray down on this little table in front of Mother's chair. I guess she wanted me to pass the cups. That's probably the only reason she let me come in.

"You have some fine old portraits here, Arthur," Mr. Hopper said. He was looking at my Charleston great-grandmother's portrait.

"Yeah, they like all this old junk, I guess. We don't have any new ones."

"Very fine," Mr. Hopper said, standing back and squinting his eyes.

"Hey, Mr. Hopper," Arthur said. "Do you know Buzz Hill? Up in New York?"

70

Mr. Hopper turned. "Hill? Is he in banking?"

"Nawwww, he goes to the same school I do. He's from New York City. There're a lotta boys up there from New York City."

"Well, New York's a very big place."

"I know it. I was just wondering if you knew Buzz Hill. He's this huge old boy. Plays football. Just about everybody in New York knows him."

"Nooo, don't believe I know him."

Arthur just kind of shook his head. "I just thought if you knew him, you could tell him you saw me down here."

"I can call him for you, if you want me to."

"Naw, that's okay. I just thought probably you knew him and all."

Mother came into the room and sat down in front of the coffee tray. "Cream and sugar, Mr. Hopper?"

"Just black, thanks." Scratch. Scratch. Scratch.

I handed him his cup, and when he sat down I decided to sit down by him. I kind of folded my hands and tried to sit like Mother had told me to. I'd forgotten that afternoon.

"You're not having any coffee, Felicia?" he asked me.

"No, I never drink coffee at night."

"She never drinks it at all," Arthur said.

I could have gladly killed Arthur, but I pretended I didn't mind and just kind of moved my shoulders up and down.

Mr. Hopper turned to Mother. "Now who is coming tonight?"

"Just a few people. I'd like them to meet you. A Mr. and Mrs. Ewing will be here and—"

"The Ewings have a swimming pool," I said. I knew he would die over that.

"Is that sooo?" he said, and started blinking his eyes.

Mother kind of smiled at him. "And I asked the—"

But then the door bell rang. Father came striding through the front hall and opened the door.

"Aaaaaalllison!" came this voice from outside. I could feel my face getting red all over. Why Mother had to go and invite Mrs. Foster at a time like this I'll *never* know. One time she said she liked to have her because she thought it was nice to have a pretty face in a gathering. Out-of-town people always like Mrs. Foster, but they don't know what she's really like.

In they came! Mrs. Foster with her huge top and Mrs. Ewing dragging her old knitting bag. Mrs. Foster had on a green dress and green shoes and Mr. Foster and Mr. Ewing were following her.

Mother started introducing them to Mr. Hopper and they all looked so excited not one soul spoke to me—not even Mr. Foster.

"A Yankee, huh?" said Mr. Ewing, shaking hands with Mr. Hopper.

Mr. Hopper laughed though. "Yes, I see I'm going to have to dig up some Southern blood from somewhere." Scratch. Scratch.

"That's all right," Mr. Ewing said. "I'm a Harvard man myself." Mr. Ewing always has to tell everybody in the very beginning he's a Harvard man.

"I'm surprised you're not in Washington then?" Mr. Hopper said.

"Damned if that's so," Mr. Ewing said. (I had hoped he wouldn't say damn in front of Mr. Hopper.)

"Don't tell me you're a Republican—down here in Georgia?"

"Oh, I've got some company," Mr. Ewing said. "Getting more and more all the time. Every time Kennedy appoints one more Negrah to something I get another Republican."

"You don't like that, eh?" Mr. Hopper said. He lit another one of his long cigarettes.

"No, sir."

"Let's not talk about that right away," Mother said very brightly. "Here, Felicia, help me pass the cups."

I went trembling around the room with the cups. I hate to pass them because they're so little you think you're going to spill all over everybody.

Mr. Hopper sat on the sofa next to Mrs. Foster. I knew he would because of you know what. And Mrs. Ewing was sitting next to Mother. Right away the knitting needles started coming out.

72

Isaiah came in with the tray of ice and bottles. He put them on this side table by the piano and everybody started getting happier looking. I guess they were afraid all they were going to get was coffee. I declare, Mother and Father's friends simply adore to drink whisky, but it's a lovely pastime, I think.

The doorbell rang again and Mother told me to go to the door. It was Miss Esther! And she had on her old black cape.

"Good evening, Felicia," was all she said.

"Good evening," I said and opened the door wider. When she got in the hall she looked tremendous. Miss Esther is very tall and big, but, even though I hate to say it, I think she has a pretty face. She wears her hair kind of pulled back and her eyebrows are very dark and even, which is nice because her eyes are dark, too, and her complexion very pale. She was wearing these very tiny diamond earrings and she also had on some lipstick. I guess she had gotten sort of dressed up to meet Mr. Hopper. That was nice of her, I thought. Mother says you ought to dress up some when you go to somebody's house because it compliments the person. I agree with that profoundly.

She didn't say anything else to me. She just took off her cape and handed it to me. It weighed two hundred pounds at least and I had to tote it to the closet with both of my arms.

Mother came out into the hall. "Miss Esther, how love-ly of you to come over!"

"I wanted to, Sarah," was all she said.

"How pretty you look tonight," Mother said, looking down at Miss Esther's black knitted dress. Miss Esther isn't fat; she's just kind of large somehow. The dress did look nice on her.

"Thank you," she said.

Everybody got up when we came back into the living room and there was this tremendous silence. It was terrible for Miss Esther, I bet, everybody just staring and listening to what she was going to say when she was introduced to Mr. Hopper.

Father introduced her.

"I'm happy to meet you, Mr. Hopper," she said. "I have read your books."

Mr. Hopper nearly passed out with joy. He scratched his laugh and actually put his arm around Miss Esther. I nearly flopped to the floor; nobody in Ashton would dare put their arm around Miss Esther!

"Where did you find my books, for heavens sake?" Mr. Hopper asked her.

"In Atlanta. In a bookstore in Atlanta," she said. "When Sarah told me you were coming, I drove over to find your books." She kind of nodded to him.

"Why, how very thoughtful of you, Miss Esther," Mother said.

I thought that was nice of her, too. Miss Esther doesn't have a new car or anything. It's this ancient, old high Buick and Father says she's had it as long as he can remember—even before the Second World War. And she'd driven all the way over to Atlanta, just to find Mr. Hopper's books.

"I think you write adequately, Mr. Hopper," she said.

See, that's what I mean about Miss Esther. That's not too nice to say to somebody that they just write adequately. You ought to tell just some kind of a little story and say, "I think you write just wonderfully!" But Miss Esther wouldn't say that for anything.

"Thank you," Mr. Hopper said and kind of looked down at the floor.

"What would you like to have, Miss Esther?" Father asked.

She sat down in this tiny little ladies' rocking chair we have. "I think I would enjoy a glass of sherry, Allison. Thank you." She glanced across the room. "Good evening, Arthur."

Arthur was still standing up. He kind of jerked his head. "Good evening, Miss Esther." And his glasses started reflecting all over the place.

"Are you enjoying your experiences in Connecticut?"

"Yes ma'm, I'm *really* enjoying my experiences."

She kind of nodded and then everybody flopped back down in their seats.

Well, I don't know whether I ought to put in about what happened later or not. It was pretty bad but since everybody in Ashton knows about it anyway, I don't guess it matters so much now if I put it in.

See, what happened was everybody in the room, all at once, started pouncing on poor Mr. Hopper. They were all pretty nice to him in the beginning, for about a half an hour. But about high-ball time, it all started.

Mr. Ewing started it by bringing up the article Mr. Hopper was going to write.

I don't know how he happened to think of the article because for a long time I thought he was pretty bored with everybody. He just sat there in the winged-back chair smoking a cigar and didn't say anything for simply ages. Then when he was about halfway through his drink he kind of leaned toward the sofa where Mr. Hopper was listening to Mrs. Foster and said, "Hopper, what're you planning to write about us down here?"

Mr. Hopper said he wasn't sure yet, that he hadn't gotten all his ideas together. Then he told about seeing Ralph McGill and Luther King in Atlanta.

"Well, tell the truth, damn it!" Mr. Ewing said. "Tell the truth!"

"I certainly plan to," Mr. Hopper said.

"Naw, you don't," Mr. Ewing said and kind of leaned back in his chair. "You're going to tell what those liberal birds over in Atlanta told you, then you're going to quote a bunch of crackers and Negroes and that'll be the end of that. I never read anything you fellows up there wrote yet that was halfway true."

Mr. Hopper was just sitting there, staring at Mr. Ewing. "What do *you* think is the truth, sir?"

But then Mother kind of motioned to me and pointed to the upstairs. I shook my head but she came over to me.

"Bedtime," she whispered.

I saw Mrs. Foster looking at me, so I knew I had to get up.

"Say goodnight to everyone," Mother said.

She didn't have to say that. I was going to anyway. But I was nicer to Mr. Hopper than anybody when I shook his hand. I told him I'd see him tomorrow morning, which was the truth. I was already planning to present some of my intellect to him because I knew it would be interesting for his article.

When I left the room, I just kind of glanced at Arthur, but he didn't glance back. So what I did was I went straight up to the top of the stairs and sat down. You could hear very well from there and naturally I didn't want to miss anything.

Well, they kept on talking about the South and colored people and Mr. Ewing's voice kept getting louder and louder.

"It's the same way it was one hundred years ago," he was saying. "You Northerners sit up there and talk religion and morals and just bring one of you—*one* of you down here to live, and you won't have as much to do with the Negro as the average clay farmer!"

"I'm not so—" Mr. Hopper started to say, but Mrs. Ewing butted in.

"Yes, there's a couple from Boston who've moved to Atlanta. They're interested in some textile plants down here, and I was talking to her the other day at the Driving Club—She said she wouldn't have colored help in her house. You should have heard the things she said. She brought her own Irish help down."

"Perhaps that was just a matter of preference," Mr. Hopper said. "I wasn't particularly talking about domestic help. I was talking about—"

"What's the difference, man?" Mr. Ewing interrupted him. "That very woman—from Boston—had sent money, mind you, down to Montgomery, Alabama, to help the Negroes in their bus strike. Yet she wouldn't have a darky in her house for love *or* money!"

"Perhaps," Mr. Hopper said. "I *know* there is prejudice in the North, plenty of it. But my point is the colored man has got to be treated like an adult—not like a toy or a child."

"Then first he must be adult!" Mr. Ewing said. "Yes, I know you're going to sit there and tell me you went to school with some Negroes and you know a couple of educated Negroes who are just as intelligent as any white man you've ever met. That's always your argument in favor of lambasting the South. But the majority of the colored *are* like children—charming children, yes! What the N.A.A.C.P. ought to do is first teach them to be adult instead of trying to force them onto the white man! They ought to learn to own their own homes before they buy the first Cadillac. They ought to take baths. They ought to stop brawling and they ought to learn to tell the *truth!* I swear—you—"

"But don't you think good schooling would remedy all that?" Mr. Hopper asked.

"What do you think the white man in the South has been trying to do for one hundred years?"

"I'm afraid, not very much," Mr. Hopper said.

"Damned if that's so!" Mr. Ewing said.

"Now, Bill," Mrs. Ewing said. "We shouldn't get angry."

But he was getting angry. "Give me another drink, Allison!"

Then Miss Esther started talking.

"Mr. Hopper just doesn't seem to understand. As you know, Mr. Hopper, we in the South have been poor. Only now are we really recovering from the aftermath of the war. We were never given a Marshall Plan to recover as Germany was. We were completely ravaged by war and we were ravaged in the years following." She was talking like she was making a speech. "But, during all that time, the colored man and the white man in the South grew up together. We had a bond that sustained us—the bond of defeat and even hunger. In most instances we learned to appreciate each other's virtues, to love each other if you will. Also we were striving to uplift ourselves, the colored *and* the white. People in the North are always pointing to the condition of Negro schools in the South, but many of them are much better than some of the white—to this very day."

Mr. Hopper kind of cleared his throat. "That's interesting, Miss Stein, but then are *you* in favor of integrating the Southern schools?"

"No, I am not."

"Why not?"

"I don't think it would help anything, and I think it would possibly harm some things."

77

"But if they don't start now—how will the Negro *ever* be ready for it?"

"First things first, Mr. Hopper. I think the colored race should put more emphasis on helping themselves first—see that their own schools are first rate, their teachers first rate and, believe me, many of them are. I would like the Negro *first* to develop pride of race, not envy of the white."

"You surprise me, Miss Stein," Mr. Hopper said.

"Oh?"

"Yes." He kind of scratched his laugh. "Pardon me, but I've never met anyone from—uh—well, the Jewish race who felt as you do."

There was this very long silence and then Mrs. Foster spoke up. "I don't see what that has to do with anything."

"Goddamn it, man," Mr. Ewing said. "There's not one person in this room who's ever stopped to think what Miss Esther's religion is!"

"Now, Bill," Mrs. Ewing said. "Your language."

"Well, he's—"

"I wasn't trying to infer anything by my remark," Mr. Hopper said. "Forgive me, Miss Stein, but I just thought your views were interesting in light of your religion. Most Jewish people I know are quite liberal along these lines."

"I've lived in the South all my life, Mr. Hopper," Miss Esther said. "The Steins have lived in Georgia long before the War Between the States. Our faith has never changed our ideas."

"And the South has been lucky to have you, too," Mr. Ewing said.

"Thank you, William," Miss Esther said.

There was another silence, but Father spoke up, "I appreciate how difficult it must be for you to understand us, Hopper. I suppose if I had lived in the North all my life I could share your views, too."

"Hell you would, Allison!" Mr. Ewing said. "Most people up there don't even *like* Negroes. They just talk. Let me ask you,

Hopper. Just let me ask you this—What have you *ever* done for a colored man? How have *you* personally ever helped him?"

"By just being his friend, I suppose. Treating him as an equal, you might say. Actually, I don't think I've had a great deal of contact with the Negro race."

"Exactly!" Mr. Ewing said. "Well, you take any person in this room—any one of us—and I'll guarantee you we have all fed, clothed, and sheltered Negroes—everyone of us—paid their hospital bills, gotten them out of jail, paid for lawyers, doctors, dentists. Right now—right this minute I'm footing the bill for three colored boys to go through college. And, believe me, Hopper, they appreciate it. They *do!*"

"That's very fine," Mr. Hopper said. "But do you want to continue to do that sort of thing?"

"Hell, no, I don't! Not *now*. Let the N.A.A.C.P. do it!"

"Then it would seem an integrated education is the only answer."

Mr. Ewing let out this huge sigh. "Mr. Hopper, you can integrate a town like this—a town just like this one—where the white man is outnumbered three to one—You can integrate us from here to breakfast and back, and there'll still be separation—and perhaps a crueler one. Just remember I told you that one day."

Mr. Hopper mumbled something then, something about all he wanted was for people to have opportunities, equal opportunities, but I couldn't hear too well. Arthur came striding through the hall, carrying the empty ice bucket. I've never seen him walk so fast in my life.

"Hey, Arthur," I kind of half whispered at him.

He just glanced up at me. "Man!" he said and hurried on back to the kitchen. I guess he didn't want to miss anything.

Then I heard Mother. "Dear me, Bob. I don't think we've been very nice to you this evening."

"Oh, I'm finding it very interesting. I really am."

"Yeh, man," Mr. Foster said. "You kinda got yoself in a beehive down here. Didn't you?"

79

"Seems that way."

"Well, all you gotta remember—Just remember, heah, the South's gone RIIIIISE agin!"

"Oh, Harry," said Mrs. Foster very annoyed, but Mr. Hopper scratched again.

"Write anything you want to about us, Hopper," Mr. Ewing said, "but you're not going to change us—not one damn iota—not in a thousand years!"

Terrible! I started crying. I don't know why. Poor Mr. Hopper. Mr. Ewing was the rudest man I've ever heard. And I knew Mr. Hopper was going away and write the worst article in the world about us. All of Arthur's friends up in Connecticut would see it and they'd hate him and think we were hicks and—Arthur came flying back through the hall with the bucket full of ice. Just the sight of him made the tears start streaming down my face. He looked so pitiful with that ice bucket.

For about one million hours I sat there on the steps with my head in my lap. And then, finally, Father came out into the hall.

"Felicia," he said, coming up the stairs two at a time. "What's the matter?"

"Nothing."

"Why are you crying?"

I looked up at him. "I don't know."

"You should be in bed."

I got up and we went on up to my room.

"Tell me, Liza Jane—" He calls me that sometime—"What's the matter now? Aren't you feeling well? Are you sick?" He sat down in the straight-back chair.

"I think you all were terrible," I said, and started sobbing all over the place again.

"Why?"

"Being rude to Mr. Hopper. He thinks we're hicks!"

"I don't think he really does," Father said very softly.

"We're not rich and all of Arthur's friends up in Connecticut are and they'll read about us and—"

"Where will they read about us?"

"In Mr. Hopper's article. He's never talked to anybody that's enjoyed our class before. He said so. He—"

Father kind of smiled. "I don't think he'll write anything we would be ashamed of. Do you?"

"Uh huh." The thought made this huge lump swell up in my throat.

"Well, I'm sure he won't."

I went over and sat on the bed. "What's Jewish?" I asked.

"Jewish?"

"Uh huh."

"It's a religion, a faith. You know that."

"I didn't know Miss Esther was Jewish."

"Well, she is."

"Is it bad—being Jewish?"

"Of course not! Some of the finest families in Ashton are Jewish. The Steins are one of the finest families in Georgia."

"I don't think Mr. Hopper likes Jewish people," I said.

"I think he does. But if he doesn't that's his privilege."

"Are the Ewings Jewish?"

"No. You know they go to our church."

"Do the Jewish people have a church?"

"Yes. You've seen it—there on the corner of Aikin Street."

"That red church? The real little one?"

"Yes. Now, Felicia, you get to bed. And stop worrying about Mr. Hopper."

"All right," I said.

"And you won't worry any more?"

"I guess not."

"Promise?"

"Uh huh."

But I did. When I got into bed I was simply a wreck. I vowed that tomorrow I'd talk to Mr. Hopper if it killed me. I was even going to *lie* if necessary. You can imagine how it was. If you had a brother that was being chastened because he came from this

81

small hick town and because he was poor and Southern, you'd want people to think you were nice, too. Sometimes I think I'd die for Arthur, but I'd never tell him. Not in a million years.

8

Well, everybody in town found out Mr. Hopper was visiting us. I guess it was Mrs. Foster that went around telling it. Father says if you tell Mrs. Foster anything it's just like publishing it in the *Reader's Digest.* She must have gotten on the phone early, because the next day at Sunday school Melissa Stewart (she's the one with four telephones in her house) said, "Hear you got a nigger lover in your house! Everybody in town's talking about it."

That made me perfectly furious and we'd just got through renouncing the pomp and the devil, too. The pomp and devil is part of the Episcopal catechism and we have to memorize the whole thing.

"You're not suppose to use that expression," I said. "It's common."

"What's common?"

"You're supposed to say Neeee—gro lover," I said, and just walked on off down the street.

I guess I shouldn't have walked away like that because then I knew I wouldn't get a ride home. Melissa and them's mothers always come in the car to get them, but Mother makes me walk. She thinks it's foolish to ride everywhere. Even if a blizzard or something would suddenly hit Georgia, there I'd be, all alone, struggling to get somewhere.

Anyway, I'm glad I left Melissa. She's my best friend, but she simply hates it if something good happens to you. Nobody famous ever visits the Stewarts; they never have any out-of-town guests at all. I guess Mrs. Foster had told everybody what Mr. Hopper thought about the South. They don't like Neeeegro lovers in Ashton. They like Neeegroes better than they do the lovers. It's most peculiar.

I got to thinking about all that while I was walking home and, too, I was wondering how was I going to get a chance to present my intellect to Mr. Hopper. Mother and Father occupied him practically all the time, and even after breakfast I didn't get a chance to see him alone. Also, I was pretty scared at the idea of talking to him. Isn't it funny that in the nighttime when you think up doing something, it seems a whole lot easier than when the morning comes. But one thing is if you get your mind up on something, like saving your brother or something, you can pretty well do it. Besides, as I say, I have a tremendous faculty for being untruthful sometimes.

Anyway, I came dragging on up the driveway to our house and right away I saw Mother and Mr. Hopper out in the garden. Mother wasn't going to church. When we have unspiritual guests in the house she doesn't usually go. She gets furious, not going, but I guess it's nicer being considerate of the guest.

Mother and Mr. Hopper were bending over looking at the Christmas roses. Mother simply adores the Christmas rose. She planted them about three years ago and they've bloomed every year just at the right time.

"Yeeeees," said Mr. Hopper. "Stunning." He straightened up. "Oh hello, Felicia."

"Hello, Mr. Hopper." Right away my heart started pounding away. I was wondering if I really dared to discuss anything with him or not. I knew I couldn't with Mother there, of course.

He walked over to our largest camellia bush. "I never realized they bloomed this time of year," he said. "Wait until I tell my friends in New York." He kind of waved his hand. "Camellias instead of snow."

It was a very nice day. There wasn't a cloud in the sky and it was almost like spring. I guess up in New York it was storming with snow.

"I love the camellias, too," Mother said, "but my favorite, of course, are the jonquils. We don't see them until March. Let me show you." We walked over to the side of the hill. "By March, the entire hillside is covered with jonquils."

"Stunning," Mr. Hopper said.

"Yes, it means spring to me," Mother said. "I love to see them when they're first pushing through the ground." She smiled at Mr. Hopper. "There's a poem I love, by Sara Henderson Hay, the poet. It's so lovely."

"Oh?" said Mr. Hopper.

"If I can remember—There're two lines I especially love:

> And bladed jonquils, pricking through,
> Can split my very soul in two.

"Yessssss, beautiful!" said Mr. Hopper.

Mother pushed back a strand of hair and sort of laughed into the breeze. "It reminds me of my two youngsters—just now at the age they are now. They're kind of pricking through."

They both looked at me. Embarrassing! I'm not like any bladed jonquil. I wish Mother wouldn't say things like that. I kind of started whistling off around the holly tree. I didn't want them to stand there smiling at me like I was a weed or something.

"It's a beau-ti-ful, beau-ti-ful garden," Mr. Hopper said.

"Thank you. Both Allison and I enjoy gardening." She turned to him. "I wish you had time to see the farm."

"That would be—"

But then Velvet called for Mother; somebody wanted her on the telephone. I could have cried with joy.

She hurried toward the house and Mr. Hopper and I were alone. *Now* was the time, I thought. My heart really started banging away.

Mr. Hopper was looking up into the holly tree. "This tree must be fifty years old, at least."

"Uh huh," I said and started yawning. "Ohhhh me."

"Sleepy?"

"Me? Oh, no. I just *do* wish my Neeeegro friends were coming over this afternoon."

84

I yawned very loudly again and Mr. Hopper looked at me pretty sharply. "Do you have Neeegro friends?"

"Of course! Most of my friends are Neeee-gro." I tried to look exceedingly bored. "I've got hundreds of them."

"Do they come *here?*" he asked. "To your home?"

"Occasionally. Not very often. Mother and Father seem more partial to my white friends. I have one Neeeegro friend, Melissa Stewart." (She'd die!) "She used to come quite frequently, but Mother and Father put a stop to it."

"Why did they do that?"

I wished he'd stop staring at me. I didn't dare look at him, so I just kind of casually started pulling a few berries off the tree. "I don't know *why* they don't like them to come. I guess it's because of Mr. and Mrs. Ewing and them."

"What do *they* have to do about it?"

"Oh, I guess they didn't think I should be seen with just colored people all the time. I think they spoke to Mother or something." Gosh, my heart was about to pop right out of me. I looked up at him. "But, I forgot, you met the Ewings last night. Didn't you?"

"Yessss, I met them all right." He had this kind of peculiar frown on his face and started looking at his fingernails. "Wouldn't you like it, actually, wouldn't you, if your Neeegro friends could go to school with you?"

I remembered he'd asked me that before, when he first came. "Yes," I said, "now that I think about it. I'd adore it if Melissa Stewart could go to school with me. People in the North go to school with Neeee-groes all the time, don't they?"

"Some do."

"How I *do* wish it were the same here! You know, I don't think I'd mind it even if I were the only white person in the room."

He didn't seem to be listening. "Perhaps *your* generation—you and your friends can do something about all this. The Neeegro just isn't treated right down here. Is he?"

"No, he's not." I started digging my heel in the ground. "And

85

poor Velvet! She suffers so. So does Isaiah. They've told me so many things."

"What have they told you?"

"Ohhhh—" I started yawning again—"Velvet says she goes home lots of times and just crieeeees because she's Neeee-gro."

"She shouldn't do that."

"No, she shouldn't. I usually try to cheer her up about it—also Isaiah. It's very pathetic."

"You're a nice girl, Felicia."

I kind of turned the corners of my mouth down. "Thank you," I said. "Thank you."

There was this kind of silence, but then Mr. Hopper started beaming around all over the place. "How would you like for me to take your picture, Felicia?"

I nearly collapsed. "Me!? For your magazine?"

"Maybe," he said. "We'll see how it turns out."

I started kind of smoothing my hair back. I knew I looked a wreck, but I had on my black and white plaid dress. "Well, sure!" I said.

"Good then. Let's see—"

"Are you going to put what I *said* in the magazine?"

"What you *said*?" His eyes kind of bulged.

"Uh huh. You know, about me and colored people and all?"

"I might. Yes, I might!"

"Well, surely you can take my picture!" I nearly floated away with delight.

"I'd like to show the Northern girls what a fine Southern girl looks like."

I couldn't help smiling, but then I had this other thought. "Do you think that—uh—" I kind of looked away for a second— "Uh—don't tell Mother or anything. She's quite peculiar. She —uh—"

"Oh, do you think she would mind?"

"Oh, no! She—uh—sometimes she thinks it's kind of vulgar being in newspapers and magazines and things. It's really quite peculiar."

86

"Haven't you ever had your picture in the newspaper?"

I started rolling my eyes upward. "Oh, I've had chances! But, you know, Mr. Hopper?" I kind of laughed. "I've been so silly. I used to think it was vulgar, too, being in newspapers and things. I got over it, though."

"Most young girls in the North *like* to have their pictures in the paper."

"So do *I*! Now, I mean. I'd just as soon have my picture plastered all over the place. It's nice to be public like that, I think."

"Well, let's see." He started looking around. "Where would a good place be? What about on the front veranda? By one of the pillars."

"All right. You don't have your camera, though!"

"I'll get it."

"Don't let Mother or anybody see you," I called after him. I was so excited I could scarcely talk.

Well, Mr. Hopper took a stunning picture. I was smiling extremely broadly and sort of had my hand touching one of the pillars. The only thing was I kept thinking about my legs. See, I'd started growing pretty fiercely and my legs are very, very thin. They don't touch in the middle where they're supposed to. I did everything to try to make them touch but I don't think they did.

Mr. Hopper said he thought he'd gotten a "fine shot." He liked the front of our house and he was sure I'd added great measures to it. He didn't know exactly when his article would appear. Probably not until late summer or fall. But when we were going in the house he told me he was certainly glad he'd come to Ashton. "It's been a gold mine. Those people last night and now my little talk with you." He smiled down at me very nicely. "Amazing," he said. "Simply a-mazing!"

During lunch I didn't say much while we were eating. I was thinking too hard about all the lies I'd told. Still, what I told Mr. Hopper wasn't all lies. I really *do* love many colored people. If, say, I saw Velvet somewhere and she was writhing away in a gutter or something, I'd just about die myself. Velvet can make me terribly mad, like out at the farm that time when she told on me, but I'd do anything for her. I really would, and if she died I'd never get over it. I'd go and put violets on her grave every Sunday. I might even do it if Freedonia died.

You don't know Freedonia, but she's Velvet's niece. She's my age and she used to wear red ribbons in her hair all the time. When we were children Velvet used to bring her by the house. We'd play, but the only thing is Freedonia and I are different. What she wanted to do was play Swinging Hips all the time. What you do is you stand by the elm tree, put your hands on your hips and then walk real crazy and fast with your hips swinging all over the place. I thought that was very boring, but Freedonia nearly killed herself laughing over it. What I wanted to do was jump the boxwoods. Do you know that to this day I can clear a five-foot boxwood without even touching it. Freedonia couldn't stand to do that. She'd try, but almost every time she'd land smack in the middle. Mother got kind of furious because Freedonia had broken about six of her best boxwoods. I don't know what ever happened to Freedonia. She moved to Detroit when we were six. Sometimes I wonder what became of her.

The only thing is I don't like mean niggers and that isn't bad to say. Velvet says it herself. I told her it wasn't cultivated to say "nigger," but she said it was all right if they were mean. "Ain't no other word for 'em," she said. "That's what they is—mean niggers!" You'd die over them and I don't think even Mr. Hopper would like them. They hate white people, mean niggers do. Velvet said so.

Anyway, after lunch Mr. Hopper said he wanted to go around and see something of the people of Ashton. He wanted to make a call on the head of the N.A.A.A.C.P. and he wanted to visit with Velvet's preacher. Velvet's preacher is widely known in Ashton and just about everybody in town has contributed money for this new church he wants to build. People have contributed for centuries. You'd think it ought to be built by now.

"Why don't you let Isaiah drive you?" Mother said.

"That would be nice. *Thank* you," Mr. Hopper said.

I knew Isaiah would flip over that. Sunday is his day off. One thing, though, I knew Isaiah was counting on a pretty big tip from Mr. Hopper. Tips are the only thing Isaiah likes about guests. He can always tell whether somebody's gonna tip pretty good or not.

"He ain't no count," he says about some people. "He jes a one-dollah man." What Isaiah likes is a "fi-dollah" man. I kind of think he thought Mr. Hopper was a "fi-dollah" man; he was being so nice to Isaiah and everything.

Mother went into the kitchen to tell Velvet about Mr. Hopper wanting to go to her church that afternoon.

"What for?" she asked with this down-in-the-mouth look she gets sometimes.

"Because he wants to meet your minister and because he's interested in all things American," Mother said.

"Why don't he write up something about his own church," Velvet mumbled to me after Mother had gone.

"Maybe he doesn't have one," I said. "He's divorced." My uncle that is divorced has simply left the church. He never goes. It worries the family no end.

"Pshaw," Velvet said. That's what she always says when she's thinking somebody's white trash.

"Will you be there, Velvet, in church?"

"If I kin ever get outta here, I will."

"You've got time," I said. Velvet's church doesn't begin until two in the afternoon. "Be sure and tell me about it!"

Mr. Hopper had his camera slung around his neck which was a very unspiritual way to go to church, I thought. Isaiah had on his driver's cap, too, the one Mother gave him for Christmas. He's only supposed to wear it when he's driving, but he wears it practically all the time. He's simply wild about it.

"I won't be gone very long," Mr. Hopper said. "I just want to have a chat with a few of these people."

"Fine," Mother said.

"See you later," Arthur said, and he followed Mr. Hopper out the back door!

I nearly fainted. I didn't know *he* was going with Mr. Hopper.

89

"Ar-thur!" Mother called to him. "Where are you going?"

"I'm just going with Mr. Hopper."

"It's all right," Mr. Hopper said.

"No, I don't believe so," Mother said.

"No, Arthur," Father said. "Not this time."

Arthur came dragging on back to the house. "Goooo-ud night, you act like I'm a child or something. You can't do anything around here."

"Mr. Hopper would rather be alone, I'm sure," Mother said. "He can speak more freely to the people."

"He *asked* me to go," Arthur said.

"I don't want us to have any part in any of Mr. Hopper's investigations," Father said.

My face started getting red. I wonder what he'd say if he knew Mr. Hopper had taken my picture and was also going to quote my intellect in his article. I decided then and there I wouldn't tell anybody about it, not even Velvet or Isaiah. After it came out, they'd all collapse with surprise.

"What time does his bus leave?" Mother asked. She looked very exhausted.

"Five," Father said. "He has an eight-o'clock plane out of Atlanta."

"Is he going back to New York?" I asked.

"No, Florida, I think."

Northerners are always going to Florida in the wintertime. We're always having visitors come by to see us on their way to Florida. Most Southerners wouldn't think of going there then because of all the cheap rich people there then. Besides, Southerners know the weather down there, and they laugh at all the Northerners that think they're going to swim and stuff when all they do is freeze to death and sit around looking cheap and brassy. Not all Northerners are like that, I guess, just most of them. They're very loud, as you know.

"Pretty difficult man, wouldn't you say?" Father asked.

Mother just flipped her hand. "Now, Allison, this is the last.

I'm just tired to death of having people here like that—people we'll *never* see again."

Father just kind of laughed.

Mr. Hopper and Isaiah didn't come back until just about bus-time. Both of them were bustling around, trying to get all his junk together.

"Fascinating. Ab-so-lute-ly fascinating," Mr. Hopper said about Velvet's preacher. "He gave me some excellent quotes and I took a charming picture—of his entire family, in their home. All of them were sitting around their table with their heads bowed."

I almost died. Me and Velvet's preacher would be in the magazine together! Just us. I kept thinking what everybody in Ashton would say. Mother would collapse. My face started getting scarlet. I shouldn't have let him take my picture. I know I shouldn't've.

"You've been simply charming," Mr. Hopper said to Mother. "Don't know when I've enjoyed anything so much. Bless you. Come to New York sometime."

"We will!" Arthur said, and I couldn't even open my mouth.

Isaiah was struggling through the door with Mr. Hopper's typewriter and stuff.

Mr. Hopper shook hands with Father. "I'll remember the quails," he said. "You'll hear from me next year."

"Good!" Father said.

"Have a good trip," Mother called after him.

Mr. Hopper grinned back at her and hustled on out to the car and Isaiah.

"Well," Mother said after he was gone. She gave out a huge sigh. "That is that!"

"I wonder what sort of information he got this afternoon," Father said.

"The Lord only knows," Mother said. "But, Allison, I certainly hope he doesn't include us in anything."

"He won't. At least he won't use our names. He assured me of that."

But the *picture,* I thought. I shouldn't have done it! I shouldn't have. I *know* I shouldn't've. And I had all the way to the fall to worry about it.

At six Isaiah came back with the car. The bus had been late. He came dragging on in and I knew he was in a horrible mood because of working on Sunday. I don't blame him much; Sunday's a day of rest.

He came on in the living room to give the keys to Father. He really looked beat up. I decided to try to cheer him up.

"How much tip did he give you, Isaiah? Was he a fi-dollah man?"

"Nothin'," was all he said.

"Whaaaat?" Mother said. "You mean he didn't even *tip* you? Did he leave anything for Velvet?"

"No'm."

Mother looked at Father. "Well, now, *really,* Allison. That makes me pretty sore. After all his high-sounding talk, too!"

Father didn't say anything. He just got up and gave Isaiah three dollars. "Give this to Velvet when you go home," he said. He gave him another three dollars.

"Goooo-ud night!" Arthur said. Even Arthur knows how to tip.

Mother asked Isaiah if he liked Mr. Hopper.

"No'm," he said.

"Why not?" Arthur asked him.

"He's hankty."

"I suppose," was all Mother said.

But I didn't say anything. I was wondering if Mother and Father could actually kill me. They could try, I know. And they probably would when the picture and article came out.

9

Two days later we saw Arthur off to Connecticut again. He had on his old coat, the one that had been sent to the cleaners too much, and I looked at him standing up there on the platform by the porter and I felt something of the sorrow I'd known the first time he'd left. The house always seemed so silent after he had gone.

This time, though, the silence didn't last very long. Arthur hadn't got lost in the station, but he had been a day late returning to school. Mr. Sykes wrote: "Arthur says this was an oversight on his part. Nevertheless, we find it necessary to inflict a penalty; Arthur will be restricted to the school grounds for a period of one month."

Poor Arthur. It was bad enough just being up there but being locked up made it really terrible. Home, though, was pretty much without joy too—at least for me. If I just hadn't lied! And, gosh, if Mr. Hopper put in there what I said about Melissa Stewart she'd kill me. I just hoped and prayed he didn't remember her name. If Mr. Stewart read where I'd called Melissa a Negro, that would be the end of me. He'd probably come over with a shotgun and slay us all. Mr. Stewart is widely known for his temper. Once he knocked a man out on Main Street just because the man called his mother a dog. The thought even made me sick in my stomach.

One thing that helped get my mind off the article was this letter from Arthur. It was almost jubilant, for him. His roommate, Bob Leyden, had not returned to school:

... He can't come back till he gets cured. And I'm glad. Now I got this new roomate. His name is Knox Campbell and he's from New York City and goes to night clubs all the time. I think his folks are real rich because he's got this picture of his house and it looks like a castle. He says his father makes those things—those kind of dummy things women fit clothes on when they so. He's in all my classes and we go around together all the time. He doesn't like Mr. Sykes either.

Well, I gotta go. . . .

He signed his name "A." And Father wanted to know why he'd signed his name like that, but Mother said it was just probably something he had learned.

It was that about night clubs that enthralled me. Ashton doesn't have any night clubs; the only one we've got is this one room in the basement of the country club. Older people stay in there literally all the time. Junior members aren't allowed, but if you're twenty-one or something you can go in there and get as madly drunk as you want to. It's a nice way to spend an evening if you're twenty-one.

I don't know why night clubs enchant me so. I've never been to one or anything, but I've seen them in the movies and I'd certainly like to go to one sometime. That's why Arthur's letter interested me so much. I was thinking Arthur'd probably start going to them up in Connecticut. People in the North are just thrilled to have their sons go to night clubs. Southerners are just stupid that way.

Anyway, thinking about night clubs and stuff sort of took my mind off Mr. Hopper. Not for long, though, because everytime I thought I'd completely forgotten, something strange would pop up about colored people again. One afternoon Melissa and I were at the country club. All afternoon we'd been in the ladies' room acting like we were at a night club. It was very immature, of course, but we'd also been smoking. Melissa can be worlds of fun when she wants to.

She'd brought some cigarettes and I'd brought three of Father's. We were sitting back there where the dressing table is, just smoking away, and I started up this conversation. I was really forgetting all about Mr. Hopper, and it was a lot of fun. I started off, "Oh, I'm so *bored* with all these Old Fashioneds all the time. Aren't you?" I was pretending I was this very rich lady in New

94

York City. "Aren't you bored with just one night club after another?"

"I'm so bored I could die," Melissa said. "Hey waiter, bring me another Old Fashioned."

I blew out this tremendous wad of smoke. "Melissa, deah, do you suppose we will get drunk?"

"Probably deah, but I need to. I've smoked so much my lungs are literally flapping around."

"Of course," I said. "Hey waiter, I wanted *three* Old Fashioneds, not just one. Aren't the waiters dumb here, though?"

"Dreadfully!" She kind of raised up one eyebrow and she really did look like somebody in a night club. Melissa's got naturally curly blond hair that she wears very short and her eyes are brown. When she gets older she'll fit in very nicely with night clubs, I think.

"Your hair is charming today, my deah," I said.

"Thank you. So is yours, but I *do* think you could have a permanent wave."

That did it! That messed up everything. I started talking my natural way again. "I wish I could have one," I said. "I really do." I put my hands on the side of my face and made this forlorn expression in my eyes. "This is the way I look all the time," I said. "I go around looking like a pathetic hound dog or something."

Melissa started laughing. "Why doncha just go and get a permanent. It'd be cute on—" But then she started waving her hands in the air. "Oh, oh! Somebody's coming."

I lunged toward the ash tray but it fell on the floor.

It was Mother's friend, Mrs. Meredith. I guess she'd been playing golf because she had on socks and this small yellow hat with a visor. I plopped back in the seat and pretended I'd just been sort of lounging around.

"Oh, hello, Felicia," she said.

I stood up. "How-do-you-do, Mrs. Meredith?" You could hardly see her for all the smoke.

She spoke to Melissa. "You girls just sitting in here?"

95

"Yes," Melissa said, "we just this minute came in."

Mrs. Meredith sat down in front of the mirror. "Whewh, it's so stu-ffy in here."

"I know," I said. "It was so stuffy we just couldn't sit any longer. Would you like for me to open a window, Mrs. Meredith?"

"Yes, thank you, Felicia." She sort of glanced at me. "Played golf with your sweet mother today—she's out on the porch now."

"She is?" I said. "Oh, good!" But I was about to die. I ran and slammed the window open and Melissa and I beat it down the stairs to the golf shop.

On the bottom step we both collapsed against the wall.

"D'you think she knew?" Melissa asked with this simply terrified face. Boy, if her mother knew she'd been smoking, she'd probably be chained to the bed. Mrs. Stewart is violently religious.

"I don't think she did," I said. "But what if it'd been Mother!"

We just leaned there against the wall, panting. I'd practically lost my breath out of just pure horror. If I'd got caught smoking too—*plus* what I'd done when Mr. Hopper was there, I might as well've just gone on home and committed suicide.

After a while Melissa said, "Hey, look at that!" She was pointing to the bulletin board over my head.

"What?"

"Read it," she said, and started smirking.

I read it, but I didn't see anything so smirky about it. All it said was:

ATTENTION: ALL LADY GOLFERS

Beginning January all lady golfers are requested to wear *skirts* while playing golf on the Ashton Country Club greens. No lady member wearing Bermuda shorts or any attire other than the proper-length skirt will be permitted on the greens.

Respectfully,
Marvin T. Lane, President

"So what?" I asked.

Melissa looked at me. "Don't you know why?"

"Uh uh. Why?"

"Because of the Negrah caddies."

"What about them?" I'd seen most of the caddies all my life. Most of them were all right except that Father said they gambled all the time.

"They don't want them looking at the lady golfers all the time. Daddy says it's horrible the way the caddies giggle and stuff at the ladies' behinds."

"Ohhhh," I said. But frankly I didn't believe it. I still don't, not really. Colored people just don't pay any attention to white people and certainly not lady golfers. That was kind of stupid of Melissa, but I didn't say so.

That night, though, Mother started talking about how she and Mrs. Meredith practically had to sit in the dark while they were having their little after golf drink. They were just sitting there by the window in the night club, she said, and Mr. Lane came over and closed the curtain. See, they have this very large picture window down there and it overlooks the patio. If you're sitting on the patio you can look in and see everything that's going on.

"Why did Lane do that?" Father asked.

"Because of the caddies again, I guess. He didn't want them to see us being served drinks."

"How stupid," I said. I thought I'd better stay on this conversation. I was pretty worried Mrs. Meredith might have told her about us smoking.

"No, it's not stupid," Father said. "It's illegal to *serve* drinks in Ashton. We're certainly not setting a very good example for anyone."

"Colored people do it, too," I said.

"Where?" Father asked.

"At the Elks Club," I said. "At the colored Elks Club. Isaiah told me."

"Well, they shouldn't do it either," Father said.

Mother sort of sighed. "Honestly, this situation is getting so we don't have any freedom at all any more." She looked at Father. "Wasn't that simply a *terrible* thing in the paper tonight?"

"Yes," Father said. "Now, Sarah, I want you to keep the doors to the house locked. All the time. Even during the day. Do you understand?"

"Oh, we do, now. Velvet sees to that. But, really, things are just getting out of hand."

"What happened in the paper?" I asked.

But they didn't have to tell me. The telephone rang. It was Melissa.

"Hey, it's me," she said. "You know what we were talking about this afternoon? About the caddies and all?"

"Uh huh."

"Well, did you read the paper?"

I got pretty interested. "Not yet! What was it?"

"You oughtta read it. Mrs. Tate got rapped!"

"Rapped?"

"Yeah, by this Negrah. He just walked in her house in the morning and rapped her."

"Mrs. *Tate?*"

"Yeah, *you* know. The one that does hair down at Miss Roper's beauty shop. The blonde one. The Negrah just knocked on her door and asked if her husband was there. She said he wasn't and he just came in and rapped her. You *know* what that is, don't you?"

"I'm not real sure. What is it?"

"Nasty," she said. "The nastiest thing that—"

"You mean?"

"Uh huh."

"Gosh," I said. I was terrified out of my mind. I could just picture that colored man.

"They didn't put her name in the paper or anything, but everybody knows who it was and all."

"Did they catch the colored man?"

"Not yet. But they've got all these police and dogs and everything looking for him. Isn't it the most horrible thing you ever heard of? Wouldn't you just die? What would you do if some Negrah tried to rap you?"

"Pass out of the picture, I guess."

98

"See, that's why they don't want you wearing shorts or anything at the club. And just think we're going to have to go to school with them."

Right away Mr. Hopper popped into my mind again. "I don't think we'll have to yet," I said. "Not in Ashton."

"Yeah, we are too. Next year. They're gonna start integratin' next year. We'll probably all get rapped. This girl up in Philadelphia, Pennsylvania, did. It was horrible. *Three* of them."

"But they don't care up there," I said.

"I guess not. But isn't it horrible?"

I didn't say anything and I could hear Melissa breathing on the other end of the phone. I never had thought of all that before. I mean about colored people.

"Mrs. Tate's in the hospital," Melissa said. "She's all hi-starical and everything."

"I don't blame her."

"Yeah. Could you do the third problem?"

"Rithmetic? I haven't tried them yet."

"Well, call me if you get it."

"Okay."

"Bye."

"Bye."

I just sat there, staring at the phone. I sure was glad Mother and Father hadn't told me what was in the paper. Wouldn't that have been embarrassing? Mother and Father sitting up there telling me about all that? After a while I went down and looked at the paper. It's only a weekly paper but the headlines were so big it took up practically the whole front page:

WHITE WOMAN HERE RAPED BY NEGRO

I didn't want to get caught reading about it, so I went on in the library. Father was sitting in his red leather chair, reading the old boring *Sewanee Review*. He doesn't much like to be disturbed after dinner when he's reading, but I just thought I would. I wanted to ask him some things, but I didn't want him to know

I'd read about Mrs. Tate. Mother and Father don't know I know about things, but I've known ever since I was nine. Melissa's mother told her about it. Melissa said it was the most embarrassing thing she's ever gone through. They went upstairs in Mrs. Stewart's bedroom and Mrs. Stewart started talking very sad and forlorn. Afterwards she showed Melissa this stupid book that Melissa had already looked through one thousand times. If Mother ever starts trying to tell me about it, I'm just going to yawn and pretend like I'm bored.

"Melissa says we're gonna get integrated next year," I said.

Father didn't even look up. "She does, does she?"

"Uh huh. Are we?"

He looked at me over the magazine. (I think he kind of knew I'd read the paper.) "I don't think you will, not at your level."

"I'll be in the seventh next year, junior high school. It's pretty near colored town."

"Yes, well, I think you've missed all that." He went back to reading again.

"Gooo-ud night." I tried to sound just like Arthur and plopped myself down on the sofa. "Why did they have to go and start up all this integration stuff for? It's just a big mess—everybody mad with everybody else and us having to keep our doors locked all the time. Velvet says she's not gonna let them integrate her grandchildren. And they're gonna start school next year!"

"I'm afraid Velvet doesn't have anything to say about it." He was *still* reading. Father can be as infuriating as Arthur sometimes.

"You mean if she doesn't want her grandchildren to go to school with white children, she can't even get out of it?"

"Afraid not." He looked up then.

"Well, I don't think that's right. Why can't they have three schools. Colored and white and one that's mixed up. Then, if people want to mix and all, they can. Looks like to me you oughtta be able to do what you wanta do."

"Who would pay for so many schools?"

"I don't know. Same people that pay for them now, I guess.

100

Seems to me you oughtta have some kind of choice and not just be made to go to school with people you don't want to."

He rested the magazine in his lap. "It builds character to do things you don't want to do."

"I don't see why," I said and slapped one of the sofa pillows in my lap. Father's always saying that about building character. I'm kind of tired of that saying. "Do you guess I'll ever go to school with colored people?"

"No."

"Why not?"

He started looking very bored. "For one thing you'll be in boarding school, and unless the colleges are thoroughly integrated by the time you get there, you'll probably have missed that experience."

My heart started pumping away. "Are you gonna send me away, too?"

"In time."

"To Connecticut?" I felt like crying.

"No, I think your mother wants you to go to a Southern school."

It was the first time I'd ever heard I was going to get sent away, too. It was extremely sad. Me, being put away somewhere like Arthur. At least, though, it wasn't Connecticut. "I don't believe I'd much like it up in Connecticut," I said in this very pale voice.

"Why not?"

"I just don't, that's all." I didn't want to tell him about what Arthur said, about everybody being different and rich and all. I just didn't want to worry him any more. "Did you know Arthur's school is integrated?" I said.

"No, I didn't," he said and kind of raised an eyebrow.

"Uh huh. Next year they're gonna bring a whole bunch of Africans over."

"Who says so?"

"Arthur."

"Oh."

101

He glanced back down at his magazine and I guess he wanted me to stop talking. But I was thinking that maybe—just maybe—if I saw he was in a good enough mood, I might could tell him about me and Mr. Hopper. "Father," I said extremely sweetly. "Are you partial to colored people?"

"Some of them, yes. You know we all love Velvet and her family."

"I know, but would you ever invite them to a party you were giving or something?"

"I don't think so. In the first place I don't think they would enjoy our parties very much."

"Wouldn't some of them? I mean like the real educated ones? Like over in the Congo and all?"

"I couldn't say." He put his feet up on the footstool. "It's rather obvious, though, isn't it, that the white man isn't particularly welcome in the Congo." He must've been getting unbored because he lighted a cigarette. "But—it's always been the same. The good white man and the good colored have always had nice relationships." He let out this huge cloud of smoke. "I'm sure, though, each of us feels easier with his own color."

"Yeah," I said, but I was thinking about smoking. I'd sort of liked to have been smoking, too. It's enjoyable talking deep with Father. He's never treated me like a moron, even when I was a child. But I really did agree with what he was saying. When I get to thinking about it, I think I'd feel pretty funny if I was all the time with just colored people. I mean if I was the only white one. One time Mother and I went to Velvet's church. Velvet's father had died and we were the only white people that went. It was terribly pitiful and everybody in the church started yelling and throwing their arms up in the air. We don't do that at funerals in the Episcopal church. When Grandfather Whitfield died, they just read out of the prayer book and in fifteen minutes, almost, it was over. Colored people came to his funeral but they didn't yell or anything. It kind of scared me, frankly, all the yelling and being the only white person in there. I don't know why, it

102

was just different, that's all. I sure did feel sorry for Velvet, though.

"But why are you worrying so about all this?" Father asked.

"I don't know. Everything's getting so sort of changed and spooky. We never have had to lock our doors in the daytime before." (I shouldn't have said that because he'd know I'd read the paper.)

"Well, I wouldn't be too worried about it."

"But, why has everything started getting so sort of dangerous and everything?"

He kind of frowned. "So much emphasis on this racial situation, I guess. When a person is suddenly given praise—and privileges he's never been quite accustomed to—he sometimes abuses those privileges."

"You mean colored people? Mean ones?"

"Some of them, yes. It was the same after the War Between the States. There were many colored people who abused the privilege of freedom. Still, there were many fine ones, too."

"Like Velvet," I said.

"Yes."

"It sure is spooky, though."

"*Surely*, Felicia. Not *sure*. Don't say that."

"Surely, I mean."

"Well, don't worry about it," he said. "And remember one thing. Just because a man is a Negro or different in *any* way from you, gives you no right to feel superior or be unkind."

"Oh, I know that," I said. "But sometimes don't you think it's unkind to make somebody ride on the back of the bus and all that?"

"As far as I'm concerned, they can ride anywhere they like. As long as a man is courteous and a gentleman, white or colored, it makes no difference to me where he rides."

"Me either," I said. "But, just for instance, say, what if you were having a hot dog or something at the dime store and this Negro man sat down *right* beside you? What would you do?"

103

He kind of laughed. "I don't think I'd be sitting there in the first place. I don't like hot dogs."

"But I mean if you *did* like them?"

"I suppose I'd just go on eating my hot dog."

"You *would?*"

"Yes."

"But you're not for going to school with colored people."

"No. No, I'm not. But I *do* want the colored schools to be better than they are. For that matter I want our white schools to be better."

"Yeah, like Nadine Miller's and them's school out in the country. Her school's the most rundown-looking thing you ever saw. They even teach three classes in one room."

"I know," he said and put out his cigarette. "But speaking of school, don't you have some homework to do?"

"Yeah, I guess so."

"Well then?" He picked up his magazine again. When he picks up a magazine, it means he's through talking.

I just sat there staring at him. I *wish* I'd had the courage to tell him about Mr. Hopper. I really wanted to. It would have been such a relief. But I'm such a coward at times. It's funny, but everybody in our family for simply centuries has had courage. I don't know what happened to me.

"Well, good night," I said.

"Good night."

All I could do was drag on up to my room and try to do my arithmetic. I couldn't do it, though. I couldn't even do the first problem. I guess I was worrying too much. I kept thinking about Mrs. Tate hysterical in the hospital and about Mr. Hopper and this fall and ladies not being able to wear Bermuda shorts and I guess I was just confounded out of my mind.

Thank goodness, we started hearing from Arthur again. We had a letter the very next day. It hurt us pretty bad, that one. But his next ones were quite stimulating. I practically hardly didn't even think about Mr. Hopper at all. Mother said she thought Arthur was developing.

PART II

10

Arthur really was developing. It was highly inspiring. Of course he hadn't matured yet or anything, but it looked like he had a chance. You have no idea of all the opportunities he was having, night clubs and everything. Frankly, it made me feel rather pathetic. You see, I'm not a very widely traveled human being. The only place I've ever been is to Florida and Charleston and once to North Carolina when I went to camp. It's perfectly insane, but I've never hardly even been out of the South.

I guess that's another reason I grew so interested in Arthur's letters. See, I was really *such* a child—simply dying to mature myself. I got so tired of Mother and Father sitting around wanting Arthur to mature that I thought I could show them how good I was, too. I guess you'd call Arthur a kind of pioneer, because actually he did mature first. I did a month later, though. Mother and Father were thrilled.

One afternoon we got this letter from him and his handwriting was completely changed; you couldn't hardly read it. It was more of a printing than anything else and he asked us how we liked it. He said he hoped we did because this was the way he was going to write all the time now. Knox, his roommate wrote that way, he said. Knox also said everybody at Harvard wrote that way, but

Father said if they did he didn't understand how anybody ever got out of Harvard.

It was the rest of the letter that hurt us so. He said his clothes weren't right:

> ... They don't wear the same kind of things up here they do down there. Knox says some of my suits are kind of hicky and he said when you get to be almost fifteen it's stupid to wear ties that have scotty dogs all over them and it is. He says his mother knows this store in New York City and if you'll just send me the money she can charge and I can pay her back. I can get my shoes hear all right. Knox knows the kind—like his. They call them white bucks but they don't have any down there in Ashton so don't go around trying to find them. Knox says he guesses I'll need about a hundred dollars for all this, that's all. Well, I gotta go.
>
> Sincerely,
A.

Pitiful. The only thing about it Mother had such a terrible time reading it that she read white "lucks" instead of "bucks."

"White *lucks!*" Father said, and he didn't sound hurt at all. "What in the world has come over that boy? A hundred dollars to make a sis out of him. I wish Arthur still had that boy who wet the bed for a roommate."

"Now, Allison," Mother said. "Perhaps the Northern boys don't dress like we do down here." But she added very sadly, I thought, that she thought Southern boys always looked nice.

"Of course they do!" Father said. And then he started telling about Mr. Morris. Mr. Morris is a bald man that runs Morris's Store in Ashton.

"Bob Morris knows what he's doing," Father said. "He and his father have been in business for more than a hundred years. If any boy doesn't think Bob Morris' clothes are good enough, he just doesn't know what he's talking about."

"Allison, really," Mother said. "Just because Mr. Morris is in

106

the Rotary Club with you. Now let's just do this for Arthur. You know *you* wouldn't want to be different either. You know you wouldn't."

"White lucks, my eye," he said, and walked out of the room. But you could tell by the way he said it he wasn't planning to send Arthur the money.

It was all just too pitiful for words to me. Arthur up there, looking poor and hicky. The next day at school I started looking at all the boys' feet. Not one of them had on white shoes. All they had on were just these tremendous, terrible-looking brown things —the same kind Arthur wears. No wonder he didn't like it up there. There he was with his horrible brown things and everybody else prancing around in nice white ones.

Anyway, during singing I got this very cheerful idea. We have singing once a week at school—all the schools in Ashton do. This one teacher, Miss Leroy, comes in and blows a whistle and we sing out of these books she brings. That day we just happened to be singing "Poor As I Am." It starts off:

> What can I give Him, poor as I am?
> If I were a shepherd I would bring a lamb
> If I were a Wise Man I would bring a—
> But, oh, oh, what can I give Him?
> Poor as I—yam.

Naturally, I started thinking of Arthur. Well. I went and thought up the most immature thing you've ever heard of. You see, I've got thirty-three dollars and fifty-two cents in the bank. I know it's very vulgar to mention your income, but my money's been piling up in the bank ever since the first grade, ever since we started up Bank Day. Every Tuesday, see, we have Bank Day in which you are forced to deposit money. The principal at the end of the day puts it in the regular bank downtown for you. So with all I'd banked, plus some my uncle gave me, amounts up to pretty much.

So you know what I did? Honestly, it showed no sense at all on my part. What I did was, see, I got one of Mother's checks at home and wrote out one for thirty-three dollars and fifty-two cents. I cashed it at the grocery store where Mother cashes some of hers. I didn't have any trouble at all. Mr. Becket—he's the grocer—said he was charmed to do it for me. When I got home I found a stamp and I just put the money in an envelope without writing a letter or anything. I wanted Arthur to be surprised and not know where in the world it came from. I mailed it that very afternoon, but I made sure the money was wadded up in a neat piece of paper.

Frankly, I was pretty happy about doing that. It's much better to give than to receive, you know. Funny thing, though, my being so nice and everything kind of made me want to cry. People that do nice things always make me want to cry. I could just see Arthur in his white shoes and I knew how happy he would be. I thought it was cruel of Father not to send the money. I know Father isn't made of money or anything and a hundred dollars is a huge amount, but it did look like he could've sent half anyway.

Well—I got caught. I'm the most stupid person in the world sometime. I'm so ignorant when it comes to economics it's simply a disgrace. I didn't know you had two kinds of ways to bank. I just thought if you had the money in the bank and wrote a check you could get it out. I still don't see why it isn't that way. See, all my money was in the savings part and I didn't have anything in the checking part, so my check came back to Mr. Becket marked I didn't have any fund in there.

Mr. Becket called up Mother and she was stunned out of her mind:

"*Why,* Felicia?" she kept asking me. "Why did you do such a thing? Where is the money?"

"In an envelope." Her mouth was all pinched together.

"Well, go get it. This minute."

I just stood there, staring back at her.

"Well?"

"I can't get it."

"Why not? Have you spent it?"

I shook my head.

"What did you do with it?" She looked exasperated.

"Sent it to Arthur."

"To Arthur! Did he ask you for it?"

I shook my head and kept on staring at her. I can stare just as hard as she can if I want to. We just stared at each other— for simply hours.

"Then why?" she asked again. "Why did you send it to him?" I thought I might as well go on and tell her. So I did.

She collapsed. "Felicia, Felicia, Felicia, I don't know what I'm going to do with you."

I started beaming. I was so relieved she wasn't foaming with madness.

Finally she said she appreciated the sentiment in my act, but that I'd gone about doing it in a very unwise way.

"I just wanted to help some," I said. "You know if Mr. Hopper writes a pretty bad article about us, it wouldn't be too good for Arthur up there." I just thought I'd kind of add that in. I thought I might tell her about what all I'd done—maybe.

"Mr. Hopper isn't going to write an article about us."

"I think he is," I said. Poor thing. She didn't know a thing about the picture.

"Well, that has absolutely nothing to do with this."

"I guess not." I didn't want her to start getting in a bad mood again.

Father, though, was pretty harassed. He didn't understand why the girls at the bank didn't first show him the check when it got there. He thought what I'd done would probably reflect back on all our character, because he said what I'd done was not quite honest. But he guessed it was because all the girls were pretty new at the bank and that, after all, it was just as well what I'd done because it also taught me a good lesson in economics. Boring. Father's very anxious I learn something about economics in case I ever get married or anything. Father thinks the worst thing in the world is for a person to marry a girl that is careless about economics.

But the main reason he was so hacked up was because he had sent Arthur the money also and, too, he had to pay me mine back. As I've told you, my father is a very nice man, but he gets quite disturbed over money. He just literally loathes it when the bills start coming in. It's pitiful. It puts him in a horrible mood. I wish I would hurry up and marry somebody rich so I could help him out in these matters. He worries too much.

Well, there was pitiful Arthur up there, simply loaded to the gills. I bet he'd never had so much money in all his life. He wrote us a very nice letter in reply. He thanked me violently for the gesture on my part. He knew it was from me, he said, because of the way I wrote the envelope. He also thanked Father and said he was really glad he'd gotten all his new things because Knox had asked him to visit in New York for mid-semester vacation. He said they'd probably be going to a lot of night clubs and he didn't want to look hicky. (Tragic.) But he also said he would write and tell us how much he would need.

That last, of course, was the worst thing he could have done.

"How much he'll *need?*" Father asked. "I guess he will."

Arthur just didn't know what kind of atmosphere was going on at home. Father said he couldn't wait to get Arthur home and show him what a dollar looked like. He said he didn't know how he'd reared up two persons like us. But Mother said to remember it was Arthur's birthday and that it was interesting, she thought, for young boys to have "experiences."

"Like night clubs?" Father asked.

"Now, Allison, you know better than that."

"Well, I don't. That Knox boy doesn't sound too bright to me. Arthur ought to be studying instead of thinking about white lucks and New York all the time."

But just imagine! Arthur up in New York City! I kept seeing him sitting in some great silver night club, and there I was—at home, sending him money and working myself to the bone. Frankly, I found all this obscene beyond imagining.

Nothing good was happening to me. Only one sort of pale thing. I got forty-two valentines on Valentine's Day. I didn't get

110

one from a boy, though. Mary Ann Akers got three from boys, but she's this very plump person. You have to be plump for the boys to like you. I didn't care, though. There wasn't a soul else in school that could run faster than me and I hadn't made any D's either.

Arthur's letter describing his visit in New York was three pieces of theme paper packed with joy. When I got home from my obnoxious music lesson, Mother had just finished reading his letter. I saw it in her hand, the folded pages all wadded up and half-sticking out of this very small envelope. Her face was flushed and she seemed happier almost than I'd ever seen her.

"We've had the *grandest* letter from Arthur!" she said. "I'll read it to you when your father comes home."

"That's all right," I said. "I'll read it now."

"No now, let's wait until he comes. Allison likes to be with us when we read Arthur's letters."

I don't know why we always have to have a ceremony every time we get a letter from Arthur. They aren't all that important, I don't think. But that night we sat down in the library and Mother read it to us. It was the longest letter Arthur had ever written and Mother said his new handwriting was improving vastly:

... First off, we went up on the train—I and Knox and another boy. The other boy was going to his house outside of New York which isn't too far from where Knox and them live. We stayed in the club car most the way and then we ate. But guess what? A chauffeur met us at the train. He was white and looks like Uncle Alex. We got in this huge black cadilac, in the back, and then we drove and drove until we got to this huge grey house made out of stone and it was Knox's house. Knox's Dad is really rich but he isn't really Knox's Dad. Knox said his real Dad was dead but he acts very nice. Mrs. Campbell is surely pretty. She's Knox's real mother. He told me about it. But I can't tell. I had a room all to myself and this high bed. We ate in the hugest dinning

111

room you ever saw. It had a fireplace in it, not like ours, but it was all made of silver. At dinner Mr. Campbell said I had a good vocabalary for a boy my age and he asked me what I was going to do and I said I guessed I'd have to be a farmer like you. Mrs. Campbell was always talking about me and how polite I was. She said she was glad Knox was getting Georgia from me. She said he needed manners. Anyway that night they got all dressed up and Mr. Campbell put on this top hat and a coat that had velvet around the collar and Mrs. Campbell put on this blue dress and fur coat and they took Knox and me to the—STORK CLUB! We sat in stripped seats and Mr. Campbell told this waiter he knows to bring us some cherry wine. Knox drank his and got blotto! But I didn't. There was a man in there that's been married 15 times—a real old man and Mrs. Campbell said he was going to get married again. The Stork Club is real small. But afterwards we went to the Kopa and it's even smaller but costs a lot of money. Mr. Campbell said Knox couldn't have another glass of cherry and I couldn't either. So we got a coke in there but Knox said they always put whisky in all the cokes anyway and he was really getting blotto, but I didn't. That was the best night.

Along about the last we had this dance. We didn't have it until then because I told them about me not being able to dance too good. But Mrs. Campbell showed me how until I got so I could do it just fine. She used to dance in a night club and really knows how. Anyway, all these girls came! Knox's girl is a real dame. Sue. But there was one there better than her. Rose. Knox said he thought she had the hots for me and she would write. I haven't gotten one yet, though. Northern girls are a whole lot different from Southern ones. They're much more grown up and they hit you all the time. Also they yawn. Knox said one thought the way I talked was cute, but I don't think she'll write. You ought to hear the letters Knox gets from his girl—at the end. Know what I mean? Anyway, Mrs. Campbell said I could come back any time at all. I think I will. I sure do like them. And, oh yeah, she was glad I knew how to tip. They've got these two women for maids—white ones. And I gave them ten dollars a peace. Mrs. Campbell said she thought that was too much of me but I told her how surprised and all we were when Mr. Hopper didn't tip Isaiah and Velvet one dime for all they'd done for him. They didn't do anything for me, the white ones, but I just thought I'd tip them anyway. Anyway, Knox says he wants me to come up in the summer but Mr. Campbell said Knox had to go to camp again. But Knox says he's not going because he's too old and I don't blame him. Well, that's all. There's a whole lot more, but I gotta go.

Love

A.

Well, we were all astounded by the letter. When Mother finished reading it, she looked up at us. "Weren't they *grand* to Arthur?"

"Ten dollars!" Father said. "They must think Arthur's a millionaire."

"Yes, we'll have to tell him to be more conservative. But weren't they lovely to him?"

Father wasn't smiling. "Used to dance in a night club," he said.

"Who?"

"That Mrs. Campbell. Isn't that what Arthur said?"

Mother glanced at Arthur's letter. "Oh, *that!* Arthur just probably got that wrong. Anyway, she was certainly nice. I'll have to write her right away." She opened Arthur's letter again and silently reread the end.

"What about all those girls?" I said.

Mother glanced at me but she didn't say anything. Then she looked past me, into space. After a while she said, "You know, Allison, I do think Arthur's developing. Don't you?"

"Developing what?"

"Oh, you know what I mean—becoming more mature somehow."

113

"More mature?"

"Oh, you know," she said and left Father and I alone.

"I do wish Arthur could make better grades," I said to Father, but I don't think he heard me. He was smiling and I knew he was getting very pleased over Arthur. He wouldn't get pleased over me even if I went to a thousand night clubs. Nothing about Arthur seemed very pitiful to me any more. Only me.

But then his next letter made me feel considerably better. It caused Mother no end of worry and Father said he thought Arthur had gone crazy.

11

Fond Parents, I sit hear in darkness, alone, and I am paralysed...."

Father bolted forward in his chair. "What?" he boomed.

"No, now just wait a minute," Mother said, waving him backward, and she began reading again:

Fond Parents,

I sit hear in darkness, alone, and I am paralysed. My heart is a cold grey stone and I am paralysed with gloom. I walk about in darkness alway and my feet go SLUSH, SLUSH, SLUSH in the melting snow. I go SLUSH, SLUSH, SLUSH and gloom o'ertakes me. No one knows about all this but me. Even when the sun goes down I watch it SINK, SINK, SINK and darkness comes. For darkness and blackness are my kin folks, like you all, and I can tell it to the like of you all. But nobody else! The moon rises up. RISE, RISE, RISE. But it's yellow and no kin. So, like the black ghost that I am, I walk with my heavy grey stone and my feet go SLUSH, SLUSH, SLUSH. Farewell.

Your Obediant Servant,
A.

For a time we just stared at each other and Mother, as she always does in times like this, took out her white handkerchief and just sat there, holding it to her nose, not crying or anything, just holding it and staring at the wall.

"Let me see that," Father said. And he took the one sheet of theme paper, and after putting on his horn-rimmed glasses, silently reread Arthur's strange letter. He must have had a hard time reading it because even though it was a better example of Arthur's new handwriting, he had placed little round circles over every *i* instead of just plain dots, and, though pretty, the circles were so large in places that it made the upper line hard to read. "Do you guess Arthur wrote that?"

"Oh, yes," Mother said in a strained high voice. "It's his new way."

"Doesn't seem to me Arthur ever put all those circles in one of his letters before."

"It's just something else he's learned," she said in the same high voice.

"Huh!" Father said, lifting one eyebrow. "Sounds like he's gone crazy."

"Oh, Allison! Don't. Don't say that!"

A horrible picture formed in my mind, of Arthur, chained to a great iron chair in the attic, howling mad. And I shuddered, vowing I'd never think of that again. But Father made it all seem better when he suggested perhaps Arthur was suffering from an unrequited love. I asked him what that was and he said it was when one party does and the other doesn't. This was a much nicer picture, I thought—Arthur madly in love, like a movie star, and walking around with his huge grey stone because of it all. So I didn't think too much more about it.

Not much was going on at home to take my mind off my worries either. One thing was we got this new rector at church. The fox-hunting rector from Virginia refused to come to Ashton so we got this very old man from Arkansas. We're not sure whether he fits in with the South or not, but we're being very loyal to him even if he does whistle his S's. He'll say, "Let us pray," and

115

right where the "us" is, this whistle comes out, but he's pretty nice and it was kind of interesting having somebody new to talk about.

The only other event was, Mother caught me doing the most humiliating thing. What happened was Mr. Creasy—he teaches tap dancing and stuff—gave this review he gives every spring. It was at the movies and everybody was in it, even very small children. I wasn't in it, because I don't take, but Melissa and I went to it anyway. It was pretty good and the best one in it was May Beth Hughes. She's in the tenth and may go to Hollywood. She's excruciatingly popular because she's short and smokes cigarettes in her car between classes. That night she wore this silver bathing suit, top hat and cane, and, after tap dancing onto the stage, sang "There's Gonna Be A Hot Time In The Old Town Tonight." Everybody nearly died and they clapped so hard she had do it again.

Well, when I went home I started doing it in front of the mirror—just standing up there in my room, screaming my lungs out and right while I was shuffling on into the bathroom, Mother came in and told me I was disturbing Father downstairs. I don't know why that was so embarrassing—Mother seeing me trying to act like May Beth Hughes—but it was. Mothers are always finding out things like that and it's terribly embarrassing. To me, it is.

So you see, home was howlingly boring. About the only other thing that happened was Arthur's explanation of his peculiar letter. The day after I'd acted like such an idiot in front of the mirror there was this letter from him. He had drawn the same round circles over the i's, and I found it, so I didn't have to sit around discussing it. It's stupid to me to always have to discuss something somebody's written. You ought to just read it, say "pretty interesting" and go on about your business.

I just went on and opened it before anybody else did. And right away I knew he was making reference to his peculiar letter because he started off:

116

Well, how did you like it? It was part of this theme we had to write for English and Mr. Woodford spoke to me about it. He said it showed a pretty good feeling on my part. And Mr. Woodford writes for magazines and stuff. Poems. He's practically famous. He said for me to keep on writing and the only reason he gave me C was because of punctation and spelling. Knox wrote one about this guy blowing his brains out and got D. Well, I gotta go.

Sincerely,
A.

I was astonished! I kept reading it over and over. Some famous poet up there telling Arthur to keep on writing like that! Finally, I went on into the library and sat in Father's red leather chair. I just sat there, staring. What if Arthur did turn out to be somebody famous, say like Mr. Hopper or somebody? The thought was entrancing. I kept having these visions of Arthur grown up. He was wearing his white lucks and going "Scratch! Scratch! Scratch!" all over the place.

It was a pretty sad vision because I kept seeing myself, also. I was this pitiful old maid that had never hardly even been out of Ashton, and I didn't have any friends or anything because I was always complaining about my gall bladder. All I could do was go walking up and down the streets with a brown paper sack of food and an old black hat on my head. Arthur would be too busy getting famous to care what happened to me. Finally, I'd take to drink and die all alone without Melissa or anybody there, because she'd end up marrying and having one million children to take care of.

That night at dinner Mother said she didn't think Arthur was going to become a writer. "There's never been one in the family—on either side."

"And thank goodness," Father said.

"Why, Allison, it might be rather interesting."

"Very," he said. "Who'd pay for his white lucks then?"

"Well, you don't know. Maybe Arthur will be successful at it."

"He gives every evidence of it now, of course." Occasionally Father can be very sarcastic—especially when it comes to Arthur. They don't have the companionship that I and Mother have. I know they like each other, but ever since Arthur was twelve they got to acting very peculiar to one another. Sort of formal or something.

"*I'm* very proud of him," Mother said. "You know. I really think—I really do—that Arthur at long last may be getting over the hill. I really do—"

"He's getting over something," Father said.

I didn't listen any more. And too, that was the end of Arthur's gloom letters. Exams were coming on, he said, and he was really studying. Also he couldn't wait to get home. "It'll be divine to be out!" he wrote.

"Divine?" Father said. "Where did he get *that* word?"

But the day Arthur finally did get "out," Mother and I had an argument. I didn't want to go to the train station to meet him. But Mother said she had never heard of such disloyalty. "Here your brother has been away for almost half a year and you don't even want to go the train to meet him!"

I said I could see him later, but she told me to go right upstairs and put on my good dress; we were leaving for the station in a few minutes.

When I think of it I guess what's really the truth is that I was almost afraid to see him. I mean he had been so many places and done so many things and I—I was still just me, untraveled and hicky. You know, it's embarrassing for the other person if he suddenly sees you're this extremely hicky individual—especially if you're his sister. Nobody wants to have a sister that way. But Mother didn't seem to be feeling like I was. At the train station she kept saying, "I wonder if he's changed, Allison? My, how exciting it is!"

Father was smiling, too, that half-smile he gets when he really means it. Then the train came in! I listened to the roar of the wheels and the sound of the whistle and it was almost as if Arthur himself was causing all that noise, coming home in a roar of glory. Finally this porter jumped down and the three of us stood there smiling as each passenger descended. But when the last passenger came down we stood there, still smiling somehow, and Mother said, "I wonder where he is?" Father, then, asked the porter if there had been a young school boy on the car. The porter said there had been. But at just that moment Arthur appeared at the door. At least I thought it was Arthur. I looked again.

12

Arthur certainly looked different. In the first place he had lost weight, a lot of it, and his hair was cut short all over. He was wearing his dark-blue suit and right away I noticed his white shoes and the newspaper tucked up under his arm. But the funny thing was he wasn't smiling or anything. He didn't even seem glad to see us. He came down the train steps, slowly, and Mother rushed up to him and hugged him. He halfway reacted to this, smiling only slightly. Then he suddeny backed away from her a few steps and looked into her face as if he were examining it. "Welll, hellllooooo therrrre, Motherrrrr," he said in the strangest accent I'd ever heard. Then he looked at Father. "How arrrre you, sirrrr?" He shook Father's hand. "And, Felicia," he said, looking at me as if I were some mere child. Then he straightened his shoulders and looked about. "Wellll, I see the little town is just about the same." He sighed an almost tired sigh.

We walked to the car in silence. Arthur sat up front with Father and I could see him slowly moving his head and looking at everything. When we passed the post office he said, "Nooo, nothing has realllly changed."

"You've gotten a new way of talking up there, haven't you, Arthur?" Father said.

119

"Why, nooo," Arthur said. "I don't realllly think so."

Mother didn't say anything and I was afraid to somehow. But just before we got to the house, Arthur took out this pipe and started knocking it on the window.

"What's *that?*" Father asked.

Arthur glanced at him. "Just a pipe."

"Arthur!" Mother said. "Do you *smoke?*"

"Once in a while," he said. "The Head smokes a pipe, you know."

"Who's that?" Mother asked.

"Who?"

"The *Head!*"

Arthur turned to her. "Realllly, Motherrrr. The Head*master*. Mr. Sykes."

"Oh," Mother said, a little pathetically, I thought.

Arthur held up this hand-painted tobacco pouch and glanced at Father again. "Two bucks at Penn Station," he said. "Good stuff, realllly!"

"Pretty fancy, isn't it?" was all Father said. It had a picture of mountains and trees on it.

"Made in Japan," Arthur said, and started cupping his hand over the bowl of the pipe to light it.

We drove the rest of the way home in a cloud of smoke. Arthur's tobacco made the worst-smelling smoke I'd ever smelled and Mother coughed once, but she tried to smother it in her handkerchief. I don't know why she didn't say anything to him then about smoking, or Father either, but Arthur was so strange I guess they didn't want to right then. He didn't have any expression on his face and he yawned all the time.

When we got to our driveway, Mother said, "Look, there's Velvet and Isaiah. They're waiting for you. How *nice* of them."

Arthur didn't say anything; he just yawned again.

"Wave at them, Arthur! They're so glad to have you home."

"Realllly, Motherrrrr," Arthur said again.

I thought that was terrible of Arthur, so *I* started waving at

120

them. They must have thought that was pretty peculiar of me because I'd just seen them twenty minutes before.

Arthur got out of the car with a trail of smoke following him. And in this sort of swaggering walk, he went up and shook hands with Velvet.

"How arrrre you, Velllllvet?" he said in that same peculiar accent.

Velvet immediately stopped grinning and started pouting out her lower lip.

"You'rrrre looking well, Velvet," he said. Then he turned to Isaiah. "And Isaiah, how arrrre *you?*"

Isaiah didn't say anything either; he just stood there, staring at Arthur's pipe.

Mother and Velvet looked at each other and both of them had this sort of peaceful look on their faces. Velvet and Mother pretty much understand each other without even saying things. Velvet has had just about as much trouble with Isaiah as Mother has had with Arthur. Velvet's got two sons, not just Isaiah. The other one's name is Extra. But Isaiah got in bad one time, gambling at the country club and that's when he came to work for us. Extra serves at the country club; everyone's quite partial to him.

Isaiah began to giggle. "What's *that* thang, Arthur?" he said, pointing to Arthur's pipe.

"Just a pipe."

"It sho do stank," Isaiah said and fell forward, clapping his hands like he does when he really thinks something's funny.

Arthur frowned for the first time, and then started yawning again.

"Let's go inside," Father said.

At the door I caught Velvet's eye and pointed my finger at Arthur and then at my brain.

"Lawdeee merceeee," Velvet said, and in we went.

While Arthur was upstairs helping Isaiah bring up his bags I asked Mother—"What's the matter with him?"

But Father answered. He said he thought Arthur was getting

121

malaria again. "He looks just the way he did when he first got malaria—drained and wrung out."

"No," Mother said. "I think he's just being sophisticated."

"Sophisticated!?" Father said. "Good Lord!"

Funny thing, as the morning went on Arthur sometimes forgot his new accent and at times sounded almost like the Arthur we had always known. I looked at him sitting in the winged-back chair and I wanted to ask him where his accent had gone, but Mother and Father were beaming so and he was talking so much I didn't have a chance. He was talking away about school and Knox Campbell and somebody else we didn't even know about. Suddenly he knocked out his pipe and said he had a kind of surprise for us.

"*Another* one?" Father asked.

Arthur looked at him questioningly and then got up from the chair. "It's an award I got."

"An *award?*" Mother said, and her eyes got very blue and wide.

"Uh huh. I'll go get it."

He ran up the stairs three at a time and we just sat there waiting. It was funny but with Arthur out of the room we couldn't think of a thing to say to each other.

"Let's see!" Mother said when he came back down all breathless. He was holding a rolled-up piece of paper and he handed it to Mother still rolled up.

"What is it?" I asked, getting up to look at it, too.

"Just a minute," Mother said and unrolled the paper. She read it slowly and then all radiant got up from the chair and with the paper still in her hand hugged Arthur. "I'm *so* proud of you, Arthur. It's just wonderful!"

"Can I have a look at it, too?" Father asked.

"Read it, Allison!" Mother said. "It's the grandest thing I ever saw."

Arthur was so excited he twirled all the way around on his

122

left foot. He glanced at me and, all grinning and gasping, seemed to be saying, "See! I did it! I did it!"

"What *is* it?" I asked.

"Well, now, Arthur, that's just fine," Father said. "I'll have to congratulate you." He got up and shook Arthur's hand and Arthur just looked down at the floor, trying to be humble.

"What *is* it?" I asked again and went over to the sofa and unrolled the piece of paper. It was written in this very old-fashioned writing and it said:

To Arthur Lagare Whitfield, who, during the School year nineteen hundred and sixty, distinguished himself by washing more windows and with the best spirit of any other single student at the Follett School. We, therefore, the Masters and Board of Trustees, hereby present him this Certificate of Merit.

I just stared at it.

"Isn't that *fine*, Felicia?" Mother asked.

I looked at Arthur. He was nodding his head in agreement.

"Yeah, it surely is," I said.

"I knew I was gonna get it before I did," Arthur said. "Mr. Woodford told me I'd been elected because I'd started showing all this spirit."

"Well, I'd rather get an award for fine spirit than anything I can think of," Mother said.

"Uh huh," Arthur agreed again. "You should have seen old Knox when I got it. Mr. and Mrs. Campbell were there and they started patting me on the back and stuff. Knox didn't get anything."

"I've started wearing stockings, Arthur," I said.

Arthur just looked at me with this kind of dazed look.

"Just on Sundays," Mother said. "For Sunday school and church."

"She can't keep them up though," Father said and laughed.

123

"Yes, I can," I said. "I tie knots in the garters. Velvet showed me how."

"I bet that looks cute," Arthur said and started reading his award again. Arthur can be extremely selfish sometimes.

"Well, we're just so *pleased* about this, Arthur," Mother said.

I just yawned. I thought it was about time we stopped talking about Arthur's award. It's thoughtless to dwell on such things too long.

"Maybe you can give Isaiah a hand in washing *our* windows," Father said. But his eyes were smiling and I knew how happy everybody was. I wondered if it was going to be this way all summer—everybody patting Arthur on the back and thinking about him as if he were some kind of king or something. I think I liked Arthur better when he stared and flipped through worthless magazines all the time.

I went outside and thought how sad the world is, how tragic it is to be hated in your own home. After a while I went back inside and stood in the hall. I heard them still talking in the living room, so I didn't go in there. But then I heard Mother saying, "But Ar-thur! You just didn't *work* at it. We're *so* disappointed in you."

I listened and I could feel my heart begin to beat faster. Arthur had failed algebra! Everybody was furious again. Poor, poor Arthur. He's such a kindly human being and he *has* suffered so. Never in his entire life has he hardly ever been able to do one thing right. It just isn't fair that he has to undergo all the tribations. I started wishing I wasn't so highly atriculated. Pitiful.

I went on back in the living room. "Gosh, Arthur," I said. "It's *so* nice to have you home again."

124

13

It was pretty hard for Arthur to be sophisticated after flunking algebra and everything. He had also made a D on European history, too, and all those teachers up there wrote notes on his grades. His history teacher, the one that curses all the time, said: "Arthur refuses to concentrate in class as evidenced by his complete failure to grasp the importance of the industrial revolution."

Mother said this was exactly what the principal of the grammar school had told her years ago, but Arthur said history was the most boring thing he had ever listened to and the only part he cared anything about was when Hitler started coming in. Arthur thought that about Hitler was "divine."

"Why don't we drop that word from our vocabulary," Father said.

"What word?" Arthur asked.

"Divine."

"Knox says it all the time."

"Maybe he does, but no man in Georgia says it."

"Yes, Arthur," Mother said. "And, too, I think you'd better start acting your natural way. You really were so silly when the boys came over this afternoon."

I knew what she meant. Arthur had got back in his sophisticated-malaria mood when Jack Findlay and the Foster twins came by to see him. We heard what Jack said later. He said Arthur had gone up North and got "daft."

Also, two days after he'd got home we had graduation exercises at the Ashton Grammar School. Arthur said he didn't want to come. "What do I want to go to *that* for?" he asked, and began yawning all over the place again.

"Because your sister is graduating," Mother said, "and she's also going to make a little speech."

I guess Arthur thought that was a pretty unsophisticated thing to have to do, go with your mother and father and watch a bunch of grammar-school people graduate. But it didn't hurt me too much. "I don't care whether he comes or not," I said. "I don't care if nobody comes."

That was pretty much the truth, too. I don't think I've ever been as scared about anything in all my life. Making the speech was a kind of honor, but just about everybody was asked to do something. My speech was the most intellectual one. It started off: "Books! What valuable information they convey! Each one carrying little messages to all parts of the world." It went on for about three more paragraphs and I practiced and practiced until I could have said it even if I'd lost my brains.

Everybody at home got quite tired of hearing me say it. I was always interrupting them to practice it. If they were sitting around having a fascinating time talking about Connecticut or something, I'd suddenly interrupt with: "Books! What valuable information they convey!" and they'd all get pretty furious. I made it to Mother almost one million times but she didn't get too mad, if I didn't interrupt anything.

"Gosh, I'm scared," I told her.

"There's no need to be," she said. "You certainly know it by now."

"I know, but all those people!"

"They don't want you to fail, Felicia. Remember that, no one sitting in an audience wants the person speaking to fail. It's just a human quality."

"I know that, but it's a pretty terrifying thing when you think about it. *Me* up there on the stage and everybody staring. What if I just completely forget?"

"You won't."

Well, I didn't, but I had the most heart-rendering experience almost you've ever heard of. Miss White, our teacher, started it off by giving the most excruciatingly sad speech you've ever heard of.

There we all were, sitting up there dressed-up on the stage, and Miss White shocked us all by first tiptoeing to the front. She hadn't done that when we were practicing. I just thought we'd first sing "Home on the Range" like she'd told us to do, and then everybody would start performing.

She looked nicer, though, than I'd ever seen her. She had on lipstick and this yellow corsage and black high-heeled shoes with black straps around the ankles. I don't know why it was so kind of pitiful seeing her so dressed up. I suppose it was because I don't think she'd ever had any other chances to dress up. It's funny, but you never really start thinking about somebody like a teacher until you see them at the end all dressed up. I'd never thought about Miss White maybe having a mother or father or anything. I don't think she'll ever have a beau either, not now anyway; she's about forty years old and, too, she chews her tongue. When nobody's looking and she's trying to think, she just sits there behind her desk, chewing her tongue.

She didn't chew at all on graduation day, though, thank goodness; but she did get this very strange, high, polite voice. It didn't sound like her in class at all, like when she says, "All right now, quit rattlin' that paper back there!" Sometimes Miss White can sound pretty harassed, but I never blamed her too much. It's absolutely ex-as-perating teaching some children. She told me that once when I stayed to help her clean off the blackboard.

Anyway, as I said, Miss White's speech was horribly sad. How *strange* life is— You know, it's most ignorant of me, but I had been so worried about my own speech that I'd never once stopped to think how really sad graduating from the Ashton Grammar School really was. Just sitting up there listening to Miss White, though, I started thinking about all these very pitiful things. I started thinking about how this was my last day at school and how I'd never come back again or walk through the halls again or anything. For six long years the Ashton School had practically been my home and, just think, I'd never come back to it again. Not as long as I lived.

I looked out in the audience and there was Mother and Father and Arthur, all surrounded by all these other people that had one time or another graduated, too. They all looked so old and tired

127

and bored, those people, and I got to thinking that in a few years I'd probably be sitting out there, too, looking old and tired and bored.

Miss White started off her speech in the most heart-rendering way. She said that everybody was gathered here today not only to say farewell to a graduating class, but to also say farewell to "childhood." I nearly died. "Too soon," she said, "these young people you see behind me will be grown. They will be adult men and women."

That's when it all started! I started getting this kind of lump in my throat. You see, and I know it's unwarranted on my part, but I'd actually never thought about soon becoming a woman. And, just frankly speaking, I'm not very partial to that word "woman." It reminds me of dark, unpleasant things like laxatives, church meetings, and trailing, black wires on heating pads. Women never have a good time. They're always sitting around talking about gall bladders and things.

Gosh, you don't know it and I don't act it most of the time, but I simply *love* gay things! I love, dearly love, happy times! For instance, one time in the morning I heard this very gay music over the radio and I did the most insane thing. You know what I did? I went out and simply ran down the jonquil hill. It was almost like flying. At the bottom of the hill I threw myself down and just lay there, laughing all to myself. I know it's odd, but I get so very happy sometimes.

"How soon our youth is over," said Miss White very sadly. "We look back on those few short years, and, looking back, they seem to have been only a day, one day of precious, gay merriment. Then they are no more."

Sad! Poor Miss White. There she was just standing up there in her yellow corsage telling everybody about her happy youth. I guess she was trying to warn us, but I wish she hadn't.

"Those were our cherished years, my friends. One long, lovely spring day and then no more. And yet—and yet—" I was afraid she was going to start crying. "We are privileged to live that day again—in our own dear children. But so short a time. So short. . . .

128

And so, to all you parents, I want to say, in fine, how very much I have enjoyed knowing these children of yours. A-mer-i-can youth! What a rare commodity!" She looked down at this piece of paper in her hand. "And may I say, too, that I hope *I* have had some small measure in their development along life's highway."

Life's highway! To me, that is a very beautiful saying. It's the saddest expression in the world, I think. I decided I would start using it quite often in the summer. Life's highway! Life's highway! How true. Poor Miss White. She hadn't had much of a highway. Always having to have operations and things.

"And to our children," she said, not turning around to us, "I would like to say farewell. Each of you, without exception, has a place in my heart—and—although I shan't be seeing much of you, I shall be watching you and applauding *mightily* with each tiny triumph that comes your way." She turned round then and started frowning. For a minute I thought she was going to chew her tongue, but she didn't. She just raised her arms, the piano struck this chord, and we all stood up and very quickly sang "Home on the Range."

It was most inspiring the way she did it, and my throat was aching so, I couldn't hardly get out one word.

Just think! My youth was all over and there wouldn't ever again be any joy. "One long, lovely spring day and then no more." It was the most excruciating thing you've ever heard. But then I got kind of terrified. What if when I got up to make my speech I started crying all over the place. Everybody out there would think I was an idiot and die of horror over me.

I decided I'd better stop thinking about not having my childhood any more or I'd mess up everything, so I started listening to how Melissa Stewart made her speech. It was a poem about shooting an arrow into the air and where it went she didn't know where. It's a very nice poem and Melissa did it very well and fast. But there I still was with my huge lump, waiting. I kept swallowing so it would go away. Finally, it did and I heard my name being called out.

"Books! What valuable information they convey...." I started

129

hearing my own voice and it was like a dream. Still, and I don't understand it, everybody was *smiling* at me! There was nothing in my speech to smile about, nothing at all. As I told you, it was the most intellectual one of all. But even Arthur was smiling! I started looking at Melissa Stewart's sister, the one that's in college, and she was beaming all over the place. My face started getting terribly hot.

Honestly, older people can be so odd at times. There we all were, up there saying good-bye to our childhood and me talking deep about books, and then them out there grinning away like maniacs. When I get older and I start going to the Ashton Grammar School graduations, I'm not going to grin when there's some pitiful girl up there saying good-bye to her childhood. I'll remember that until the day I die. I mean it.

I did all right, though. I didn't miss a word. When it was all over, I had many congratulations on it. But you know what? I didn't even say good-bye to Miss White. I know I should have and Mother urged me to. She said I was being absolutely unappreciative not doing it. But, I was afraid I'd start crying and the last thing in the world I wanted to do was stand up there bawling in front of Miss White and everything.

In the car Mother said, "Honestly, Felicia, you are the strangest child sometimes. Don't you think Felicia should have said a little something to Miss White, Allison?"

"Certainly do."

"Let's not talk about it any more," I said.

"Well, all right," Mother said, "but I do think you should have expressed your appreciation in some way. It was a lovely little talk she gave. She must be a dear person."

"I said *let's not talk about it any more!*"

"Don't use that tone of voice to your mother!" Father said.

I just let out this huge sigh.

"I thought you did pretty good up there," Arthur said.

I turned around to him. "I saw you out there. What were you grinning so for?"

"I wasn't grinning for hellsakes!"

130

"Arthur!" Mother said.

"Well, I wasn't grinning."

"Yes, you were too, everybody was." I turned back to Mother. "Did I do all right?"

"Yes! I thought you were excellent."

"Why was everybody grinning then?"

"They weren't grinning. They were just smiling because they were so happy for you."

"Oh!"

But I wasn't happy. We had lunch, and afterwards I went out and sat on the bench underneath the chinaberry tree. I just wanted to think for a while. It's very odd about me, but I have to think quite often. Father does, too. I guess I inherited it from him. Anyway, I got to thinking about how I'd better start acting grown. My childhood was over now and there weren't many pleasures left for me. Soon, I'd have to start sitting around talking about the price of cotton and colored people. I guess I'd also have to join a study club and have a bunch of women over to eat salads. It was all so vastly boring. I just kept sitting there thinking about it all and finally I got to literally hating myself. I hated myself so much I could have just thrown myself down on the ground and started beating my head on a rock.

That night, though, Father said we were going back to Ponte Vedra again and I could have died of joy. I love the ocean and I have enjoyed my most enjoyable pastimes of my entire life there. The only thing is the Woods from Richmond, Virginia, are always there when we are and they're extremely rich and snobbish people. I just hoped we wouldn't have to see them!

14

Well, I got to be thirteen right smack dab in the middle of Ponte Vedra. Ponte Vedra is this place outside Jacksonville, Florida. Rich Northerners go there in the wintertime and rich Southerners in the summertime. That's the reason we can only stay one week. Most people stay two weeks and there're some that even stay three. Anyway, I had my birthday there and that night this orchestra they have in the Cactus Room played "Happy Birthday" and everybody stared. Afterwards, I went out on this sort of terrace and thought about how soon I would be able to wear lipstick and ride around waving at everybody. That's what Sue Pate and Mary Lou Fitts do. They're the most popular girls in Ashton, but they don't speak.

The stars were out and you could hear the ocean roar. I guess Ponte Vedra is my most favorite place in the world. I was glad we had five more days. That morning I saw these sad people bring out their bags and pack up to go home. I felt extremely sorry for them, but then I knew our time would come, too. It's like dying, I guess. Everybody knows you've got to, but you never think about it. I do, though, sometimes. I don't talk about it; I just think, and I think it's simply terrible the way they put you in those caskets and everything. When I die I've already decided what I want. I want thousands of violets growing around me and this very small black iron cross with just my first name on it. I don't know where they'll get the cross. Maybe in England somewhere or I guess Mother and Father will have to have it made. All they do for you in Ashton is put this huge cement piece of sidewalk on top of you.

I didn't think about dying long, because Mother came out and told me it was time to go to bed. Arthur was still inside looking at this cheap movie they show after dinner sometimes. It was just as well he was by himself because Arthur had practically ruined our entire vacation. Almost every night we were having some kind of argument.

See, what happened was Arthur developed false pride. He developed it about eight miles out of Ponte Vedra. We had been driving all day and it was terribly hot. It's a pretty long drive from Ashton to Ponte Vedra, and I couldn't wait to get there because soon as you get to the ocean it is really quite cool. Sometimes at night you even have to put blankets over you. Anyway, Ponte Vedra is about eighteen miles from Jacksonville and you think you'll never get there. But right in the middle of Route A1A, Arthur had to go and develop false pride. It was about five o'clock and we were trying to hurry so we could swim before dinner. As usual Arthur was sitting up front with Father, and all of a sudden he said we had to stop.

"You just went an hour ago," Mother said. (You know what she was talking about.)

"No," Arthur said. "I just want to get my suitcase out, that's all."

"Why?" I said. "We'll be there in ten minutes!"

"I just want to," Arthur said. "I want to put on my other suit." He looked at Father who looked very hot and wrinkled. "I think we all should change."

"Really, now, Arthur," Mother said. "No one's going to notice us."

"Yes, they are," Arthur said. "They're always hanging around in the Inn, waiting to see a bunch of hicks walk in." He glanced at Father. "There's a hamburger place up here not too far and we can all just go in there and change."

"Nobody," Father said in this very pinched-mouth way. "*Nobody* is going to stop this car now for anything!"

"D'ya want everybody to think we're a bunch of jerks?"

"I don't think anyone will," Mother said. "They know we've been traveling."

"Nobody knows it but us," Arthur said.

"Don't have such false pride, Arthur," Mother said. "It's what's inside a person that counts."

133

Arthur turned all the way around. "Nobody'll know what you've got inside, if you go around looking like a jerk all the time."

"Don't speak to your mother that way," Father said. "Nobody's going to look at you anyway."

Arthur didn't say anything else until we got to the Inn and then we drove up under this porte-cochere sort of thing and there was old June, the nicest colored man you ever saw. He was smiling and welcoming us back. But the thing was, Arthur didn't even have to go inside. Only Father, just to register, because we had been put down at the lower patio, right on the ocean, where it's private and nobody has to see you.

"Whewhhhhh!" Arthur sighed, leaning back all relaxed on the car seat. "We didn't have to go in!"

"You're just being silly, Arthur," Mother said. "Now, see, you went to all that worry for nothing."

But then when we got to the patio, Arthur started up again. He refused to go swimming, which was the strangest thing in the world. Usually, Arthur is the first one into the ocean. But when we were all ready, he was just sitting in a chair in his room looking through this pamphlet they put in there for you.

"Aren't you coming, Arthur?" Mother asked him. We were all standing at his door with these striped robes we've got on.

Arthur glanced up from his pamphlet. "No, I don't think I will this time."

"Why not?" I asked.

"Hurry up, Arthur," Father said. "We don't have much time before dinner."

Arthur just went back to flipping through his pamphlet again.

Mother motioned for us to go on, and she went and sat down on the other twin bed.

Father and I went on down to the ocean. It was pretty cold, but not too rough. Every year whenever I first go in I keep thinking about crabs and sharks and things. It doesn't last long, and toward the last I never think about them at all. The time I like Father almost the best is when we're in the ocean. He's a lot of fun and he helps me over the biggest waves, even though I can swim better than anybody in Ashton. The only place I have to swim, though, is the Ewings swimming pool and Mother won't let me go until I'm invited because she thinks people are always taking advantage of the Ewings. I went practically every day last summer. The country club's going to build a swimming pool next year and I can hardly wait.

I thought Mother would positively never come, but she finally did.

"Well, I finally got it out of him," she said to Father.

"What's his trouble now?" Father asked.

"He says we're white."

"We're—*whaaaat?*" Father said, frowning at her.

"White," Mother said.

I just looked at her.

"He says you can always tell new people because they're so much whiter than anybody else. He wants to wait until he gets tanner before he comes out."

"How's he going to do that?" I asked.

"It seems he bought some lotion at the drugstore before he left. You put it on and you can tan—even without the sun." She glanced back at the patio. "He's up there now, putting it on."

Father just shook his head, and then the three of us went further out into the ocean and it was wonderful. Mother adores the ocean, too.

I can't tell you how good you feel after swimming. It makes you happy all over—so happy you almost feel like crying. I could have cried while we were walking back to the rooms, but I wasn't in the mood. It's just when things are boring that you feel like crying.

We all got dressed for dinner and while we were sitting around waiting for Mother and Father to finish their highball, Arthur started getting orange. He kept getting oranger and oranger, and the only thing white about him was these two white circles round his eyes. His neck looked funny, too.

"Arthur!" I said. "Look at your face!"

He went over to the bureau mirror and stood looking at himself, turning his face from left to right. "Uh huh," he said. He actually sounded proud.

But then when it was time to go to dinner, Arthur said he wasn't hungry.

"Now, Arthur!" Mother said. "We're all getting just a little tired of this! Felicia, you shouldn't have told him his face was orange. It isn't, really. He looks quite nice. Up you go now. It's late."

"It's not orange, Arthur," I said. I was starving.

"I'm just not hungry," he said, and then I noticed him looking up and down at *us*. I wondered if he were ashamed of us or anything. I knew he couldn't be ashamed of Mother. She was wearing a black dress and she really looked pretty. Father looked nice too—for a man. He was wearing a dark-blue suit and he wasn't as tired looking as he is in Ashton.

I started backing away, sort of. I guess it was me Arthur was ashamed of. As I say, I'm not pretty. I have these very long, thin legs that look like sticks and my hair is too blonde and no eyebrows hardly. Also I inherited Grandfather Whitfield's nose. It's not too bad, I guess, but it doesn't turn up enough. Mother says I look all right. She says I have a fine twinkle in my eye and that my face has character. But who wants to have that! To be popular you have to be short and plump and have a turned-up nose. One whole month I kept putting adhesive tape on my nose, attaching it to one end and clamping the other to my forehead, so I'd have a turned up nose, kind of like Melissa Stewart's. But it kept coming off in bed and didn't do anything.

"Well, I'm pretty hungry," Father said. "Let's go!"

Mother looked at Arthur again. "Are you sure you don't want to come, Arthur?"

"Yep," was all he said, and we left him there.

I didn't say anything all the way over to the Inn. I kept wishing I didn't look the way I did. Father said if Arthur got hungry enough, he'd come.

Dinner was wonderful and all these people kept coming up to

136

our table. Mother and Father are these very well-liked people at Ponte Vedra and even though we do live in such a small town, some of the people we see there come from afar to visit us.

I had pompano and right in the middle of it, Arthur came walking all orange into the dining room! The only thing was he was wearing dark glasses like a blind man and he also had this cigarette holder dangling from his hand.

Right away I felt the blood rush to my face. *"Do* something, Mother," I said. "Tell him to go back."

"Heavens," Mother said, and I knew everybody was staring. Arthur plopped down in a chair and didn't say anything.

"Arthur," Mother whispered in this almost rasping voice. "Put that away!"

"What?" he asked very innocently.

"You know what," Father said. "Give it to me!"

"My holder?"

"Give it to me!"

Arthur handed over the cigarette holder, and then our waiter came over. Arthur looked up into his face and I wondered if he could see anything. It was dark in the dining room anyway.

"The pompano is very good," Mother said. I guess she was trying to help him out. It was impossible for him to read the menu.

I declare, I can't understand why Arthur does these batty things all the time.

Anyway, when we got to the dessert, Arthur changed his dark glasses for his normal ones and in the soft light you could hardly tell he had those white circles round his eyes. The rest of dinner was great, except later, when they served coffee in the lounge, we spotted the Woods from Richmond! I saw them first, because I saw Margaret and Jonathan. Margaret and Jonathan are the daughter and son of Mr. and Mrs. Woods. I despise them. Margaret is Arthur's age and Jonathan is in college now. They surely had changed—just in one year!

"How lovely," Mrs. Woods said when Mother went up to speak to her. They never come over and speak to us first. Margaret and Jonathan were talking to some people their age, but Mrs. Woods went right on telling us about them anyway—without our even asking. Margaret was at Miss Porter's School in Farmington, Connecticut, this year, she said, and of course Jonathan was at Princeton. "We're quite proud of him. He made Henry's club, you know."

"What club were you, Henry?" Mother asked Mr. Woods.

"Ahvy," Mr. Woods said as if he were about to throw up. He has these very large nostrils. He meant "Ivy."

Mother invited them *all* over for cocktails the next night and I could have died. But she said the Woods were always having us and she thought we should do something for them this time. I hate, hate the Woods!

15

The reason I hate the Woods is because of what they did to Arthur. I don't mean Mr. and Mrs. Woods especially. What I mean is Margaret and Jonathan. Peg. "Everyone calls me Peg at Farmington," she said in this slurpy voice she'd gotten up.

Let me tell you about Jonathan and Peg. They are these very handsome people, both of them. Jonathan is tall and blond with this bored, bony face and white teeth. At Ponte Vedra he gets very tan and his eyebrows very light. His nose never gets red. The only thing that gets red about him is his cheekbones, and they don't get too red because he tans so much. He's always known how good looking he is and you ought to see him on the beach. He wears these black and white checked bathing trunks and comes walking out and never speaks to anybody. He doesn't even make any splash when he goes in the ocean.

It's funny, but Peg is a brunette. Her hair is never messed up and she wears it straight and under, except for this one wave she has on the side. She has green eyes and her mother's nose—straight and not too long. Even when she was ten you would have thought she was fifty. Neither Peg or Jonathan have ever laughed.

138

Years ago when they used to come to Ponte Vedra they had a white governess. She never laughed either, and Mother used to make Arthur and I go over and have a tea party on the lawn with them. Jonathan never would let anybody else have any cookies, and he sat there gulping them all down and that governess never said one word to him. She hated Arthur and I because we didn't live in Virginia.

The really odd thing is both Peg and Jonathan always have an awful lot of friends at Ponte Vedra. I don't see why, but they're always going around with a bunch of people. Jonathan is this big golfer and he and his father are always boring everybody about it. I think that's the most tiresome thing in the world— people that sit around talking about *their* golf game all the time. No one on earth is interested in it except themselves. Peg plays tennis and I saw her one day. She has this white tennis dress and she serves the ball like she was doing a ballet dance. She's also very lazy, and when she gets through playing, her face never gets red or anything like mine does. She just very gracefully goes over and plops herself down in a chair. Peg is extremely popular, but I don't know why because she never laughs and she's always looking like she was half bored to death. I guess that's the way you have to be to be popular.

Anyway, while Mother and I were bringing glasses out onto the patio and getting ready for the Woods, I just happened to say that if I went to Princeton the one club I wouldn't want to be in would be Ivy. She asked me why and I told her.

"Why, Felicia, I think Jonathan is a charming boy. His mother told me he was doing so well in college."

"Just because he got in that club," I said. "What's so good about that?"

"It's just a very interesting club, that's all," Mother said.

"I bet it's filled up to here with snobs," I said, holding my hand up to my throat.

Mother put down a glass on the tray and looked at me. "Felicia, since when have you gotten so interested in the word snob?"

139

"I've always been interested in it. There're about one million at school."

"They're not snobbish to you, are they?"

"No, but they're snobbish to just about everybody else. If you happen to be poor and live in some little grey wooden house, they think you're absolutely horrible."

"Well, that of course isn't very nice of them." She counted out some paper napkins and put them on the table. "But you be nice to Jonathan and Margaret. Remember *you're* entertaining."

"*I'm* not," I said. "I'll just be sitting here and staring like I always do. Nobody cares whether I'm here or not."

And they didn't. About six o'clock they came piling onto the patio, all dressed up. Mrs. Woods is a brunette with these streaks of grey in it. She's also very tan and has Jonathan's white teeth. She's the only one in the whole family that laughs, but every time she does you know she doesn't mean it. She was wearing a dark-blue polka-dot dress with long white beads. I guess she wanted us to see how tan she was.

The sun was going down and we all stood there like idiots watching the sun sink into the water. Jonathan and Peg were very bored, and then Arthur came out with his white coat on. I thought he looked very nice because he was smiling and shaking hands with everybody except Peg. He pretended she wasn't there. And then he dragged this chair up and sat by Mrs. Woods. I heard him say to her: "Mrs. Woods, do you go to the Stork Club? I mean, have you ever been there?"

I guess that sort of surprised Mrs. Woods because she started batting her eyes and said, "Why, no, Arthur. Mr. Woods and I don't enjoy night clubs very much."

"You *don't?*" Arthur asked and glanced up at Jonathan who was still standing and looking down at Arthur in a very inferior way, "I go all the time," Arthur said. "I've been to the Stork Club and the Copa and even down in Greenwitch Village."

"*Gran*itch," Jonathan said. "Granitch Village, for godsakes." He gave out this extremely sneering laugh.

Mrs. Woods turned to Mother, which I thought was very rude

of her because Arthur had even drug up a chair to sit beside her.

Peg came over and leaned on this chair near Arthur. She was wearing a green dress and the left side of her hair was held back from her face. "I'm literally dying for a drink," she said to Jonathan.

"Do you drink?" Arthur asked her and his eyes grew quite wide.

"Occasionally. Don't you?"

"I do when I'm in New York," Arthur said. "I don't do it too much in Georgia."

"Oh?" Peg said and kind of pushed her hair back some. She went over to Mother. "Missus Whitfield, this is terribly cute of you to have us over and everything, but I think I'm just going to have to dash. We're meeting some people for dinner."

"Oh, I'm sorry, Margaret," Mother said. "But you were sweet to come by."

"Well, I literally couldn't have stood it if I didn't get just a tiny glimpse of you and Mr. Whitfield." She looked very bored back at Jonathan who was drinking this very pale drink Father had poured for him. "Jawny, I really think we've *got* to dash!"

Jonathan glanced at his watch. "Yes, we're meeting some people, I guess." He went over to Father and shook hands. "Thank you for the drink, Mr. Whitfield. Peachy."

"Sorry you have to go, Jonathan," Father said.

Jonathan didn't say anything and went over and thanked Mother. He told her he thought it had been peachy, too.

Nobody said anything to Arthur and I and they started down the patio steps.

"Jawny," Mrs. Woods said. "I think Arthur would like to go with you."

Both of them turned and stared at Arthur as if they'd never seen him before.

"Oh, I don't have to go," Arthur said.

"Of course, you do," Mrs. Woods said. She turned to Mother. "There's an awfully nice group of young people here this year."

141

"Would you like to come?" Peg asked Arthur in this very quiet voice.

"Yes, he would," Mrs. Woods said, as if she were doing some huge favor for Arthur.

"Why don't you go with them, Arthur?" Mother said. "Arthur hasn't met any young people yet," she said to Mrs. Woods. (I guess it didn't make any difference that I hadn't met any either.)

"Okay then," Arthur said, and right away Jonathan and Peg started walking away. There was only room enough for two on the walkway, so Arthur trailed behind them, grinning. I knew how happy he was, and I hadn't minded too much not being asked. I guess nobody even thought of me because I'm such a goon.

"So cute, aren't they?" Mrs. Woods said, watching them as they turned to go up to the back patio. You knew, though, she was only talking about Jonathan and Peg.

I thought we positively never would go to dinner. After Arthur and them left, we sat for hours talking about Barry Goldwater. Boring. Boring. Boring. Mr. Woods with his half-bald head and tremendous nostrils thought Barry Goldwater was practically the saviour of the universe. He thought people that didn't like Goldwater were Communists.

Father didn't say what I knew he was thinking, but he thinks Barry Goldwater is inferior. I've heard him at home talking to Mother, and I know for a fact Father is not inclined to Communism. He's quite partial to President Kennedy because he reads books and tries to keep up with what's going on. Mr. Woods, though, thought Kennedy wanted to give the government away. Boring.

Mother and Mrs. Woods were extremely nice to each other. Mrs. Woods kept talking about her ancestors all the time. She had this relative that was in Millard Filmore's cabinet when he was President and now she has his portrait hanging in her house. She said it was so interesting because the man looked exactly like

142

Jonathan. People were always coming in her house and saying it was a spitting image of Jonathan. For the life of me I can't understand why anybody would want something that looked like Jonathan sitting up on their wall. Mother, though, thought that was just a lovely thing for Mrs. Woods to have. At least she said so.

I didn't get to say a thing, as is my custom. I just sat there, staring at the ocean and drinking Coca-Colas. I drank three and on the last one I thought I was getting drunk. Lial Anderson— this friend at home, said she drank six once and got so drunk she couldn't even stagger home. Mother had this little plate of peanuts on the table and every time I got a chance I'd grab a handful and eat one at a time. I didn't have to pass because everybody just grabbed.

Mr. Woods started getting louder and louder with his talk about Barry Goldwater, and Mrs. Woods finally said she thought it was time for us to go to the dining room. I guess she thought Mr. Woods was getting drunk. He did sort of sound like it but I guess it was just his Virginia accent. The Woods said "aboot" for "about" and "hoose" for "house." It's kind of nice in a way. I thought about maybe developing a Virginia accent.

They were all very jolly going over to the Inn, and I just kind of trailed behind them. Sometimes I remind myself of a slave. Thank goodness, though, the Woods sat at their own table and we at ours. Across the room was this long table where Arthur and about seven other people were sitting. I kept looking at them and I thought they should have given Arthur a better seat. He was all squashed in between these two older boys and nobody was saying anything to him. Everybody there looked like they were about Jonathan's age, but it didn't make any difference to Peg. She and this blonde girl were talking to all the other boys and Arthur was looking down at his plate. I told Mother I thought it wasn't very nice of them to squeeze Arthur in like that. "How can he eat?"

"I suppose they already had the table planned," Mother said. "They couldn't have known Arthur was coming."

143

"They all look so *old*," I said.

"The girls are his age," Mother said, and then I saw her slowly put her fork down. She was looking at Arthur's table.

I turned, too, and the terrible thing was everybody was leaving the table. Everybody but Arthur! They all got up, even Jonathan and Peg, and not one soul said one word to Arthur. Not even good-bye!

"Where're they going?" I asked.

"I don't know," Mother said. "They seem to have left Arthur."

Poor Arthur. There he was, just sitting at that long table all by himself. Other people were looking at him, too, and he wasn't eating or anything. He was just sitting there, looking down at his plate with his shoulders all humped up.

"That's mean of them," I said. "They didn't even say good-bye."

I don't know why Arthur didn't get up or anything. Maybe he just didn't want to, with everybody staring and everything.

"Darn it!" Father said. And then he got up and went over to Arthur. I thought Father was mad or something, but he wasn't. He kind of put his arm around Arthur's shoulder and leaned down and said something.

Arthur didn't look up, so Father sat down beside him and started talking. After a while they both got up and came over to our table.

"Arthur and I are going out on the town," Father said. "We're going to a movie and then afterward we're going to stop somewhere and have a bite to eat."

"Where did the other people go?" I asked.

"Dancing," Arthur said.

"Didn't they ask you?" Mother said.

Arthur shook his head.

"No one asked you?" she said.

Arthur just kind of looked away.

"That doesn't make any difference," Father said. "We'll show them. Won't we, Arthur? We'll show them!"

Arthur nodded and I could have cried.

After dinner Mother said she believed she wanted to just go

144

on back to the room. I guess she was feeling so sorry for Arthur she just didn't have the heart to stand around in the lounge being nice to people.

I'm certainly glad we went back, though, because just about as soon as we got to the patio the phone started ringing. It was my Aunt Ann calling long distance from Charleston. Aunt Ann is Mother's sister and Mother's very partial to her.

"Oh, Ann!" Mother said. "What's the matter? Is something wrong with Pett? Oh, you had me frightened for a minute.... Why, yes, Ann! We'd *love* to have her. Will she fly down? Fine. I know. I know. Yes, I know. We'll do the best we can. Felicia will be so happy to see her ... I don't know. I guess we'll come over maybe in the fall. I want Felicia to come, too. Oh, lovely! Yes, yes...."

"Who's coming?" I asked when she put down the receiver.

"Winky," Mother said. "Ann thinks she needs a change. I guess it's that boy she's interested in. Ann is simply frantic she may marry him."

I nearly passed out with delight. Winky coming to Ponte Vedra! She is my most favorite cousin in all the world. See, she's tragic. She's twenty-seven years old and still not married. It's the most pitiful thing in the world because she's had offers to marry and everything, but for the life of her she just can't seem to find anybody with the right connections. *You* know, somebody from Charleston.

"Gosh, how long will she stay?" I asked, beaming violently.

"Just for the weekend. It'll be lovely to have her, won't it?"

"Sure *will*." Winky's a thousand times nicer than the Woods. She went to Wellesley and she's the most unsnobbish person you ever saw. Also, I thought I might could tell her what I'd done when Mr. Hopper was at home. She wouldn't tell a soul. That's the kind of human being she is. She's exceedingly inspirational.

16

Winky's plane didn't get in until the next afternoon, so that gave me plenty of time to get myself together. Mother said Winky was going to stay in my room with me which, as you can imagine, was a fine pleasure for me. I got up quite early Saturday morning and put on stockings. This was quite a shock to everyone at breakfast. I came walking in the dining room and everyone was vastly surprised. All anybody else ever has on for breakfast are Bermuda shorts and things, but I came walking in with my stockings and lovely dark-blue dress on.

"What in the world, Felicia?" Mother asked.

"What?" I asked back.

"Why are you so dressed up?"

"I don't know. Just tired of going around looking so haggard, I guess."

"Why, I think you've looked very nice."

"Not really. I think everyone ought to look decent sometimes."

"All right, but, remember, that's your best dress."

"I know." Sometimes Mother doesn't even think I have a brain.

It *was* rather boring sitting around all dressed up. After breakfast I went in the lounge and sat watching everybody. I watched until about ten-thirty. You would think that if you were the only person sitting in a huge room like the lounge, *some*body would speak to you, but nobody did. Most of the people just kind of smiled and I kind of smiled back.

Finally, I decided I'd better go on back to the room and go swimming. That would kill a lot of time until Winky got there and, besides, I could dress up again after lunch.

I'm certainly glad I went back when I did. Because, I got in on the beginning of this terrible thing Arthur did. I'm not so sure I really ought to tell about it. Mother made me promise I wouldn't say anything about it in Ashton. And I'm not—not the really bad part. Everybody at Ponte Vedra thought it was funny,

146

but we didn't. Arthur wouldn't even come out of his room for the last two days we were there.

What happened was—see—Arthur didn't meet any girls his age. He met this one the junior hostess tried to push off on him. But she was this very tall, giggly girl that did nothing but walk around with her hand dangling in the air. They did play bingo one night but she giggled all the way through the game and neither of them ever "bingoed." Arthur had to pay two dollars and fifty cents a card, too. Ponte Vedra gets quite expensive like that, in a thousand different ways.

Anyway, that morning at breakfast Arthur was glooming around because they were having the Saturday-night dance at the Surf Club. Mother said Arthur could go to it this year on account of he was getting so old.

"You can be with us," she said.

Arthur didn't say anything, but the last thing in the world I knew he wanted was to sit up there with Mother and Father.

"Why don't you ask Peg Woods to go with you?" I asked.

"Heavens," Mother said. "I certainly wouldn't do *that*—not after the way she treated you."

"She wasn't so bad," Arthur said. I knew he didn't want to act humiliated in front of us.

"Besides, I'm sure she already has an engagement," Mother said.

Arthur just mumbled something.

"Go on and call her," I said. It was exciting. I wanted to see what would happen. I could just see Arthur and Peg.

We didn't talk about it any more then. But when I got back to the room to go swimming I heard him talking on the phone in his room.

"...You've gotta wash your *hair?*" he was saying. "What do you have to do that for? Yeah? Well, why don't you wash it now?" There was a long silence. "Well, Peg, look! We can just stay for a half hour. Your mother wouldn't think that was too much.... You came down here to rest? Well, look, go ask her if you can't go for just a half hour?" Another long pause. "She did? By ten-thirty? Sure! We don't even have to stay that long if you don't want to. Okay, look, I'll see you about eight o'clock. Eight-thirty? Okay. Bye."

Well, I was amazed. To tell the truth I didn't think Arthur had that much nerve, to call up somebody like Peg Woods. It's terrible for boys to have to call up girls, I think. But sometimes Arthur can surprise you. I think he inherited a lot of his nerve from Uncle Alex that is divorced. Uncle Alex was also a well-known spy during World War II.

I was glad for Arthur, though I thought it was quite interesting for him to partake of a good time, since his life has been so unfulfilled and everything.

After lunch, Winky came driving up with a one-eyed taxi driver. Naturally we were overjoyed to see her and we showed a great deal of emotion on our part. She looked very nice in a seersucker suit. Winky's pretty tall and actually I guess when I get older I'll probably look something like her myself. She's blonde, but the only thing about her is she has these two teeth that kind of cross in the front. It doesn't look too bad but I'm glad I don't have them. Also she plays golf all the time.

She and Mother started embracing madly. Terrible!

"Awnt Seyruh!" she said to Mother. I forgot to tell you, that's how they talk in Charleston. They say "Seyruh" for Sarah and "bo-ut" for boat and "pyehpuh" for paper. I think they get it from refined colored people. Somebody told me that, I think.

"Felicia!" she said. "How gro-wan you are!"

"Thank you," I said, and started kind of hitting the sides of my legs. I guess she noticed my stockings.

"Where's Allison?" she asked all breathy and beaming.

"Playing golf," Mother said. "He'll be in later. I don't know *where* Arthur is."

"He's in the lounge reading that book again," I said.

"What book?" Mother asked.

"The one by that French girl—the one you said was well written but trash."

"Oh dear," Mother said, and Winky laughed.

148

Mother put her arm around Winky. "Well, come, Winky. I hope you don't mind staying in the room with Felicia."

"Nooo. I *hoped* I would!"

Wasn't that *nice* of her to say that? That's the way she is, and she really meant it, too. I know.

When we got in the room she ran to the window. "Oah, this wonderful ocean! Such a lovely breeze." She turned to Mother. "Let's take a walk, Awnt Seyruh, right now. Up the beach."

Winky is absolutely harassed with energy. She's always wanting to take walks and things.

"Fine," Mother said. "But don't you want to unpack first?"

"I'll do that later. Come on, Felicia!"

Winky always starts up fun-things, right away.

"Would you like to take a walk, too, Felicia?" Mother asked.

"Just dying to," I said and started toward the door.

"I think you'd better change first, don't you?" Mother said. "Felicia's started wearing stockings, you know, Winky."

Winky looked down at my pitiful thin legs. "I see," was all she said.

I wish Mother hadn't said that. It isn't nice to tell somebody that somebody else has started doing something new. It makes you feel stupid.

We all got dressed in shorts and then went strolling up the beach very slowly. I walked beside them and not in back like I usually do. I love being with Winky and Mother. They treat me so elderly. I wished Winky had been with us for the whole time.

When we'd got a little ways from the patio, Mother said, "Now, Winky, tell me about this *boy!*"

I was thrilled. That's the kind of conversation I'm very partial to.

"Tom, you mean?" Winky asked. "I see Mother has been bothering you about it, too."

"She's mentioned him," Mother said.

"I suppose she told you he's a Yankee?"

"Yes, she told me that immediately."

Winky laughed. "You should *hear* Awnt Pett. She's absolutely

149

beside herself. A Petrie marrying a damn Yankee! She's positive I'm going to marry him."

"Well, *are* you?" Mother asked.

"I don't know." But by the way she said it you knew she was teasing.

"He's rich, isn't he, Winky?" I said. "Cheap rich?"

Both Mother and her laughed uproariously. I just wanted to know.

"I see Mother really *has* been talking," Winky said. "They've bought the old La Jeune plantation, you know. You can imagine how Awnt Pett feels about that. 'Yankee trash, living in that beautiful old place.' Really, you ought to hear her!"

"I can imagine," Mother said. "But, Winky, are you really interested in him?"

"Oh, I don't think so. Not really. He's just somebody to— Everybody's married, you know. Literally everybody I—"

"Well, I think that's very nice for you, Winky," Mother said. "Why does Ann object to him so?"

"Family, I guess. They *are* a bit much and, too, Tom doesn't do anything and he's kind of fat."

"*Fat?*" Mother and I asked together.

"Not really—but you'll see him. Mother says you're coming over this fall."

"I'd like to," Mother said. "Either this fall or spring. I want Felicia to see more of Charleston now that she's getting a little older."

Winky glanced at me. "Yes, since you're getting so gro-wan." She kind of patted me on the shoulder.

"When are we going, Mother?" I asked. Frankly, it kind of scared me, the thought of going to a place as snobbish as Charleston. I mean I'd learned all about how snobs are and I knew they'd hate me! My Aunt Pett won't even speak to you unless you've got about one million ancestors. They all have to be Southerners, too. I know all about Charleston. Don't go there unless you really have nice ancestors. If you don't and go anyway, people might be nice to you, but they'll think you're common just the same.

It's pretty terrible, and the worst thing about me is I'm bored to distraction over ancestors. I just have no inclination toward them at all. I might get over it, though.

Mother said she wasn't sure when we were going, that it depended on school and Arthur and many things.

"Well, I'll see to it you meet Tom," Winky said. "I think you'd like him. He's so fun-ny."

Poor Winky. She did want to be married so. Still, I just couldn't imagine her married to a cheap-rich Northerner. I think, myself, I'd almost even rather be an old maid. But not in Charleston.

"Do you still hear from the one in New York?" Mother asked. "The one you were so interested in in college?"

"Oh yes," Winky said. "He says he may be coming down this fall."

"He's the only one you've ever really been interested in. Isn't he?"

Winky started looking very serious. "Yes," she said, "unfortunately."

Mother let out this sigh. "It's all so trying, isn't it?"

"I don't think he ever really cared anything about me. He—"

"Well, why don't you just forget him then?"

"I'm trying."

We didn't say anything more for a long time. We just walked very slowly and tragically. I think it's terrible that somebody as nice as Winky has to go and suffer so much. She's always so cheerful about her plot, too. If I were twenty-seven and still not married, I don't think I'd be cheerful at all. I probably won't be married then either. I'll probably go on until I'm fifty thousand and then marry somebody old like Velvet said I would. That is, if I marry at all.

"Oah," Winky said. "I forgot to tell you! I've got some friends down here. They have a house. The Tarletons. They're in the tobacco business from Greensboro. I called Alice at the airport and she wants me to go to some dance or something with them tonight. All right?"

151

"Why, lovely," Mother said. "The dance is down at the Surf Club."

"That's where Arthur's going to be, too," I said. "He's going to the dance, too."

"Arthur is?" Mother asked. "Does he have a date to go?"

"Uh huh, with Peg Woods."

"Peg *Woods?*" Mother asked.

"Uh huh. He asked her this morning and she first said she had to wash her hair. But she's going."

"Oh dear."

Winky looked at Mother. "Why, is something wrong with Peg Woods?"

"No. No," Mother said. "I just think she's a little more advanced than Arthur."

"They're the same age," I said.

"I know, but girls mature so much faster."

"I know," I said and looked at Winky. "We just don't think Arthur will ever mature."

Winky laughed. "I don't think any of us will, frankly. But, really, Arthur going to a dance! I can't believe it."

"He goes all the time up in New York," I said.

"Now, Felicia," Mother said. That's what she's always telling me when she thinks I'm exaggerating. She thinks I exaggerate all the time. Exaggerating means lying. To her, I mean. I thought of Mr. Hopper.

"Time, time, time," Winky said. "It makes such a loud noise rushing by."

Beautiful saying! See, that's the way Winky is. She's always going around saying beautiful things like that. I like that. Time, time, time. It's so poetic.

We walked for miles up the beach and talked deep the whole way. When we got back to the room, Arthur was already dressed up. Also Father. They were just sitting in the room, dressed up and staring at each other. It's very peculiar, but when it's just Arthur and Father alone they can't ever think up much to say to each other.

152

Winky kissed both of them on the cheek and they seemed exceedingly glad to see her.

"Where have you three been?" Father asked.

"For a walk," Mother said.

"Well, it's five-thirty. Arthur wants to have an early dinner tonight. Seems he has a date."

Arthur had on his dark-blue suit—the one he had bought up in New York and his hair was all slicked down. He looked like he had been dressing for hours. How strange life is. We used to have terrible troubles with Arthur; he wouldn't even take a bath. That went on for simply years.

"We won't be a minute," Winky said. "Come on, Felicia. Let's get dressed."

"Okay," I said but I was thinking that now might be the time I could confess to her about Mr. Hopper. It's funny, but I'd never thought about the magazine coming out and people in Charleston reading it, too. They'd all commit suicide—me saying I didn't like anybody but Negroes and that I wanted to go to school with nothing but Negroes in the room. Aunt Pett and them would never speak to me again. Even Aunt Ann and Uncle Petrie wouldn't.

While Winky was combing her hair, I said "Winky, I've got something to tell you. It's the most terrible thing in the world. Really awful."

"What is it?" she asked, but she didn't look around from the mirror or anything.

"Well, it's about this Northern newspaperman. He came down to visit us and I—"

But the telephone rang. I answered it and it was for Winky.

"Scuse me, Felicia," she said. It was her friends from North Carolina. They were coming right away to get her. She banged down the receiver and kind of let out a yelp. "I've got to hurry!"

I watched her flying around the room, getting junk together and putting them in her pocketbook. I guess she'd forgotten about me having something terrible to tell her. She didn't even ask me about it.

"Are you going to be pretty late coming back, Winky?"

"I don't know, but you go on to sleep. I hope I won't disturb you coming in."

"Oh, you won't!"

I started to say I could tell her later, but she wasn't in the mood to listen, I guess. I knew I wasn't going to get another chance to tell her because she'd be playing golf the next day and then after that we'd be going home. When Mother and I got to Charleston the article would be out and I'd already be a common disgrace.

Mother and Father and Arthur and I, all alone, had dinner together at the Surf Club—out in the open. It was a very beautiful night. You could hear the roar of the ocean and the stars were out so you could see the palm trees outlined against the sky. The stars are so close to you in Florida.

Winky and her friends sat at another table and Winky was extremely happy looking. She was laughing and talking and I just sat there, watching her. She was the only person in the world I could have told what I'd done to. It wouldn't have worried her as much as somebody like Mother or Father and, too, I know she wouldn't have told Aunt Pett and them. What she could have done was stolen the magazine when it came out so nobody would see it.

Arthur made us hurry up and finish our dessert because I guess he wanted us to leave. Father asked Mother if she didn't want to stay for the dancing, but Arthur started getting very nervous so Mother said "no," that she was a little tired from so much walking and believed she would just like to go back to the room. Mother and Father usually stay a while for the dancing, but I guess they didn't want to humiliate Arthur.

"Then it looks as if this is going to be *your* night, Arthur," Father said and scraped back his chair.

On the way back to our rooms Father said he thought Arthur had started getting ashamed of us. He sort of laughed, so I guess he wasn't hurt or anything. I was glad it wasn't just me Arthur was ashamed of.

154

Anyway, while he was dancing we sat around in Mother and Father's room and talked about Uncle Alex. Uncle Alex owns a newspaper down in southern Georgia. I like him tremendously but, of course, he's the one that's divorced! Nobody else, on either side of the family, has ever been divorced before, and when Uncle Alex did it, you would have thought he had axed up somebody or something. He only married his wife because he was lonely. He went to school in England.

I started yawning. It's depressing, I think, to sit up and talk about somebody in your own family that's divorced. But Mother said every family in the world has some trouble in it and she thinks we've been pretty lucky so far.

"I guess I'll go on to bed," I said.

"Yes," Father said. "I think we all should."

Mother looked at her watch. "Almost ten. Arthur should be in soon. I *do* want to hear about it."

I got in bed and started reading a story in a magazine I'd found. It wasn't very good and I started to turn out the light but I heard this knocking on my door. "Missus Whitfield. Missus Whitfield." It was Peg!

I jumped out of bed and ran into Mother's room. "Peg Woods is outside," I said. "She's calling for you."

"For me?" Mother said. She went to the door. "Why, Peg dear, what is it?"

"Missus Whitfield," Peg said. "Arthur's drunk and something pretty awful has happened."

For a moment I thought Mother was going to faint, but she didn't. She just said, "Allison! Allison! Come here immediately!"

Father right away went down to the Surf Club to see what had happened, and Mother and I just sat there with our hearts thumping. Arthur drunk! It was like the stars dropping out of the sky—one by one.

Mother didn't say much. She just sat there, her mouth one thin line and her fingers resting in her lap. We thought Father would positively never come back. He must have been gone over an hour at least. Mother told me to go to bed, but I said I couldn't sleep

155

anyway. She said, "All right. All right. Why don't they come?"

Then—in they came! Arthur had a huge bandage over his nose and his glasses were all crooked. We just stood there, staring at him. Father didn't say anything; he led Arthur into his room and shut the door.

"He's hurt," I said. Arthur had such a funny look in his eyes I wanted to cry.

"His nose—" Mother said in this very pathetic voice. Then Father came out.

"What happened?" Mother asked.

"I don't know exactly," Father said. It *seemed* that Arthur had ordered a bottle of cherry wine, which he thought was Sherry wine. He had told the waiter it was for Father. But the waiter had brought Cherry Heering instead and Arthur had drunk too much. He got sick, practically crawled into the men's room and the toilet seat fell on his nose.

"Where was Winky?" Mother asked.

"Gone, I guess," Father said. "They weren't there when I got there."

"Heavens." Poor Mother looked so pale.

"We've been up and down the beach trying to find a doctor," Father said. "We finally found one."

"Is his nose broken?" Mother asked.

"It isn't a bad break."

Mother just sort of collapsed into a chair. "On a *toilet* seat," she said. "And he's the last of the Whitfields, too. The very last."

We all nearly died.

PART III

17

I never did get a chance to talk to Winky. Just as I knew she would, she played golf all the next day and she never asked me what it was I had to tell her. I guess she was too interested in Arthur and his huge bandage on his nose. She kept telling him he ought not to be embarrassed, but he was. He wouldn't even go in the dining room so we had to send trays and things over to him. False pride. We do hope he will triumph over that.

Poor old Arthur. I don't think his vacation had been a very enjoyable one. But mine sure had. It was the saddest thing in the world saying good-bye to Ponte Vedra. Also to Winky, but Mother kept telling her we'd see her soon. "Yes," I thought, "after I'm exposed as the most tremendous liar in the entire universe." I started up worrying again, terribly this time.

So that's the way we returned from vacation—me, half worried to death and Arthur with his bandage. Thank goodness, though, Arthur got only a slight hump on his nose. We were worried he would have to go back to school with a large one, but he didn't. It was pretty sad, seeing him go again. The night before he left we had a kind of celebration dinner and we all gave him presents. I gave him a tie Mother had got in Atlanta. Father was kind of mad about our going to Atlanta to shop. He still wanted us to be "loyal" and go to Morris' Store in Ashton because Mr. Morris was in the Rotary Club with him. Anyway, Mother gave him a sweater, dark grey. But Father did this very peculiar thing. He gave Arthur a New Testament, with his name on it. I don't know what Arthur thought because he didn't say very much. Inside, Father had written: "To Arthur Whitfield from his father: September 20, 1960." And underneath was written: "Remember Now Thy Creator In The Days Of Thy Youth." I read it and felt a huge sorrow—worse than when we left Ponte Vedra. I don't know why I felt that way, but when somebody's leaving and then your father does something like that, it just sort of makes you really want to cry. I kept thinking, "What if we don't ever see Arthur again?" Connecticut is so far away and everybody's so different and you can't ever tell what might happen when someone's away. That's what Mother always says.

"That's lovely, Allison," Mother said when she finished examining the New Testament.

"Now that's the most important thing you have, Arthur," Father said.

"Yes, sir," Arthur mumbled, and he just sat there with his head hanging down, looking at his gold name on the outside.

The next day we all went down to the station to see him off again—even Isaiah and Velvet. Sometimes when I think about it, it seems I've spent my entire life in the train station. We're always going down there meeting somebody or seeing somebody off. Across the tracks from the station there's this colored house and these colored children are always racing around drinking great big bottles of orange. Everytime you go down there, one or other of the children has grown some more. I watch them all the time and think about everybody growing old—us and they.

But there was Arthur. It's terrible to always be the one going. I mean we could all be safe together at home, but not Arthur. I guess it's sort of like going into the army. There you are, getting on the train to have your brains blown out and everybody else is just standing there, forcing this terrible cheerfulness.

"Now you won't get lost this time," Mother said. "You know

158

how to go through the station in New York, don't you, Arthur?"

"Certainly!" Arthur said, and I thought I heard a tinge of his sophisticated accent again. I guess he was getting ready for up there.

And then the train came in. Mother and Velvet hugged Arthur good-bye and Isaiah and Father only shook hands with him.

"Now study hard," Father said. "Let's see some A's this year— including algebra."

"Okay," Arthur said, grinning, a little too much, I thought. He just glanced at me. "Bye, Felicia."

"Bye," I said.

He looked very nice this time. He had on his dark-grey suit, and even though he was a little too chubby from the summer, I bet he looked just as nice as anybody else on the train. The only thing was I like Arthur's hair better when he doesn't put too much water on it. When it gets dry, he looks better.

Velvet started waving her apron and cutting up like she does sometimes. Arthur was laughing, but I knew he didn't feel much like it. I know I didn't. It's pitiful when a member of your own family goes away and you know they're going to stay for months and months.

The train jerked and the porter hopped on the platform and slammed the door shut. There was another jerk and the train began to go. Arthur was leaning out the door, still waving. You could tell what he was saying but you couldn't hear. He was saying, "Good-bye. Good-bye. Good-bye." You would have died.

When the train disappeared we were all still standing there, grinning. "Oh, I *do* hope something grand happens to him," Mother said. "I just pray it will."

"A-men," Velvet said, and we all walked back to the car with our heads hanging down.

But *I* walked back into stark-raving tragedy! I don't much like to talk about it, but since it's part of last year I guess I'd better put it in. For the life of me I don't know how it all happened, but what happened was I grew one million feet tall. Just overnight, almost. It must have happened in the summer or something. Nobody else much had grown and Mother had a fit because I had to have all these new clothes and things. It was a dreadful entrance into the Ashton Junior High School. See, junior-high school is attached to high school and there're all these boys— older ones and everything.

Literally everything about me started getting long—arms, neck, legs—even my fingers. I got to be even taller than Mother. At gym one day we all had to measure and weigh, and this teacher that has cross-eyes and goes around bouncing the basketball all over the place looked at me when my time came and said "whoops" and stretched the measuring part of the scales so high I could have cried. I was five feet seven and a half inches tall!

I don't know why that had to go and happen to me. Everybody else got extremely beautiful and popular. Mother said that when I get older I'll be thankful to be tall but she doesn't know anything. Sometimes I'd lie in the bathtub and think if I could only cut off about five inches off my legs, then attach my feet back on again I'd be all right. You don't know what it's like walking down the hall with somebody like Melissa Stewart who is short and exceedingly beautiful, and there you are this huge, thin giant of a human being.

It was so terrible I couldn't even listen to any of Arthur's letters. I remember he did write something about not rooming with Knox Campbell this year because both of them had forgotten to sign up. Knox had to room with Bob Leyden who was back and cured, and Arthur was rooming with a thin, excruciatingly intelligent human being from Lake Forest, Illinois, that never took baths.

Mother and Father were always trying to get me to join in in reading Arthur's letters, but all I could think about was slam books and dances. See, that's what started up that fall. Slam books are these notebooks, and you put everybody's name at the top, then everybody flips through and writes down what they really think of you. It's strange, but if it's *your* book everybody writes "cute," "pretty hair," and "nice clothes" all over your

160

name, but if it's somebody *else's* they write what they really think of you. In Marilyn Summer's book somebody wrote under my name "to tall, bean pole." There wasn't one single "cute" and only four "nices."

In my diary I made a list:

POPULAR:
Melissa Stewart
Marilyn Summers
Margaret Ann Akers
Eloise Adams
Virginia Sue Markham
Betty Rice

UNPOPULAR:
Felicia Whitfield!!!
Jane Farris
Katharine Armstrong
Charlotte Harrison
Sally Ann Greer
Mary Elizabeth Harmon

These meant boys, not girls! I still had hundreds of friends, but no boys. Girls were always bounding around all over the house. Melissa said that if I started eating—eating everything in sight—I'd start getting fatter and then I wouldn't look so tall. I tried it, but it didn't work. Nothing worked. This new girl moved to Ashton—Carolyn Dunwoody. She was a half a grade above all of us, but she immediately became the most popular person you ever saw. She had green eyes and long, straight brown hair that she wore with a silver clip. Boys were *always* going to her house—even on Sunday afternoons.

Every one of us bought silver clips for our hair, too, but it didn't work with me. I started letting my hair grow frantically long, but Mother made me have it cut. Mother kept saying, "Felicia, you're going to be all right. You have a lovely complexion and your hair is a fine color of blonde."

"But that doesn't help," I said. "You've got to be short and have brown hair and a turned-up nose."

"Ohhhhh me," she kept groaning. I heard her telling Mrs. Ewing that I was at the difficult age which is strange because once I heard Mrs. Ewing say that *Mr.* Ewing was at the difficult age.

Actually, I didn't like to talk very much to Mother about my

161

tragedy. I don't know why exactly. I guess I didn't want her to know how pitiful I was. As you know, no mother wants to know they've brought some goon into the world. It's just too humiliating for them. Besides, Mother was always exceedingly popular when she was my age.

That's pretty much the way it was. Except for dances. *They* started up because this dancing teacher started them. But then later Melissa and all of them started *giving* dances. Mother at first didn't think I ought to go. She said she thought thirteen was too young. "It's ridiculous, Allison," she said. "They just start things too early in Ashton."

"Everybody else is going," I said.

"I know, I know," Mother said.

"Well, why did you let me take from the dancing teacher then if I'm not ever going to dance."

"I think it's a good idea to know *how*," Mother said. "But there's plenty of time for that yet."

I stood up. "I hate you! I hate you! I hate you!"

Mother and Father looked at me as if they had been shot. I don't know why I said that. Mother was just getting on my nervous system, that's all.

"Felicia, *what* has come over you this year?" she said. "You've always been such a pleasant child."

"I'm just tired of always being different, that's all. Everybody else buys their clothes and I still have to go up there to Miss Hodges. She sticks pins in you on purpose. Everything's different. All the time!"

"Well, your father and I are doing the best we can for you. Now, you just get some control!"

"And stop that whining," Father said. "I don't want to hear any more of it."

I just went on up in my room and thought about dying. When I was dead they'd be sorry. Everybody would come to my funeral —even boys—and people would never forget it because of all the violets and everything. I cried for hours it was so pathetically sad.

See, it was Melissa Stewart that was giving the dance. It was

162

the first private one any of us had ever given. Literally everybody was invited, older ones, too. It was going to be in the basement of the Coca-Cola plant. When we get older I guess we'll start having them at the country club so we can get drunk. But the basement of the Coca-Cola plant is pretty good, too. There're cokes all over the place and Mr. Stewart, who owns a fleet of restaurants in Ashton, knows how to buy records that are really good.

Well, anyway, there I was up in my room crying away about being dead and in Mother came. She said she and Father had been talking it over and they guessed I could go to the dance. She didn't really approve of it because it was "just silly, that's all— at your age."

"But I can go?"

"I suppose so." She didn't share my joy at all.

"Hot spit!" I said and started bouncing up and down on the bed.

But, later, after Mother left, I got to *really* thinking about it. The dance. I was scared out of my mind.

18

The first thing that happened was Mrs. Ewing came bounding over all thrilled to death because she had found some dresses for me. They weren't new, but they were party dresses! She had gotten them in the summer when she was up North in a place called Litchfield. Her "dear friend" had given them to her. Her "dear friend's" daughter that was at Smith had simply just grown out of them.

"I don't think she's worn them more than a few times," Mrs. Ewing said as she hilariously unwrapped the box.

"That's the nicest thing I ever *heard* of," Mother said. "Felicia

163

wants to go to a little dance and the dressmaker is down with her gall bladder again."

I just stood there with my hands behind my back, waiting. I don't know why Mother is so partial to people giving me their old worn-out clothes. I've told her a thousand times I think it's sort of downtrodden. But she thinks it's simply grand and sensible, wearing other people's clothes.

"Flo was just going to give them away," Mrs. Ewing said, "but I told her I had a little friend in Ashton and I *knew* she would love to have them."

"How sweet," Mother said. "Really, that is, Margaret."

"Her daughter's a charmer," Mrs. Ewing said, opening the tissue paper. "A perfect little charmer."

And out they came! You positively would have committed suicide.

"Why, why, they're absolutely love-ly!" Mother said. *"Just* Felicia's type."

"Gosh," I said, and I meant it. Taffeta! Not a single ruffle anywhere. One was a plaid—orange and black—and the other—dark blue!

"The little plaid is so handsomely tailored," Mrs. Ewing said. "Here, Felicia." She held the dress up to me and practically broke my collarbone with her two thumbs. "So nice with her fair hair."

"Just *exactly* the sort of thing I had in mind. Isn't it, Felicia?"

"Yesssss," I said, trying to sound overjoyed with pleasure. Somebody as rich as Mrs. Ewing, you can't hurt her feelings.

"Honestly, Margaret," Mother said, "this is the nicest thing I've ever heard of." She really was happy. "Here, let's try the dark blue."

They held it up, too, and I had to just stand there like an idiot.

"I almost think that's better than the other one," Mrs. Ewing said. "Felicia *is* the tailored type. And see, Sarah," she caught hold of the back of the dress, "the little pleats to give it just enough flair."

Mother really was happy. She's been telling me and telling me I'm the tailored type. She adores clothes that you don't notice too

164

much. She thinks there's nothing worser in the world than some girl that looks all dress coming down the street.

"Margaret, how lovely of you to think of Felicia—especially when you were away like that." She had this sad smile on her face as if she were going to cry. Mother is also very partial to people being appreciative. Being appreciative is the gateway to Heaven, she's always saying. She looked at me.

"They certainly are nice, Mrs. Ewing," I said. But I positively couldn't wait until she left. I wasn't going to wear one of those dresses if they put me in iron chains and tried to drag me there. I had already seen Melissa's and Marilyn's. They were the most gorgeous things you've ever seen. Melissa's was blue and ruffled all the way down from the waist. She also had a hoop to wear under it so she looked like War Between the States days. Marilyn's was peach colored and had miles and miles of stuck-out skirt. What if I walked in in that pitiful dark-blue dress with just those pleats in the back. If Mother made me do that I'd never speak to her again.

"Well, I've got to run," Mrs. Ewing said, looking at her watch. "Bill's got to have a little operation tomorrow and—"

"An operation!" Mother said. "Bill Ewing?"

"Nothing serious," Mrs. Ewing said. She put her finger to her mouth. "Hemorrhoids. We don't like to say much about it, but he's been *so* uncomfortable—in real pain."

"Ohhh, I'm so sorry, Margaret. Give him my love, won't you?"

Aren't women peculiar? They can sit up and talk about something like hemorrhoids for hours and hours and never bat an eye.

"Bye, Felicia," Mrs. Ewing said. "Have a nice time at the dance."

"I surely do appreciate your thoughtfulness, Mrs. Ewing."

"Not a-tall. Not a-tall."

"Thank you, Margaret," Mother said. "You were a dear to think of us. I do hope Bill gets along all right."

"Oh, he will. He'll just go in and come right out again."

Mother waved at her and I didn't say anything. I shut the door.

165

"Now wasn't that *grand* of Margaret to think of you?"

"I wish she hadn't," I said. But I don't think Mother heard me. She went back to the box of dresses. "Velvet can take these in for you. I think they need to come in just a—" She held up the plaid one. "Here, Felicia, run up and let's try them on."

"There's no point in it," I said.

"Why?"

"Be-*cause* I just will not wear them."

"What do you mean?"

"I mean I'm not going to walk into the Coca-Cola plant looking like a Yankee goon."

Mother was exasperated. She sat down in the chair. "Felicia, I just don't know *what* I'm going to do with you. In the first place we don't call Northern people Yankees. Some of the loveliest people in the world live in the North. Many of them have excellent taste in clothes and these—those dresses—were bought in New York. You're always talking about wanting to go to New York. I just don't understand you at all."

"*Those* weren't made in New York."

"They certainly were." She got up and examined the label. "Bests. Now you see. It's a fine store for young girls."

"In New York they wear dresses with sparkles all over them."

"No decent person does."

"Yes, they do."

"Felicia, now, pu-leeeese don't try to be silly."

"I'm not!"

"Go right upstairs and try them on." She started walking back to the kitchen. "Vel-vet. Vel-vet. Can you come here a second, please?"

So, *that* is the way I marched into the Coca-Cola plant! I wore the plaid one because at least it had some color in it. It also had a bow in the back, but you couldn't see it too well because it was so large and low it looked like the rest of the dress. Also I had to wear these sad low-heeled black shoes with straps over the instep and I looked like the most tragic person you've ever seen.

166

"You really look lovely," Mother said. "Not like some little overdressed silly. Doesn't she, Allison?"

"What?" Father said. He wasn't even paying any attention. He was reading the old boring *Sewanee Review* again.

"Doesn't Felicia look nice?" Mother said.

He glanced up at me. "Is she wearing lipstick?"

"I think that's all right," Mother said. "For a dance. Just a little."

I felt five thousand feet tall, standing there, and my heart was pounding away. When my heart starts pounding, my face starts getting red and I look terrible. I wish I could get over it.

"She looks all right," Father said.

Mother straightened the strand of pearls. "What time is Mrs. Summers coming for you?"

"Ina minute." I could scarcely talk, and for some reason I went around slapping all the pieces of furniture in the living room.

"There they are now," Mother said. "You'd better wear your coat, Felicia. Here." She put the coat over my shoulders. "And your gloves. Now have a good time."

"Okay," I said and walked out into the night. It was like walking to the guillotine, like Marie Antoinette did in that old movie on television.

Mrs. Summers was driving and she looked sort of beat up compared to everybody else. In the back were Margaret Ann Akers and Betty Rice (Popular). Marilyn was up front with her mother. Margaret Ann and Betty were all spread out with their ruffled dresses. There was hardly any room to sit.

"Is there enough room?" Mrs. Summers asked. "You girls with your skirts," she said.

"There's room," I said. Neither Margaret Ann or Betty moved. I sat all scrunched in by the window, but I noticed my knees were taller than anybody else's. My face started banging away. It was like my heart was inside of my cheeks or something. I thought I just might throw up. I guess it's worse, though, if you have to go to a dance with a boy!

Actually, I don't even remember walking into the Cola-Cola

plant. I do remember seeing some of the machines and things, but what I remember most is the girls' powder room. Everybody was there. Even Carolyn Dunwoody—the new one that's so popular. She was sitting in front of the mirror, combing her hair, and everybody was flocking around her. She looked very beautiful in this white ruffled dress with a blue bow in the back. Everybody, except a few that had on net dresses, had on hooped skirts. One girl's was so large she could hardly make it through the door. She was fat, too.

I just stood up against the wall with my arms crossed and felt like the Empire State Building. It's funny but nobody seemed particularly happy. Nobody was laughing or anything. They all looked dreadfully conceited and bored. Every now and then they'd stare at themselves in the mirror. I would have given anything in the world to have been Carolyn Dunwoody. She used to live in Griffin, Georgia, and that's where she started getting popular. I think she's more popular in Ashton, though, than she was even in Griffin. Mother and Father don't know the Dunwoodys because they're obscure. I wish Mother and Father were.

Anyway, you couldn't stay in the powder room all night, so I went on out to the dance floor. Nothing had begun yet. All these boys were sliding up and down on the floor. That's what they do all the time, start running and then slide as far as they can. Clumps of girls were standing around. Even Harriet Lane and Elizabeth Hill were there. They're in the high ninth and are always being sponsors at football games and things, even in the high ninth. They also chew gum and talk very fast. Most popular people do.

I went on up and stood by Betty Rice and Marilyn. They didn't say much and nobody mentioned my dress. I tried to stand more on my left foot so I wouldn't look so tall. Melissa Stewart was going around giggling to everybody. She knew *she* was safe because she was giving it. They'd all *have* to dance with her.

At the Coca-Cola plant they have these benches that line the wall, all the way around the room. The girls sit on the right side of the room and the boys on the left. What you do is, you sit there and then these boys come racing across the room at you and the one that stands in front of you dances with you. It's horrifying.

Mrs. Stewart went over and plugged in this huge record player that had bubbles going up and down in it, then she said we were going to have three dances where the boys could *choose* their partners. She started clapping her hands and told this one boy that was trying to be funny—he was walking around the floor on his knees—to go sit down and behave with the other boys. Everybody thought that was excruciatingly funny.

"Now when I blow this whistle," Mrs. Stewart said, smiling all over the place because it was her and Melissa's party, "that means that another dance has started."

I was sitting on the bench by Sally Whitehead. She has red hair and her mother is a friend of Mother's. Sally's fourteen and the thinnest person you ever saw. She had on a dress sort of like mine, no ruffles or anything. I guess she didn't want to say too much to me because I'm a grade behind her.

Well, Mrs. Stewart blew the whistle and it was like an *army* attack. Waves and waves of boys came literally dashing across the room. Up the line from where Sally and I were you could hear all this commotion. I think every boy in the room tried to get to Carolyn Dunwoody first. I looked up and she was already dancing. Marilyn and Betty had been chosen, too. Nobody was standing near Sally and I. My face started getting hotter and hotter and then, finally, old Cecil Bowers tapped me on the shoulder.

"Wanna dance?" he said.

I stood up right away. "Yeah!" I looked back down at Sally. She was still sitting there, alone. There was just this one other girl—way down at the other end—and there weren't any other boys. I started to say something, but Cecil was getting all ready to dance, looking down at his feet with his elbows stretched out.

Cecil's in my grade but he's a half a head shorter than I. He's also pretty dumb. All the way through grammar school all he did was sit at his desk and draw castles. His test papers were always on the bottom when they were hung up for everybody to see.

169

"I've been eatin' onion," Cecil said, doing this one step we all knew—slide, slide together, back; slide, slide together, front.

"What for?" I asked him.

"I dunno. I eat 'em all the time."

"Me, too," I said. That's the way to be popular. If a boy says he eats onions, you say you do, too.

We didn't say much else. I looked back at Sally. She and the other left-out girl were sitting side by side. Sally had her arms crossed and her legs stretched out in front of her. It was rude, I thought, of Mrs. Stewart not to see that there were enough boys. Carolyn Dunwoody and this blond boy started doing these other steps that nobody else knew. Everybody was speaking to her—

"Hey, Carolyn. Hey, Carolyn. Hey, Carolyn."

She didn't even smile at them. "Hey," she'd say in this very bored way. Carolyn Dunwoody usually dances with her eyes shut. She's the only one.

I started getting a very bored look on my face. It was pretty hard to do because Cecil Bowers was not very good to dance with. He kept looking down at his feet which made him shrink up even more.

Mrs. Stewart blew the whistle and we had to go sit back down. I don't know *why* I went and sat down by Sally again.

"Well, *you* got asked," she said as if that was the most unheard of thing in the world.

"Uh huh," I said and looked across the room at the boys. They were getting all set to spring across and attack again. I guess they were all trying to reach Carolyn and them first. I put on my bored expression again.

But nobody asked me to dance the second time. Nobody asked Sally either. There we were, just sitting there, and every now and then everybody looked sort of pitifully over at us.

"Well, goddamn," Sally said. She really said that and let out this huge sigh. "If they don't wanta dance with me, I'm going home!"

The blood rushed to my face. I didn't want to be the *only* one left. "You can't, Sally! You can't go."

170

"I think you ought to, too," she said.

"Why?"

"Just because."

My face started burning again and my fingers were cold when I touched my face.

Mrs. Stewart came over to us. "Are you girls having a nice time?" she asked exceedingly cheerfully. She has these tiny brown eyes.

"Yes'm, we really are!" I said. "Melissa surely looks nice, Mrs. Stewart."

She sat down beside us. "Melissa *is* pretty, isn't she?"

Sally didn't say anything and, anyway, all these ladies started coming in—friends of Mrs. Stewart's—so she got up and went over to greet them. I knew what they were going to do. They were going to sit in chairs and watch us. They adore to do that. They simply love to sit there and watch how unpopular you are.

Finally, we formed these circles—the boys inside and the girls outside. Mr. Stewart and this other man with a palm tree painted on his tie also got in the circle so it would be even. What you were supposed to do is walk around the room in the circle until the music stops and the one in front of you—dances with you.

Guess who stopped in front of me? Bobby Phillips. He's in the high ninth and practically the most popular boy in the entire town. He has blond hair and brown eyes and thousands of teeth. He also has this habit of kind of sucking in his cheeks all the time which is pretty attractive also. When I looked and saw it was him that was going to dance with me, I nearly died. But the only thing was he kept looking at everybody else. While we were dancing I might as well of not even been there. Even Carolyn Dunwoody kept looking at us. She was dancing with Henry Johnston—this fat boy.

Bobby also kept hitting all these other boys while we were dancing. Extremely rude. I decided I hated him, and when the music stopped he didn't even say "thank you" or anything. He just went dashing over to his side. Wonder why it is boys are like that? If I were a boy and saw some tall girl was just sitting

171

around, I'd go over and dance every dance with her. I would, too.

Well, this is the part I really don't much want to tell about, but I guess I will since life is so strange. See, Sally went on home. She called up her mother and told her to come and get her. I wouldn't have done that for anything. Besides, I don't know whether Mother would have come for me or not. She believes in sticking things out. Even if you were in the army and a bunch of Chinamen were coming at you to kill you, she'd believe in sticking it out.

So I did. But then punch time came around. Mrs. Stewart blew her whistle for the one-thousandth time and then told everybody to choose their partners for refreshments. The boys started letting out this whoop and then came racing across the floor for partners. That's the most important time at any dance because you really get to know people.

All these women were hovering around the punch table and the line started forming. Then, just like that, it came blasting to me that I had been left out! *Every* girl had been chosen—every one but me! I started desperately looking around the room. There wasn't another boy left. My face, even my arms, started getting this really terrible burning. I didn't know what to do. I couldn't just sit there on the bench. Who was I going to have punch with? I'd probably have to sit over by the piano all alone with everybody staring. You couldn't join up with anybody else, not without a boy. Nobody does that. So, what I did was, I just went to the line and stood at the end all by myself. This other couple you don't know was standing in front of me, but they didn't turn around to talk or anything. Even my throat started aching and I knew my face was scarlet. I kept looking down at the floor because I wanted to go somewhere where I could cry. I kept wondering where I would sit when I finally did get the punch. Everybody else was all going back to the benches and I couldn't just go walking to the bench alone—the last one, carrying my punch, alone. My brains started whirling and then this voice said: "Felicia? Felicia, do you feel well?"

172

It was Mrs. Summers, Marilyn's mother, that had brought us in the car.

"No'm," I said. "I think I have scarlet fever."

"Let me feel your forehead." She put her hand to my face. "You do feel warm. Would you like to go home? I can take you."

"Yes'm," I said. "I really don't feel well."

"Let's see if I have my keys." She started digging around in her pocketbook. "Yes, here they are! Do you have your coat?"

I never looked back at the line. I don't know what everybody thought—me, trailing out of the room after Mrs. Summers. I kept wondering if she had seen and was just being nice. Or if she thought I really was sick.

In the car I kept sighing. "I hope it isn't anything contagious —you know, like polio, or anything."

"Oh, I don't think so," she said. "You probably just got overheated."

"Maybe so," I said and let out this slight groan.

At the house I told her good-bye. She sounded like she was feeling sorry for me when she said she hoped I'd be feeling better. I didn't want anybody to feel sorry for me, so I very cheerily said, "Don't worry, Mrs. Summers. I'll be okay. Tell Marilyn to call me."

As I walked up to the house, I could see Mother's light on in her bedroom. I knew she would be in bed, reading. I didn't want to tell her what had really happened.

"Why are you so early, Felicia?"

I got this terrible frown on my face. "Mrs. Summers brought me on home because she said I looked sick. I am too, really."

"Heavens," she said. "Here, let me see?" She felt my forehead. "You're not warm. Are you really sick?"

"Uh huh. Kind of in my stomach. I think I have to throw up."

"Felicia," she said in this now-tell-me-the-truth voice. "What happened?"

"Whatdoya mean?"

"At the dance?"

173

"Nothing. It was just won-der-ful! Bobby Phillips and every-body danced with me." I started frowning again. "But I really don't feel very well. Doya guess it's polio?"

"Well, I think you'd better go to bed. We'll see how you are in the morning."

"Okay then. Nite."

"Good night." But I knew she knew I wasn't sick. She *knows* when I'm sick and when I'm not. I guess I've ruined Mother's life.

I got on into bed and just lay there, thinking. I had been saved! Mrs. Summers had saved me from the most humiliatingly horrible experience of my life. Then I started crying, *really*. I kept saying: "I'm going again! I'm going to the *next* one and the *next* one and the *next* one! I will! I will...!"

But, oh, it was so terrible.

19

I guess I shouldn't of told you about all that. You'll think I'm this dreadful goon and won't go on and hear about the end. Be-sides, my father says that just the most selfish people in the world are always dwelling upon themselves. He thinks that if you do that too much you'll go insane. People in Ashton are always going insane. They're pitiful. I sometimes feel so sorry for them I could die. But Father believes you've got to have some "get up and come on" in life. And he doesn't have too much patience with people that're dwelling upon themselves too much. I don't blame him.

Really, though, I don't talk about myself very much. A lot of people do and I'm always listening. Older women especially like to talk to me. If I'm waiting in the dentist office or something and there's this older woman in there, she'll tell me all about her daughter-in-law and how she's just got one kidney and this dry socket and all. I don't know why it is people are always telling me things. It embarrasses me to talk out loud about me or Mother or Father or Arthur or anybody. You know the other person is bored to death because I am, usually, listening to them tell about what all somebody did yesterday. That's what Marilyn and Melissa do *all* the time.

After the dance Marilyn called me up and asked me just *once* if I didn't think the dance was just the most heavenly thing I'd ever been to. When I said "yes," then she went into all about herself and what this boy said and what that one said. I just rested the telephone on my shoulder and when it was silent I'd say "gosh" every now and then and that was all. I guess she hadn't heard about me leaving and everything. I don't guess anybody did because nobody said anything to me about it. You'd have thought Mrs. Summers would have told Marilyn at least, but I guess she didn't, thank goodness.

When I got through talking to Marilyn I went on outside and thought about the dance for a while. I figured one of the reasons I wasn't popular was because I didn't talk or laugh loud enough. You take everybody there that was popular—they all talked and laughed tremendously loudly—everybody except Carolyn Dunwoody and she didn't say hardly a thing. But the rest of them just carried on almost like boys were girls or something.

I don't know why but boys kind of scare me. They're so tough and they're always going around in groups and things. Also, I think many boys are terribly boring. All they like to talk about is cars. I'll never understand to my dying day how somebody can sit up and talk about nothing but a car for one hundred hours. You have to act interested, though, if you want to be popular.

I didn't think about the dance too long, because it was Saturday and I thought I better do something. I decided to go on back in the house and call up Melissa and maybe play tennis or see if she just wanted to hang around the country club or something. I went moseying on into the house and right away I heard Mother talking on the telephone.

"*Felicia's* picture? Whaaaat?"

My mouth went dry and my whole body just froze up. The magazine! The *News Review*! It was out!

"Yes. Yes. The way Bill talked? Why, Margaret...."

It was Mrs. Ewing Mother was talking to. Mrs. Ewing had already read the article.

"I just can't i-*mag*-ine, Margaret. I don't think Felicia even talked to him. No, I—Oh dear. Why, I think he just made it up. No, I know she wouldn't. At least, I don't think so...."

I just silently closed the back door and went back outside. I thought I was going to have a heart attack. My legs started shaking so I couldn't hardly walk. I saw Velvet and went giggling up to her like a moron.

"Hey, Velvet," I whispered. "The magazine's out."

"Whut magazine?"

I couldn't hardly even swallow. "The one with Mr. Hopper's article in it."

"Who's Mr. Hopper?"

"You know that man that—"

Mother called me. "Felici—a!"

"Huh?"

"Come here a minute, please."

"Huh?"

"I said come here, please."

I can lie, I thought. *It's the only thing to do. I'll just tell her I didn't even talk to him. That's what I'll do.*

Mother was standing near the telephone with her car keys in her hand. "We're going down town to buy the *News Review*." Her mouth was set in one thin line.

"What for?" I asked. "I thought we got it in the mail."

"It hasn't come yet." She was staring at me like she was trying to *drag* the truth out of me. "Felicia, did Mr. Hopper take your picture?"

"My picture?"

"Yes."

"Ohhhh *that!*" I laughed exceedingly gaily. "He said he wanted

176

a picture of the front of our house and asked me to stand there. Why?"

"Let's go downtown," was all she said.

Well, Mr. Hopper's article was *simply* terrible! As soon as we got home, Mother and I went and sat in the library. I started not to, but she made me anyway. She practically ripped open the magazine and right away there I was. It wasn't a big picture or anything. The biggest one was of Velvet's preacher and his family—all sitting around the table praying for integration. At least, that's what it said under the picture. But under mine, it said: "... And A Little Child Shall Lead Them...." A child! I could have died, but my legs didn't look too bad.

Our house looked very pretty, too, but Mother was beside herself with fury. "The nerve of that man! Taking a picture of you without our permission. I'd like to sue him! I'll bet Allison will."

As I say, she was mad then, but she was insane after she got through reading the article. So was I, from just plain fear. To tell you the truth, Mr. Hopper just out and out disgraced us. In the first place he made us all sound like sharecroppers, especially Mr. Ewing. Everytime he quoted something Mr. Ewing said he made him sound like a moron with a Southern accent, but every time Velvet's preacher said anything he sounded like Prince Philip of England!

Mr. Ewing never in his entire life has said, "Ah'll tell you, suh." Nobody in the South says "Ah" for "I" and nobody says "you all" when they're just talking to one person. I've never heard Mr. Ewing say "Madam" to Mother either, and he certainly didn't say, "Ah'm sendin' a buncha niggahs to college, too, you heah me?" Mr. Ewing says his "ings"; I was there and I *heard* how he said it. Mr. Hopper didn't even mention that Mr. Ewing had gone to Harvard, and one of the strange things about it is Mother's always said Bill Ewing has a "very nice way of speaking." He does have a Southern accent, I guess—all of us do, but we're not crackers, and children don't go around saying

177

"ain't"—nice ones, anyway. Mr. Hopper made poor Mr. Ewing sound like he'd never come out of the cotton patch.

He didn't get around to us, though, until about the middle of the article. First he talked on about Ralph McGill and the Reverend Luther King. He said Luther King was one of the most inspiring men he'd ever met and that Ralph McGill, against "great opposition," was continuing with his quiet crusade to awaken the "backward South." He said a bunch of other things just as boring and then he got around to us!

He told about Ashton and how small it was (I knew Arthur would die) and then started talking about us. "Here is where one first discovers the strange paradox which is the core of the South today." He told about our house and the farm and about us once having our plantation and owning slaves and things.

"Yet being entertained in this home is a unique experience in modern-day America," he wrote. "One had only to close one's eyes to believe that this was a centennial year and not one hundred years ago. True, the Negro servants come and go as they will now; they are not slaves today, not in the true sense, but in another sense, yes." He told how Velvet still wears a bandanna on her head (she does it for her headaches) and says "Yes ma'm" to Mother, "even though she's much older than the white mistress of the house." He also went into how Isaiah bows when he serves drinks. "Graciousness?" he asked. "Yes. But graciousness built on hopeless wrong. Everything is separate in this town: drinking fountains, restaurants, the seating in movies, buses; libraries are separated, most public facilities and, of course, the schools." The wages paid these "second-class citizens" were so pathetically small, he said, that he was shocked—"twenty dollars a week for a cook."

Then he got on to Mother and Father. He said they were "well-intentioned, charming people" but "of course, as most Southerners, pathetically provincial in their thinking." That made me perfectly furious. Provincial, as you know, means "hicks." He thought Mother and Father were charming hicks!

"He doesn't have any right to say that," I said.

"Apparently he does," Mother said and went right on reading.

"... One reads fear in the eyes of these people, fear that their 'way of life' is going—but mainly fear of the Negro himself. This, it seemed to me, was the answer to these peoples' blatant prejudice. They cited statistics to me—endless ones—in which criminal offenses by the Negro were disproportionately high.

" 'And yawl up theah wanta loose *this* upon us! Have our chirrun go to school with that kind of element! No, suh!' explained one of the more audible guests." (I guess he was talking about poor, timid Mr. Foster.)

Mr. Hopper didn't even like Miss Esther, and she'd driven all the way to Atlanta to buy his books, too. He said Miss Esther was a member of what Southerners refer to as a "fine old Jewish family," but she was still the possessor of some of the South's "fine old bromides." "... The argument, of course, has been repeated and repeated. We've all heard it: the poverty of the South, no Marshall Plan to recover after the Civil War, discriminatory distribution of Federal funds and on and on. Ironically, this fine lady finally ended up in a diatribe of how the true Southerner really loves the Negro. Strange land! Strange paradox! There is a frightening kind of schizophrenia here."

Velvet's preacher, though, the Reverend Moses Lincoln, was a "wise and courageous clergyman," Mr. Hopper thought. I didn't know it myself, but Mr. Hopper said that Reverend Lincoln had sung "Rock of Ages" walking down the streets in Atlanta so he could get a hot dog at the dime store there. Reverend Lincoln was a big fan of an organization called the Southern Christian Educational Fund, Inc. Mr. Hopper'd learned all this when he went to church and afterwards visited Reverend Lincoln's house. He said Mrs. Lincoln was a gracious hostess and that the house was spotlessly clean and the children beautifully dressed. (He didn't say a thing about how Arthur and me were dressed.)

"... It was here that Mrs. Lincoln, though not in the range of the children's hearing, told me of not being able to vote. It was this one small act of citizenship that this proud woman wanted more than any other."

179

"Why can't she vote?" I asked Mother. "Velvet does."

"Perhaps she hasn't paid her poll tax," Mother said.

"I guess Velvet must have paid hers, huh?"

"Your father gave both Velvet and Isaiah the money to pay it."

I started to say something else, but Mother went on reading and I got violently interested because the next part was about me!

Mr. Hopper thought I was full of pathos. "It is the children who constitute the real tragedy of this section. From birth they are conditioned by the well-intentioned, but prejudiced, thinking of their parents." By mere chance, Mr. Hopper said, he'd found an opportunity to speak frankly with me. Before this, I had been kept purposely, he thought, in the background. Yet when he did talk to me, all his first suspicions had been "gratified."

"Here was a kid (Mother simply loathes that expression, kid) like any other normal kid you might meet, wanting the companionship of friends, black or white, and yet she was being denied the privilege of choosing merely because of the color of someone's skin." He went into how I'd said I wanted to go to school with colored people, that my best friend was colored, but that my parents and elders would not allow me to see this girl. "The kid was actually grieving. She told me of a friendship she had with another Negro girl but was forced to practice this otherwise normal relationship in private because of brutal censorship in the community."

Mother didn't read any more. Her voice just sort of trailed off and she let the magazine relax in her lap. Finally, she looked up at me and just stared. "Felicia," was all she said.

There was a look on her face I'd never seen before—like a terrible hurt, too hurt even to cry. It frightened me somehow and yet I wanted to help her, too. I can't explain my feelings, but I started shaking my head violently. "He must have gotten that all wrong. I didn't even talk to him. I didn't. Honestly."

She dampened her lips and looked down at the magazine. She didn't say anything for simply ages. "There must be some truth in it, Felicia. There's basis for everything else he's said."

180

My throat was aching. "Not for that. Not for what he *said* I said. I didn't hardly even see him. You all had him occupied all the time."

She looked at me again with terribly blue eyes. "Felicia, this is very serious. It isn't so much *what* you said to Mr. Hopper, it's the fact that you *lied*. You—"

But the back door slammed. It was Father. He came into the library and he still had on his hat and coat. His hat was tilted on the back of his head and a copy of the magazine was hanging open from his hand.

"You've read this then," Mother said very softly.

"Yep," he said and kind of fell into his red leather chair. He didn't take his coat off or anything and he just sat there looking at Mother.

Nobody said anything for simply ages and I kept making these awful frowning faces and pinching tiny little pleats in my skirt. I wished they'd hurry up and start hollering at me. Hollering would have been a whole lot better than just silence. For some reason I let out this one, loud kind of giggle. I don't know why. Nerves, I guess.

"Well, Felicia?" Father said finally.

"Huh?" I went back to pinching my skirt and making those faces again.

"What do you have to say for yourself?"

"Whatdoya mean?"

"I think you know."

I looked up at him. "Mother said I lied to Mr. Hopper, but I didn't even hardly talk to him."

"Now, Felicia," Mother said.

"Well, I didn't."

"Tell us the truth," Father said.

"I—"

But there was this loud bang at the front door.

"No, I want to see Mr. Whitfield." It was Mr. Ewing talking to Isaiah.

He came striding on into the library and immediately I saw

181

the rolled-up magazine in his hand. He looked terribly pale, but I guess that was because he'd just got through with his hemorrhoids.

"Where's that pansy newspaperman? Where can I get in touch with him?" He was practically shouting so you knew he was mad, but I thought that was very strange calling somebody a flower when he was mad. "Goddamn it, Allison! I've never been so sore in all my life!"

Father got up from his chair. "Sit down, Bill," he said quietly. "Sorry you had to get in on this. Kind of gave us a raking over, didn't he?"

"Well, *he's* going to get a raking over when I get through. I'm going to sue him! He'll be singing 'Rock of Ages' himself when I get through with him!"

Mother let out this tremendous sigh. "I just can't understand it. In many ways I thought he was such a nice man."

"Nice, hell!" Mr. Ewing said. "He's nothing but one of those pansy-writer types. Knew it the first time I laid eyes on him!"

"Let's have a drink," Father said. "I think we need it."

"Not for me, Allison," Mother said. She looked at me. The reason she didn't have one is because she was getting ready to chasten me. She never has one when she gets ready for that.

"I'll have one!" Mr. Ewing said. "Might even have the whole damn bottle!"

While Father was getting the drinks, Mr. Ewing kept flipping through the article. He was breathing violently loudly. I didn't know people breathed that loud.

"Look at that!" he said. "Lincoln up there with his head bowed. I'd like to have every dollar I've given that so-called church he's always saying he's building. He pocketed every damn dime of it or else gave it to those troublemakers over in Atlanta! 'Rock of Ages,' my aaa—foot!"

"It's just sympathy, Bill," Mother said. "A lot of the North falls for it. It's the colored man's greatest weapon nowadays. They *want* people to feel sorry for them, pity them. Even the most intelligent of them; it's their way of being noticed."

182

"Hell, I know it!" Mr. Ewing said. "Martyrs! They love it! Always want the ride, but refuse to buy the ticket."

Mother sort of leaned back on the sofa. "But, you know—and I really mean it now. For the first time in my life I feel as if I'm free."

"Whatdoya mean, Sarah?"

"I mean I'm free of the Negro now. I don't have to worry about him any more. We've always been so closed in by him. They've been like a wall around us, something to care for, to mend, and always there." She sort of lifted the magazine. "But it's this sort of thing—this continual hitting at the South—that's making me almost hate the colored now. I've never hated before in my life."

"I know. I know. Put somebody on the defensive and he's bound to fight."

Mother sighed. "It's sad in a way. In many ways we had such a lovely relationship with the Negro."

"Yes, well, there's a new bunch now, Sarah. Remember that! The old conservative Negro has *gone*. This new crop is hotheaded and—and irresponsible. They thrive on excitement, dramatics—" He sat up straighter—"Just staying in school and quietly trying to improve themselves isn't exciting enough. They want to martyr themselves. Well, I say—let them *be* martyrs!"

Mother didn't say anything.

Then Father came back with two drinks and bowed very deeply when he handed Mr. Ewing his glass. "Suh," he said, imitating Mr. Hopper's article, "for *you* were a king in Babylon and *I* but a Christian slave."

Mr. Ewing just kind of jerked his shoulder up.

"Slaves," he said. "Sometimes I wonder just who are the slaves down here." He got up from the sofa and went and sat in the chair by Father. "I mean it, Allison. I'm going to sue that magazine, for every penny it's worth."

"On what grounds, Bill?"

"Libel, that's what! Public ridicule. You can sue them for taking your child's picture."

"I don't think so."

183

"Well, we'll discuss that later," Mother said. "About Felicia."

I started making my faces again. Gosh, I was hoping Mr. Ewing would stay forever. I was sick in my stomach. My throat was aching, too, and all I wanted to do was just run somewhere, anywhere, so I could cry. I was aching to cry.

Father said he didn't think it would be very wise to sue because that would only mean more publicity.

"Yes, we have Felicia and Arthur to think about, too," Mother said.

"I don't care how much publicity it gives me," Mr. Ewing said. "And I don't have any children to think about. I'm so damn tired of these Northern newspapers and magazines—television, too, with their damn editing—trying to throw off their so-called morality on us! They sit up there in their air-conditioned offices and pant about the poor Southern Negro, and most of them don't give a damn about the Negro; they're just having a circulation fight up there and they're scared to death—scared of the Negro! They're like politicians. And the South's as safe a target as any."

"Still, there's no way to fight back," Father said. "They won't even print our ads. Freedom of the press! Who was it who referred to the Northern press as the paper curtain?"

"I don't know, but it's an apt expression."

"One thing for sure, they're not being very wise," Father said and he used a word I haven't attained yet. (I think it meant insane.) "They're not helping the Negro and they're only making the white man angrier. It's a kind of sins of the fathers all over again."

"Exactly." Mr. Ewing kind of scraped his chair. "And the North always wants to know what the rest of the world thinks of the South. Hah! They ought to ask themselves some questions."

Father sipped his drink slowly. "But it's the poor white who's going to get the brunt of this—not us: Sometimes I don't blame them for their madness. It's the only way they know to fight."

I kind of thought about that for a while. It was people like Nadine Miller and them that'd end up going to school with colored people. In some ways it really isn't fair. I don't think it's

184

such a terrible thing, not wanting to mix with people you don't want to mix with. Colored people are the same way.

Nobody said anything for a while, then Mother said, "I was just telling Bill, Allison, that it's this sort of thing that actually stirs up hatred."

"What?"

"Magazine articles like this."

"Well, it shouldn't," Father said. "Nothing's worth hatred. Nothing. But if they're trying to ruin the South in other ways, they're doing a good job of it."

Mr. Ewing drained his glass in one big gulp and stood up. "Maybe I'll calm down one of these days, but right now I don't think so."

"It's all very unfortunate," Mother said.

"To say the *least!*" Mr. Ewing said. He waved at Father. "Go'night, Allison!"

"Go'night, Bill."

I heard him slam the front door and there we were alone in the library again. I just sat there, waiting.

"Now," Father said. "Felicia, I want you to tell us the truth. You were not truthful to Mr. Hopper, were you?"

He was standing over me, and when I looked up at him I thought he looked suddenly very tired. He looked older, too, and I guess it was this—the way he looked and everything—that started me acting like an insane person. I don't know what happened, but I had worried so long.... Just all at once almost, everything started getting blank or something and I started sobbing like I was a four-year-old. I threw myself down on the sofa. "Yes, I lied," I said. "I betrayed you all! They called you all hicks. If it hadn't of been for me, you would've—he woulda said nice things...." My breath started jerking and I started sobbing louder and louder. Everything just kind of broke inside.

From somewhere that seemed almost far away, I heard Father say, "No, Sarah, just let her cry it out. Just leave her be."

I guess they went away. I don't know. All I know was that I wanted to be dead and I kept thinking that if I could just make

185

it until I was old, that's all I had to do. Just live out the years. Go to bed, get up. Go to bed, get up. And at the end of many days I'd die and it would all be over. I got to thinking about my life that had gone—the dance, people at school getting popular, and me this tall giant of a person that nothing good would ever happen to, not as long as I lived. Now I'd betrayed my own parents and Arthur, too. Finally the ache inside was so dreadful and I was so afraid, that the only thing I knew was to pray. So, biting the pillow, I prayed:

> Now I lay me down to sleep,
> I pray the Lord my soul to keep.
> If I should die before I wake,
> I pray the Lord my soul to take.

And I *hope* He heard me.

20

...Man, am I glad Mr. Hopper didn't mention me in his article. Mr. Woodford, the one that teaches English, he read it and said for you all not to worry about anybody calling you all provincials. He said just about everybody was which is the truth. Practically everybody in New York's one. Old Jimerson, though, he teaches history and after he read it he said he'd always known the South had a lot of bigguts in it. That's just like old Jimerson, though. He was in the army in Georgia and he didn't like it because he caught malaria and had to stay in the hospital practically the whole time. He said that Georgia ought to be a challenge for me to try and influence. He and these Harvard boys are going to march around the South this summer and sit at dime stores. He said they'd probably get put in jail but they thought it would be a first hand experience.

I thought your picture was pretty good, Felicia. Everybody up hear thought our house was a good example of arcitecture. This boy got kicked out of school last week for cheating. I gotta go.

With Personal Regards,
A.

P.S. Knox and them said they thought Mr. Hopper sounded kind of flitty.

Thank goodness, I didn't have to sit around and discuss Arthur's letter. Mother and Father'd read it at lunch and I'd had lunch at school again. I'd started up having lunch at school quite often because junior-high school is so far away from home it makes a nervous wreck out of me beating it back to class on time. Mother thought I'd started getting nervous. She thought my experience with Mr. Hopper kind of made me that way, which was perfectly insane.

The next day we had a call from Aunt Pett in Charleston and she was confounded out of her mind about the article. She wanted Mother and I to come to Charleston right away for comfort, but Mother said she would rather wait and have us come over in the spring because she thought I'd been through enough already. That was very kind of Mother, I thought, because by spring I was sure everybody would have pretty much forgotten about the magazine. Besides, I was pretty much dreading Charleston. I did want to hear about Winky, but I just didn't want to appear a hick, not now, not after everything, and especially not in Charleston.

One good thing that happened was Mr. Ewing didn't sue. Mother said she thought perhaps it was because he was too busy. Mr. Ewing has a terrible time with the Japanese and labor unions. They're trying to run him out of business, so he's always having to revitalize. It's very difficult for him and it keeps him violently harassed.

Still, it was a good thing he didn't sue. We just couldn't afford to have any more publicity. But you should have seen the *rest* of the town! They were out of their minds with fury! Mr. Henry,

187

the editor of the paper, wrote this front-page editorial that blasted the fool out of Mr. Hopper and the entire North. He said Mr. Hopper ought to empty his garbage in his own back yard instead of coming down here trying to make public ridicule out of the "finest flowers" of the South. The "finest flowers" was us and Father extended his gratitude violently.

The only thing was Father had to confess about me, because Mr. Henry said in his editorial that he knew a girl brought up in the home background that I was, would never say such a thing about colored people. That was simply terrible, I mean Father having to tell my "little indiscretion" that way. "Little indiscretion" is the way we refer to it now. Still, I was pretty humiliated, everybody talking about what I'd done.

The next day after the article came out, Mother dragged me out to the farm. I guess she wanted to hide me, but it was terrible being out there with nothing to take my mind off things. All I did was go dragging along by the cotton fields thinking myself to death. Sunday morning I went by the Millers' house, and there was Nadine, pouting and picking feathers off a chicken. She was sitting on the back-porch steps and she didn't have any lipstick on, so I thought she'd probably speak.

"Hey, Nadine," I said violently friendly. "What'rya doing?"

She glanced up at me like she hadn't already seen me coming down the path. "Uh," was all she said. I don't know why Nadine doesn't like me any more. I think it's because she thinks I'm rich and it's embarrassing for her not being.

"I do that all the time," I said and kind of put my arm around this grey post on the porch.

"What?"

"Pluck chickens. I hate it, don't you?"

"It ain't so bad." She went right on plucking.

Nadine sometimes can be exceedingly rude. She doesn't even try to continue a conversation.

"Want me to help you?" I asked.

"I kin manage." She didn't even look up and there was this awful silence which made me feel very unwanted.

188

"Hey, Nadine," I said. "I was just going to the gas station to get something to drink. D'you wanta go?"

"Uh uh."

I decided to sit down on the steps beside her. She didn't ask me, and the silence was pretty bad. Finally, I said, "Oh, me, it's terribly boring today, isn't it?"

"Whar your nigger friends?" she asked me.

I looked at her and my face bolted red.

"I read all about that. I read whatya said."

"Ohhh, that!" I let out this very happy tone. "Did you read it? D'yall take the *News Review?*"

"Papa went in town and bought it."

"We did, too. Mother went to town and bought it."

She plucked this tremendous wad of feathers off the chicken's tail. "I ain't goin' to school with no niggers."

"Me *neither!*" I said with profound anger.

She glanced over at me then. "How come you said so then?"

"I didn't." I sat down on the bottom step so I could see her better. "Nadine, that man was simply a disgrace. He lied all over the magazine."

"Mama figgered he did."

"Yeah, can't you see me in school with niggers?" I could hardly get out that last word, but I said it out of loyalty to Nadine. It isn't very nice to have a nice pronunciation when you're talking to somebody that doesn't.

She picked this great black hair off the chicken's leg. "They start puttin' niggers in the school out chere and they'll be a couple of deaduns lyin' round, too."

"Same thing in town," I said very sincerely, but I kind of started examining Nadine's face. I wondered if she really would kill them. There was a white ring round her mouth. She might if she got mad enough. It's better to be nice to people like Nadine, because they've got terrible tempers, like those women that throw rocks and things. They might throw them at you even, I mean if they felt like it.

189

"We're organized out chere. Ain't gone be no niggers in my school."

"We're organized, too," I said, but just frankly speaking I didn't know what she was talking about.

"School-ins, sit-ins—" she started turning her mouth down— "next thing they'll be wantin' marry-ins and after that there'll be some bury-ins. That's what there'll be—bury-ins—all nigger."

Nadine had grown into a very morbid individual. It kind of scared you, so I thought I'd better change the subject.

"Wasn't that terrible of that man to lie so, though?"

"What man?"

"The man that wrote the article in the magazine."

She looked up from the chicken at me. "Yankee trash, wasn't he?"

"Uh huh. He was simply terrible."

"All of 'em are—ruttin' round with niggers all the time."

I started to yawn but Mrs. Miller let out this yell from inside the house and nearly jolted my heart up into my mouth. She was calling for Nadine.

"Whaaaaaat?" Nadine called back just as loud.

"Come 'ere and git this kettle off the stove."

"Aww," she practically dumped the chicken when she stood up.

"I guess I gotta go," I said. "See you real soon, Nadine."

"Okay." She didn't glance at me when she went in the house.

I started walking back to the cabin very swiftly. Gosh, even Nadine had heard about the article! I was a public disgrace— everywhere! Everybody knew about it! All over the world. The old lump started coming in my throat again and right soon the tears started literally pouring down my face. School was what I was worrying about the most. They were probably all at home now, hating me, getting organized to hate me until I died. I started walking like a maniac, with my fists all wadded up and my face so wet I looked like a mad woman. I saw Mother out in front of the cabin so I kind of went over by this tree and stood behind it until the jerking in my breath stopped. I didn't want her to see I'd been crying, because she'd ask me why and we'd have to talk some more about the article.

Well, what happened was, Monday morning came on and I told Mother I didn't believe I'd go to school, but she told me not to be silly and to get some "get up and come on" and just walk proudly in. So I grabbed my poor sad books off the piano and started dragging the long way to school again. I thought it was pretty unthinking of Mother not to drive me, but—like I said—she positively adores to have me walk myself to death. Actually, I thought *somebody* would give me a ride, but nobody did. There I was just dragging on and on and then this car passed by—an old one with a bunch of boys in it. I looked up and saw the Foster twins. One of them started beating on the side of the car and this red-haired boy let out this yell: "See you la-ter, in-te-gra-ter!" And there were these roars of laughter as they sped on.

My heart started pounding away and I practically flew all the rest of the way to school. But when I turned the corner I saw everybody hanging around outside waiting for the bell. I started to wait but I just went on and got some get up and come on and walked as proud as I could. Well, I nearly fainted out of just pure shock. *Every*body, literally *everybody*, started saying "Hey, Felicia! Hey, Felicia!" Even this very popular girl that's older. She's never said anything to me in her life. And she said, "Hey, Felicia Whitfield." I said "hey" back in this extremely gay voice. (I may start going around with her.)

Anyhow, I was famous! You ought to have heard what everybody said. They loved my picture and Melissa thought that was hysterical about them calling me a "child." I told her I could have thrown up over that. But the main thing about it was none of them had read the article. I asked Melissa if she had and she said she hadn't but that her parents had and they were irate over it. She said the whole town was "irate" but that her father said it wasn't our fault, the article, that it was just a bunch of damn Yankees kicking up their rears again.

Gosh, though, you don't know how happy I was over being

191

famous. The Ashton Junior High School is the most tremendous place you ever saw and just everybody started speaking. I was famous for two straight days, and wherever I'd go all these girls started flocking around asking me things about Mr. Hopper.

"You really have to be able to talk deep to talk to him," I said and they all just stared.

Well, fame doesn't last very long. Before you know it you're back in your old boring life again. One day you're everything and three days later, nothing. Everybody, I guess, thinks you're flying around in all this glory but they forget about you and go on just having fun by themselves. Also, you get your comeuppance in this world, too. You betray somebody and before you know it somebody'll turn around and betray you. That's what happened to me.

I don't know when it all started up exactly, sometime after the dance, I think, but, anyway, Marilyn and Melissa started becoming these very, very popular people. They never had been before, not with boys and things, but just very suddenly almost they started becoming excruciatingly popular.

On Saturdays they were always at each other's house and all these boys would come by. It used to be that they were always at my house but not any more. They'd go for days without even calling on the telephone. I called them about one thousand times, but they were always doing something.

Then they started going around with Carolyn Dunwoody! Just the three of them. They thought that was about the most terrific thing that had ever happened to them. You'd always see them walking down the street, going to the movies or something. And if you just happened to be in there yourself, you couldn't even look at the movie because there they'd be, sitting all hunched down in the seats and pretending not to notice all these boys throwing popcorn at them.

They also started wearing lipstick and carrying these huge pocketbooks around with them. In the ladies' room at the movies they'd hardly speak. All three of them would be talking to each other and putting on lipstick and they wouldn't even hardly speak. I don't think all that would have happened if Mother had let me wear lipstick. She absolutely refused and there I was—nothing—always nothing.

All the rest of my friends, though, were pretty loyal and when we'd spend the night, we'd sit for hours talking about friendship and how people betray you. That's one thing about me. As long as I live I'll always be loyal to my friends. Even if suddenly I started becoming this popular human being I wouldn't stop calling up somebody like Margaret Ann Akers just because one of her eyes goes out of joint sometimes. I'd never be that way!

Margaret Ann said her mother said there were a whole bunch of rich snobs in Ashton but that my Mother and Father had never been that way. I told her nobody in my family would be a snob even if it killed them. She said, "I know it," and we sat and stared about that for hours. She, too, had been betrayed. I think Margaret Ann Akers is about the nicest human being in the entire universe. Her father owns the transfer business and I wouldn't care even if Arthur married her some day.

Mother said for me not to worry about about Melissa and Marilyn—that some people have their time now and others later. "Marilyn and Melissa are having theirs now, that's all."

"Well, when is *mine* coming?"

"It will, if you'll just be decent and honorable and kind."

Throw up! I don't know why that kind of irritated me. What I want to be is be a drunkard. I want to have dates and ride out to the Green Lantern and get madly drunk—every night. That's what some of the seniors in high school do. Sometimes you can lie in your bed at night and hear them racing around in cars, laughing. You always know what fun they're having, and there you are, this unpopular person, just lying there. It certainly would be fun to go to the Green Lantern and get drunk and be popular.

Mother started talking more and more about sending me away to boarding school. She's not very partial to the atmosphere at the Ashton High School. She and Father would sit up and talk about sending me away for hours. They *adored* it! They have definitely decided on this one school in Virginia instead of Ashley Hall in Charleston. Mother would prefer I go to Ashley Hall because they won't let any cheap-rich people in there, but she thinks I need to soak up Virginia now since I already know Charleston. Mother said the one in Virginia is a nice school, too. No cheap-rich people go there either. That's the kind of school Mother is partial to—a small one that has profound emphasis on the Episcopal Church.

But, actually, it doesn't matter to me too much any more, getting sent away from my own home. Once I thought about writing Melissa and Marilyn a letter. I'd write it after I got to boarding school. It would be excruciatingly sad, all about friendship and how I was the kind of human being that would never turn my back on them. They'd read it and cry for hours, and when I came home for Christmas they'd come dashing over and tell me how horrified they were at what they'd done. I'd just smile at them and say, "You're forgiven." Things are so gloomy in this world.

Things didn't even get any better when Arthur came home for Christmas. He didn't pay any attention to me at all. He had become exceedingly intellectual, always going around talking about Robert Browning's "sanguinary period." He was writing a theme in English on it, and I thought if I heard about Robert Browning's "sanguinary period" one more time I'd scream. Dinners were ghastly with Arthur sitting up there asking us questions all the time. ". . . Betchah don't know who wrote 'Fair as a star when only one is shining in the sky.' Okay, betchah don't know who wrote 'I grieve to think what man has made of man.' " Mother said she had forgotten that one, but Arthur said it was Robert Browning, of course. "But it wasn't during his sanguinary period!"

Boring. Mother was beside herself with joy! Arthur was certainly developing, she kept saying. His report card didn't show it too much, though. He didn't make a single B. I made many, but that didn't make any difference. If I'd been proclaimed the most intellectual person in the entire world, it wouldn't have made any difference.

Also, Arthur had a date with Carolyn Dunwoody! I could have shot him dead. They went to a movie, and when Mother and I just happened to be riding by on our way to the drugstore we saw them walking. She told me not to even look at them. But I did, once, and there was Arthur all straight and trying to be taller and Carolyn sauntering along beside him in this very wide, plaid skirt and white jacket. I told Arthur I didn't think Carolyn had much character, but he wouldn't listen and called her up again!

I would literally die of horror if Arthur married Carolyn Dunwoody. But he probably will. One thing is, Arthur hasn't developed any real appreciation for the right kind of girls. We are simply dying for Arthur to marry someone with her feet on the ground. Mother says she just wants Arthur to marry somebody sensible. "Just as long as she has her feet on the ground and has some *practical* sense." Mother thinks Arthur's quite inclined to going around in the clouds a lot. So is Carolyn Dunwoody.

One night I heard him in the kitchen. He'd just come back from a date with Carolyn and was stopping off in the kitchen. I declare, Arthur has the most tremendous appetite you ever saw. He can drink two quarts of milk in one day. It's good Father has the farm or we'd go broke for sure.

I came walking in the kitchen with my hip out of joint. That is an act of mine which simply irritates Arthur out of his mind.

"I wish you could see yourself when you do that," he said. He was munching on this huge sandwich.

I laughed very hysterically. "I'm the only person I know of that can do it."

"Well, it isn't funny."

He just went on munching.

"How was Carolyn Dunwoody?"

"Okay."

I sat down in one of the chairs and tilted it up against the wall. "Are you in love with her?" Nauseating. But I just thought I'd ask it. I was in an exceedingly nauseating mood.

"Love?" he asked.

"Uh huh. You're getting on in age now, you know. You could probably even get married if you wanted to."

"What do I wanta do that for?" He looked at me over his huge sandwich.

"I don't know. Can't you just see you and Carolyn somewhere? You wouldn't be able to live in the house with us. You'd have to live in this one room somewhere and there'd be clotheslines outside and these dirty babies running all over the place. You couldn't go to college or anything and you'd have to work in a filling station for the rest of your life because you'd be so ignorant you couldn't get a job in the bank."

He just stared at me with this tremendous bite of sandwich in his mouth, then he went on chewing. "You surely are peculiar sometimes."

"Why?" I asked, and sat forward in the chair.

"Anybody that can sit up and think up all that. You oughtta start wearing lipstick and getting your hair curled."

"*I* know it. Mother won't let me."

"Shoot, you oughtta see Northern girls when they're thirteen. Most of them look like they're twenty or something."

"I know it." I let out this huge sigh. "We're just a very peculiar family, that's all." I watched him drain his glass of milk. "Arthur, why do you like Carolyn Dunwoody?"

"I dunno. She's a pretty good old girl."

"No, I mean, why do you guess she's so popular with boys?"

"I dunno. She's not silly or anything and she's pretty fast."

Embarrassing! But I pretended I didn't know. "Whatdoya mean, *fast?*"

"Hell, I don't know! Why don't you ask some of those stupid friends of yours."

I looked down at the floor sideways. My flip mood had gone. Arthur can be very unthinking sometimes. "I don't have any friends any more," I said.

"Why don't you?" He didn't sound concerned at all.

"They just don't like me any more, that's all."

"There's always somebody over here—girls all over the place screaming and stuff."

196

"Not Marilyn and Melissa. Not any more. They go around with Carolyn Dunwoody all the time."

"They're stupid anyway."

"Who?"

"Marilyn and Melissa."

"I know but—" I started frowning. "They were my best friends, Arthur."

He looked back in the refrigerator. "Carolyn likes ya," he said into the refrigerator.

"Carolyn Dunwoody?! How do you know?"

"She told me. She said she thought you were cute."

"Me?" I started beaming all over.

"Uh huh."

"Really, Arthur? Are you telling the truth? You're not just making that up?"

"Uh uh. I'm not making it up."

I got to thinking about that. She did speak to me in the hall the other day. Maybe she really did think I was—"Gosh," I said.

Arthur slammed the refrigerator door. "Go-night."

"Hey, Arthur," I said. I didn't want him to go to bed. I was much too fascinated to go to bed. "What did people up at school say about Mr. Hopper's article? I mean, really?"

"Nothing."

"They must've said something. You wrote two of them had read it."

"They didn't say anything. Mother said you ought not to talk about it."

"Did she tell you that?"

"Uh huh."

"Why?"

"I dunno."

"Well, did they think we were horrible? Hicks and stuff?"

He kind of leaned up against the refrigerator. "Aw, they think you're a hick anyway."

"Why?"

197

"If you don't live in New York and go to Bermuda and stuff, they think you're kind of a jerk."

"Yeah," I said. "Hey, Arthur, what's flitty mean?"

"Huh?" And then he started bumping up against the refrigerator and howling with laughter. "Man, Felicia, you're crazy!"

I couldn't help but smile, too. Arthur doesn't laugh very much but when he does everybody else laughs, too. "But what does it mean? Mother didn't know either."

"I knew she wouldn't. I didn't know either when I wrote it, but *man,* I know now! Ask somebody else." He kind of straightened up, all red faced. "Hey, I gotta go to bed."

I got up from the chair. I honestly didn't want to go to bed. "I tell you what, Arthur. Let's go in the library and have a cigarette. Mother and Father both have gone to bed."

"Do *you* smoke?"

"Of course. I started up about two years ago."

He kind of shrugged his shoulders.

We went on in the library and turned on the lights. The cigarette box was literally jammed with cigarettes.

"I can't smoke these," he said.

"Why not?"

"They don't have any filters. I can't possibly smoke without a filter. It'll give you lung cancer."

"*I* can," I said.

"O—kay then, but I'm not."

"Well, just wait till I have one then. I'm terribly nervous tonight. One would do me worlds of good."

"Ner-vous," Arthur said. "You're a crazy kid."

"Mother despises that word, 'kid.' It's a Northern expression, isn't it?"

"Yeah, but it's all right. Everybody says it."

"Just colored people down here say it." I lit the cigarette and started giggling all over the place.

"You don't even in-*hale.*"

"Yeah, I do."

198

"No, you're not. Just leaving the smoke in your mouth isn't inhaling. You're supposed to suck it on down in your lungs." He started to go.

"Hey, Arthur," I said. "Is school any better this year? I mean, do you like it better?"

He started yawning. "It's more contemplative, I guess."

"Whatdoya mean?" I blew out a great wad.

"I don't know. They keep you busy writing these long themes and essays and things."

"Like on Robert Browning's sanguinary period?"

"Uh huh. And old Walden."

"Who's he?"

"Just this man, a writer. He was all the time going out staring at his pond."

"You mean you do that at school?"

"There isn't any pond, but you can go to the football field and sit and think. I do that lots, at night." He looked very tragic with his glasses.

"What do you think about?"

"Oh, death and all."

I spewed out the smoke. "Arthur, you wouldn't ever commit suicide or anything. Would you?"

He looked up at the ceiling. "Maybe."

"Oh, *Ar*-thur!" I just stared at him.

"I've thought about it a lot. My id's all the time getting messed up."

"What's your id?"

"This thing inside you."

"Like your intestines?"

"No. It's up in your brain."

I looked at his brain. "Do you *really* think about committing suicide?"

"Hell, most people do. Really intellectual people."

"Well, stop being intellectual then. Mother and Father would absolutely die."

"They'd get over it."

"No, they wouldn't." I put out my cigarette violently. "Arthur, you're very unthinking. You're—"

"Aw, Felicia. For hellsakes, I'm not gonna commit suicide."

"Well, I should hope *not!* That's certainly an immature thing to do. Can't you see us, though? We'd all be sitting around and this wire would come and there you'd be, up in Connecticut, with your brains blown out."

He kind of started laughing. "You think up the most peculiar things."

"I know it."

"Well, you oughtta cut it out. It isn't sanguinary. Come on, I gotta go to bed."

When we were going up the stairs I said, "Ohhh me, I have to go to a cocktail party."

He jerked around. *"You?"*

"Uh huh, in Charleston. Mother says I *have* to go this year. It's such a bore."

"Y'all going to Charleston? You and Mother?"

"Uh huh. This spring. Mother wants to be loyal to Aunt Ann ona count of Winky."

"What's Winky done?"

"You know! That trashy boy she may have to marry."

"Oh that! That's stupid."

"No, it isn't stupid, Arthur. One should be most selective when choosing one's mate. We're all *very* concerned over who you'll marry."

"Hell, *I'm* not gonna get married!"

"In time you will. We'll visit you in your one room with dirty babies running all over the place and—"

"Hell," he said and went on up to his room on the third floor.

21

The day before we left for Charleston, Mother started talking around about that she thought it would be a good idea for us to go to Connecticut in June.

"We've never really seen that part of the country and I think it would be interesting for Arthur to see more of New England, too. We could take a little trip after school is out."

"Gosh," I said, and I meant it. It was bad enough just going to Charleston, but to have to go up to *Connecticut* and have Arthur ashamed of us, was just about the worst.

"Why don't we just let him come home on the train?" I said.

"Why, Felicia, don't you want to see Arthur's school?"

"Not particularly. I'm sure Arthur'd rather come home on the train. That's such a long ride in the car."

"We can drive leisurely."

"Okay, but you're not gonna like it up there."

"Well, we'll see. Now, Felicia, have you finished packing?"

"Uh huh. I packed two weeks ago."

Mother laughed and kind of put her arm around my shoulder. "You *have* been looking forward to Charleston, haven't you?"

"Yaaaas," I said, which was a distinct lie. One reason was I wasn't looking so hot. It's funny about me but some weeks I can really look pretty good and then let something come along like going to Charleston and I look perfectly insane. Everybody in Charleston is highly advanced. Girls start wearing stockings when they're eleven even.

Father had wanted to come along with us, too, but since it was spring he said he had too much to do out at the farm. So it was just Mother and me. We had a hilarious time, driving in the car. It was the first time just us had ever been anywhere together and it was lovely to drive along in the warm air and sort of talk deep. I kept asking her why so many people in Charleston were snobbish and she said they weren't really, they were just used to their own ways, that's all.

"But I mean—just *say* I might have turned out this girl with sort of pathetic parents and all—they wouldn't even let me in the back door of the St. Cecelia Ball, would they?"

I was talking about this ball they give every February. It's mainly for debutantes but you're supposed to have about one million ancestors before you can go. Some inferior people sneak in sometimes, but not too many.

"In that case, I guess you couldn't go then."

"Do you think that's fair of them?"

"Yes, I think it is. I'm sure the other girls have a dance they enjoy just as much."

"I bet they don't. I bet every girl in Charleston would want to go to the St. Cecelia Ball. To me, it's pitiful. They can't help who their ancestors were."

"I don't know. Decency also enters into it. If you're divorced, for instance, you can't go."

"Just because you're di*vorced?*"

"Uh huh."

"I guess Uncle Alex couldn't go then, could he?"

"No, I guess he couldn't." Mother kept looking straight ahead at the road, but I couldn't tell what she was thinking because of her dark glasses.

"You went, didn't you? Didn't you make your debut at the St. Cecelia Ball?"

"Yes."

"Well, didn't you feel kinda sorry for all the other girls that couldn't go?"

She sighed. "I don't think I really thought about it then, but I suppose if it weren't the St. Cecelia, it would probably be something else. When you give a party you only invite your friends. The Ball is the same."

"Ohhhh me." I leaned back on the car seat and thought about how if *I* ever gave another party I'd invite even some of those people that live down near the train station. I'd be nicer to them

202

than anybody and Marilyn and Melissa would turn out these excruciating snobs.

At junior-high school there're lots of poor people. There weren't hardly any in grammar school, but once you get to junior-high school just everybody goes there.

"I do wonder how Pett is," Mother said. I guess she was tired of talking about snobs. "Petrie wrote she hadn't been feeling well lately."

"I hope she's all right," I said and sat up straighter. "But, look, Mother—when she has her little glass of sherry at night, let's don't—*you* know—get her to talking about how Charleston's changing and all. That's kind of boring to me."

"You use that word too much, Felicia."

"What word?"

"Boring. You say it much too much."

We were just whizzing down the highway. "Well, I'm bored pretty much of the time. Things are all the time boring me."

"They shouldn't! If you're bored, it's just a sign you're not a very interesting person."

"Well, I'm not. I'm not interesting at all."

"I think you are."

I looked at her. "Do you? Do you, really?"

"Yes, you have a fine spirit about things."

"Oh, *that*." Irritating! Who wants a fine spirit about things? That's not very interesting.

"An interesting person always has inner resources. I've never heard your father use the word 'boring.'"

"Maybe so," I said, but what I really think is that Father *does* get bored. I've seen him talking to some of the women around Ashton. He's listening all right, but *I* know he's probably thinking about the farm or going hunting or something. You can just tell.

Mother started talking about Aunt Pett again. "Most people in Charleston think she's fascinating."

"I know but—I don't mean she's boring all the time, but I get kind of tired listening to all that about Charleston—about who's

203

nice and who isn't. Some of those she thinks are so nice don't look so hot to me."

"Yes, well, that's one of the reasons for this trip. You're getting old enough to appreciate Charleston now."

"Like snobs and all?"

"Of course not! The history and charm of the city. You're very very fortunate to have an aunt and uncle like Petrie and Ann—and a great-aunt like Pett, too. You can learn a great deal."

"I know, but—" Oh well, it didn't make any difference. When Mother doesn't want to understand you, she doesn't even try. I really *do* like Aunt Ann and Uncle Petrie, but at night there's nobody there my age and you know how it is. Winky's always gone out and they really don't care whether *you're* there or not.

You'd like Aunt Ann, though, I think. She's this *grand* work-horse. At least that's what a friend of hers told us the last time we were in Charleston. Aunt Ann's always wearing sports clothes and tearing around working herself to death for the church and for these house tours they give every spring. She also plays a lot of golf, but not as much as she wants to because she's always having to drive Aunt Pett and this other extremely feeble aunt of Uncle Petrie's around. She's pretty, too, I think, with dark hair and blue eyes, but a lot of the time she looks tired because she's just got through working herself to death. Everybody likes her.

Uncle Petrie's different. He's very tall and about Father's age but he never has made much money. He just simply can't make any, that's all. He's an insurance man and he never has ever really liked it. Nobody ever understood why he went into it. Father says Uncle Petrie should have been a minister or a teacher or something. What he cares most about is Charleston—gardens, old churches, and history. Things like that.

Uncle Petrie and Aunt Ann had enough money to send Winky to schools and stuff, but they don't have anything like what Aunt Pett has. Aunt Pett lives in the house with them and she even has this trained nurse that goes literally everywhere with her.

Miss Boggs. Even when the telephone rings, Miss Boggs answers it and finds out first if it's somebody with ancestors Aunt Pett wants to talk to. Miss Boggs knows about everybody, too—even who your great-great-grandfather was. She learned it from Aunt Pett, but she also has a red nose.

The thing that everybody in Charleston really likes, though, is Aunt Ann and them's house. It's very large and has *two* drawing rooms! In the upstairs drawing room they have these two Chippendale chairs of Aunt Pett's that everybody's always slurping around about. They also carry on about the paintings in the dining room. In the biggest drawing room there's this harp! Aunt Pett says that I may inherit the harp some day, but I don't much want it. To me, it's pretty ugly, but Aunt Pett's always talking about this famous harpist that played on it once. That's the kind of people Aunt Pett likes—famous generals and harpists and stuff. You ought to hear all the famous generals and politicians Aunt Pett's related to. Practically the entire Confederate army! She's got all their swords and portraits and things. The Whitfields have a drunkard in their background. (Boy, I shouldn've put *that* in!) But we don't talk about it when we go to Charleston.

Well, we didn't get there until late afternoon which was unfortunate. See, people in Charleston, the nice ones, have their dinner in the middle of the day but not until about three o'clock in the afternoon. If you miss that, it's too bad, because all you get at night is some pitiful salad or something. People in Charleston have been eating their dinners at two and three in the afternoons practically since the Wise Men. It's very peculiar and I don't know how it all got started. If you really want to know you can ask Mr. Stoney—Mr. Sam Stoney. He knows everything about Charleston. He's this walking book of knowledge and he's also got ancestors. But when you visit somebody you nearly die of hunger until three o'clock comes. They do give you a little snack around eleven in the morning, but it doesn't help too much.

Gosh, but it was nice driving along the Battery. It was warm and there was a slight breeze coming in from the water. We passed the Fort Sumter Hotel and went riding along by the water. That's what I always think of when I think of Charleston—East Bay, the water, and sailing. Also trees with moss, flowers, old streets, and brass doorknobs. A lot of people even live in alleys, not the kind with garbage cans, but St. Michael's Alley and Price's Alley. A lot of Aunt Ann's friends live there. The houses are very nice, but not like ones in Ashton.

"Well, here we are," Mother said. We parked in front because Aunt Ann and them don't have a driveway. See, their house has a huge brick wall in front of it and this wrought-iron gate you walk through. Inside is this kind of court with all Uncle Petrie's flowers and shrubbery and stuff. There's also a small fountain. After that you go through another kind of gate and there's the house. It's very ancient brick and has a black-green door with a shiny brass knocker. Everybody keeps their brass shining in Charleston, even the doorbell on the outside wall. It's a mark of decency to do so, you know.

We rang the doorbell inside and guess who met us? Winky! Right away she and Mother started kissing each other. How I do wish you could just shake hands!

"Felicia!" Winky finally said to me. And we just kind of put our cheeks together. Embarrassing! "Gosh, you've grow-an some more!"

I didn't think Winky would've said that. As I told you, she's tall herself. I just grinned. You can't just suddenly shrink up or anything. I did feel pretty tall in the hall, though. I just kept holding onto this one suitcase and grinning. I simply never know what to do when I first come into their house. Mother's always carrying on with everybody and I'm usually just standing there.

Winky started calling for Aunt Ann and Uncle Petrie. They came down from upstairs and there was *more* joy! Aunt Ann looked tireder than I'd ever seen her, even though she was pretty tanned. Uncle Petrie always looks tired. He kind of stoops some and has wrinkles round his eyes. They acted overjoyed to see us, though.

206

Then Miss Boggs—the nurse I told you about—came from somewhere in the back! "That child's the tallest thing I ever saw!" she said to Mother about me. "When did it happen?"

"Oh, it just happened," Mother said, and put her arm around my shoulder. That was nice of Mother. But I could have killed Miss Boggs, naturally. I have discovered that many women that have worked a long time in other people's houses are very rude.

My jaws were aching from grinning so much. But then we heard Aunt Pett's deep voice from the east parlor. "Seyruh! Seyruh! Is that you?"

"Oah, it's Awnt Pett," Winky said. "She's been waiting all afternoon. Didn't even take her nap."

We went into the parlor and there was Aunt Pett, sitting all dressed up in her chair looking exactly like Franklin Roosevelt. She had on a grey dress and pearls, and you've never seen anybody that looks so much like Roosevelt. I have this feeling they're related, except he was a Northerner.

"Pett, you lovely darling," Mother said. She's practically wild over Aunt Pett. Mother can say things like "lovely darling" and it sounds all right. But if I said it, everybody'd really think I was insane.

"You're looking well, Seyruh," Aunt Pett said. "I see those Georgians haven't changed you too much."

Zung! Right away I thought of the article in the magazine. I hoped she'd forgotten about it. I hadn't even mentioned it to Mother on the way over because I didn't even want *her* to talk about it.

"Now, Pett, let's not get started on Georgia right away," Mother said.

Thank goodness, she didn't say anything about the article. But there I was, waiting for my time to come.

"Felicia! Felicia, is that you?" she said.

"Uh huh," I said. "How are you, Aunt Pett?" I went up and didn't do a real curtsy, only the jerk one.

207

She took hold of my hand. "Let me see you."

I tried to stick my face out better.

"Character!" she said. "Seyruh, she has character."

I guess that's all she could think of to say. "Thank you," I said, but I was pretty disappointed.

"She's a Whitfield." She started chuckling. "Through and through, a Whitfield."

That wasn't much of a compliment. In her mind it's a whole lot better to look like *her* side than the Whitfield side.

"You had a sweet grandmother, Felicia."

"Grandmother Whitfield?"

"Yes, she was a sweet woman. Used to come to Charleston to visit. She had nice connections here. Always came with her colored girl."

I guess maybe she didn't think the Whitfield side was too bad after all. But that's the thing about Aunt Pett. She gets you to looking at her and then tells you these things about your family as if she were telling you history. All you can do is just stand there and nod your head violently every now and then.

At least, though, she didn't mention the article and she didn't say anything about me growing or how tall I was. She's not at all mean or anything. She just isn't very partial to "simple people." That's what she says about you if you don't have any ancestors. *"Good* people, yes, but simple people. Just a *simple little family."*

Thank the Lord I heard Aunt Ann saying something about going upstairs.

"I guess I am a bit tired," Mother said. "Come, Felicia, you can see Aunt Pett later." As if I were just *dying* to stand there, holding Aunt Pett's hand all afternoon.

We started up the stairway and Aunt Ann followed us. Halfway up she told us she was giving the cocktail party tomorrow. I glanced back at her.

"For both of you," she said.

"Oh, Ann, that's too much trouble now," Mother said.

"Nooo. Just a few in after church."

208

"After *church?*" Mother said. "Honestly, sometimes I forget the way we do in Charleston."

I didn't say anything but I nearly fainted down the stairway with joy. She was really going to give it. She really was! *Me,* at a cocktail party! In Charleston! Hot spit!

22

Poor Winky. We didn't know until that night it was her birthday. We were all sitting in the upstairs drawing room and she came in all dressed up in a black cotton dress. Her cheap-rich Northern beau was giving a party for her, "and I'm in kind of a hurry," she said.

"Winky, not *again,*" Aunt Ann said. "You're not going to Tom's apartment again? It just doesn't look right."

She was standing up there by the door and we were all staring.

"The party's for me and I can't exactly *not* go," she said. You could tell she was pretty furious with Aunt Ann.

"I don't like you to go driving about alone at night," Uncle Petrie said.

"I'll be all right."

"Why doesn't Tom come and call for you here?" Aunt Ann said. "I don't think that boy ever heard of manners."

"Well, you just sit there and fume about *that* for a while," Winky said. "I'm late now."

We heard the downstairs door close and Aunt Ann let out this loud sigh. "Twenty-eight years old and *still* not married."

I didn't think that was too nice of Aunt Ann, saying that in front of us. You shouldn't expose that someone's an old maid.

"I don't think it's so important to marry so young," Mother said. "The English girls don't marry until later, and their marriages always seem more successful than ours. Winky seems a fairly happy girl."

"Well, she's not," Aunt Ann said. She looked at Uncle Petrie. "I really don't like her going to that boy's apartment that way, Petrie."

"Trash," Aunt Pett said. "I tell you Charleston is changing. Jets flying over all day, and our girls marrying the-Lord-knows-who. You ought to see some of the families the girls are marrying into. Nothing's been the same since Taber died. Nothing, absolutely nothing."

Taber was the colored doorman at the St. Cecelia Ball. Mother used to tell me about him. He was always dressed in a high silk hat, long coat, and white gloves. He knew every guest by name and had even opened carriage doors for the debutantes' grandparents. He died a few years ago.

"Everything's changing except Sam Stoney."

I just kind of leaned on the arm of the settee and started staring at the old harp I was going to inherit. If we were going to sit there and talk about Charleston changing and all, at least I was going to get comfortable. I got scrunched down and waited for the long, boring talk to come on. Thank goodness, though, Aunt Ann didn't want to hear about Charleston changing either. She looked at Mother.

"Seyruh, they're simply *terrible* people," she said.

"Who?" Mother asked.

"Those—Gibbings or whatever there names are, the parents of this Tom."

"Yes," Aunt Pett said. (She doesn't care whether anybody's talking to her or not. She just speaks up anyway.) "They came down here from one of those places up there. Probably crept out of a mine or something. Wanted Charleston to absolutely fall at their feet because of their money!" She moved her shoulders. "Those people think money's everything, you know."

"They bought the old La Jeune plantation," Uncle Petrie said.

"Yes, Winky told us."

"But now, really, Pett," Uncle Petrie went on. "The father—Gibbings—must be a rather gifted fellow. They wouldn't have made him president of the company if he hadn't been."

"Industrial trash!" Aunt Pett said. "Seyruh, Charleston is being absolutely ruined by these—these people moving in. You've never seen anything like some of these Northern women."

"I thought you always enjoyed going to Canada in the summer, Pett," Mother said. "You always said there were some lovely people there."

"Mostly Southerners," Aunt Pett said. "And from Boston. Boston has some breeding."

"Well, what's so wrong with the boy's family?" Mother asked.

"They sit on the floor," Aunt Pett said.

"Now, Pett," Uncle Petrie said.

"Letitia told me. She sat right where you're sitting, Seyruh, and told me all about it. Letitia's just as bad as Ann—both of them going around with the-Lord-knows-who, just to get people to work for the church."

"They *are* good workers, some of the new people," Aunt Ann said. "And some of them are really quite nice."

"Letitia sat right there and told me all about going there for dinner," Aunt Pett said.

Uncle Petrie wanted to know if that was when they sat on the floor, but he kind of chuckled.

"They certainly did! All got drunk, and after dinner that Gibbings man sat his large self right down on the floor."

"Did Letitia sit on the floor, too?" Mother asked.

"Of course not! They played jazz records and danced like common taxi drivers. Letitia told me all about it."

"Where in the world did Letitia *meet* them?" Mother asked. For some reason she thought all that was pretty funny.

"In the church," Aunt Pett said. "They joined Grace Church when they moved here. Probably never heard of the Episcopal Church before. That's what they all do, these *Northerners,* come down here and think they can get in with everybody by joining the Episcopal Church!"

"That's a mighty spiritual feeling you have, Pett," Uncle Petrie said and winked at Mother.

Aunt Pett must not have seen the wink. "I tell you, Seyruh,

211

everything's changing. Mr. Waring down there at the newspaper telling everybody to be Republicans and—"

Uncle Petrie said he didn't think Tom Waring was wrong. He asked Aunt Pett if she wanted to cast her vote with all that Democratic rabble in the North.

"They're no different now than they've always been." She held up her empty sherry glass. "Here, Petrie, give me another one."

Uncle Petrie got up and took her glass. "Would you two like something, some Scotch maybe?" He was asking Mother and Aunt Ann. He just ignored me.

"Fine, Petrie," Aunt Ann said. "How about you, Seyruh?"

"Yes, that might be nice. Just a little, Petrie, please."

They all seemed much happier after it was decided there'd be some booze on the scene. People always are, you know.

"Is Winky going to marry that boy?" I thought then was the time to ask.

"Heavens, just don't *speak* of it," Aunt Ann said. She looked at Mother. "It worries me so, Seyruh. Really, it does. You know for years Winky never went with anybody but Roman Catholics. One right after the other. I was sick, really sick. And now this—"

I guess I didn't tell you that people in Charleston aren't very partial to Roman Catholics. If you're French, the best thing you can be is be a Huguenot—not Catholic. I don't know why they think that's so terrible, being Catholic. I wouldn't mind being one too much. I think it would be kind of nice, going into a church with this veil on your head. You'd be all alone with this lighted candle and everything. Some boy would see you and know right then and there you were the kind of human being he wanted to marry. You'd have to wear a blue veil, though, sort of like the one the Virgin Mary was always going around wearing.

"Well, I wouldn't worry too much about Winky," Mother said. "Has she ever indicated she was really serious?" I guess Mother didn't want Aunt Ann to know Winky had already talked to us about it. Mother can be very loyal like that sometimes.

"No, but she sees him all the time," Aunt Ann said. "They go

212

over there to his apartment and cook dinners and listen to records and all that foolishness."

"I told you," Aunt Pett said, "I told you if you sent her to that college up there she'd get all sorts of foolhardy notions."

"Where did the boy go to school?" Mother asked.

"Yale," Aunt Ann said.

"Humph," Aunt Pett said. "Just like them. Always have to send their children to a *name* school. Trying to hide behind the name of a college. They don't have anything else. Trash. Common."

"He's also fat," Aunt Ann said, and let out this really tremendous sigh. "But he does have a rather nice face—a bit ordinary, but nice features."

"Winky thinks he's amusing," Aunt Pett said. "I told her— I said never marry a funny man. Funny men never succeed in life. Always too busy trying to be the center of things. Never saw a funny man yet who ever succeeded in anything."

Uncle Petrie came in with the tray of drinks. "Lavinia's broken three more glasses, Ann."

"Oh dear, these colored people you get nowadays. Nothing's been the same since my dear Millie died. I miss her to death."

"It's the N.A.A.C.P.," Aunt Pett said. "Absolutely ruined every one of them. They don't half work, and all they're interested in is sitting at the dime store. They're—Seyruh! That article was a dis*grace!* I was so ashamed I tore it right up. What in the world were you thinking about?"

I knew it! I knew it! I knew we'd get around to it. I sat up.

"Yes, it was extremely unfortunate," Mother said.

"And letting your child's *picture* be displayed like that!"

"We didn't know anything about that," Mother said.

They all looked at me.

"He just took it," I said, and blurted out this horrible laugh. Nobody else laughed. They just looked back at Mother.

"Thank heaven, they didn't use your *name*," Aunt Pett said.

"But, of course, everyone who knows us knew who it was. After all, there was Felicia's picture."

"Most disgraceful thing I ever heard of," Aunt Pett said. "Made every one of you sound like darkies."

"No," Mother said, "he said Allison and I were 'charming, well-intentioned people.' Don't you remember?"

"Well-intentioned!" Aunt Pett said. "Just because you don't go around waiting on your servants. What's the matter with those people up there? They're all alike. Never had any background, never been anywhere decent. They're—"

"They're so conscientious now," Uncle Petrie said. "Suddenly after seventy-five years of saying nothing, the North has finally decided to get quite saintly about conditions here—but only here, in the South."

"Exactly," Mother said. "You know I read so much nowadays, so much criticism and, really, hypocrisy, that it's—well, I told Allison it's turning me against the colored man."

"I know," Uncle Petrie said. "It's very sad, this feeling that is developing." He lifted his glass. "We're the minority in this country now. The Southern white man. Thank the Lord for a newspaperman like Tom Waring!"

"Yes," Aunt Pett said. "They had all that fuss around here about Fort Sumter last month. People making speeches—*fine* speeches. Fireworks. All that. And where are we? We're just about where we were one hundred years ago, mad enough to secede."

"With two exceptions, Pett," Uncle Petrie said. "The Russians and the moon."

"Savages!" Aunt Pett said. "I'm tired of having to fool with savages! All this fuss about the Russians!"

"You don't want them coming over here, do you?" Uncle Petrie asked her. "As conquerors?"

"Wouldn't be any worse than the Yankees! Wouldn't be a bit worse than what the Yankees did to us during the War!"

Mother laughed. "Ah, Pett, there'll never be another like you."

"Well, it's the truth if I ever said it! Those New Englanders brought the darkies down here, expected us to civilize them in one generation, when for a *thousand* generations they'd been eating people in the jungle. New Englanders never have understood us and we don't want to understand *them*."

Boring. Aunt Pett didn't care a thing about the Russians and everybody going up in space. That's pretty interesting to me, but it's also pretty scary. I can just see all these Russians running around in Ashton. I'd die. Anyway, though, we weren't talking about the magazine article any more. Thank goodness, Mother didn't say anything about me lying. She'd probably tell Aunt Ann and Uncle Petrie about it later. That's what she usually does.

"I wish we *had* seceded," Aunt Pett said. "It wouldn't have made any difference. We're like another country anyway."

"That's what Allison's always saying," Mother said.

"Why, yes! We're—"

I got up and started walking toward the door. I *almost* put my hip out of joint but I remembered where I was. I've got to stop doing that because I may really forget some day and do it at a cocktail party or something.

"Where're you going, Felicia?" Mother asked.

"Downstairs. Out in the garden."

"All right, but don't stay long. We're all going to bed soon. You want to be alert for the party tomorrow, remember."

"All right." Frankly, I wasn't feeling very alert right then. It's the most peculiar thing about me but I can just be sitting up in a drawing room somewhere, listening to other people talk, and I can almost go to sleep. Sometimes I really have to fight almost to keep my eyes open. I think I've probably developed some kind of disease, but then I'm always thinking that. You can just mention you've got something and right away I start aching all over and feeling horrible.

I felt much more alert, though, when I got outside. It was a warm night and the wisteria on the side of the house was blooming violently. I walked around the garden for a while and it wasn't too spooky because the lights from the house kind of lighted things up some.

After a while I got to thinking about what all Aunt Pett had

215

said. She doesn't really hate colored people. I don't know why she carries on like that. She's all the time doing things for colored people and once when Minnie, her cook for simply centuries, nearly died from this contagious disease she got, Aunt Pett stayed with her for three whole days and nights and never once left her side. None of Minnie's family would do it because they said they'd heard "death bells." When colored people hear "death bells," they just go on and give up the ghost, but Aunt Pett didn't and Minnie got well. Aunt Pett's all the time doing things like that, but she wouldn't've ever invited Minnie to a cocktail party. Minnie thought drinking whisky was sinful anyway.

What I think is the truth is that Aunt Pett is just paying "hombrage" to the glorious Southern war dead. Which is nice of her, I think. Most people go flying around and forget what somebody did once. The Northerners really were terrible to us during the War, just like Aunt Pett said, and they weren't cultivated people at all, as you know. The North just doesn't understand and, too, when they freed the colored people, many of the colored were simply a disgrace because they didn't know how to conduct themselves. We had to put up with all that and, too, when you think of it, colored people really haven't been cultivated very long—I mean in our ways. I guess they had their own ways over in the jungle. I think it was terrible of the New Englanders to make them leave their home in the jungle in the first place. Sometimes when you think about that you could almost die of pity for them. I certainly do. But I don't pity them now, because I wouldn't want anybody to go around pitying me.

Anyway, I don't want to talk about that any more. Charleston in the spring is the nicest place in the entire universe. This very warm breeze came floating in from the water and I did the craziest thing. I just held out my arms to it, as if I could somehow encircle the whole night—the bay, the water, steeples, all of it—and I got to thinking about growing up and being a part of everything, going on trips maybe and coming back. Always coming back. Have you ever done anything like that? I mean when

216

you were alone? Sort of felt like crying and yet you were violently happy? It's really peculiar.

I went over to the little stone bench by the old oak tree and I don't know how long I sat there. After a while, though, I heard a car door slam. I jerked around. Winky or somebody was coming through the gate. It *was* Winky. But she just stood there for a spell, and then I saw her put this handkerchief to her eyes. She was crying.

"Winky?"

She jerked the handkerchief away.

"Winky?" I asked again.

She came over toward me. I couldn't see her too well, but I knew by her voice she really had been crying.

"What're you doing out here, Felicia?"

"I don't know," I said in this very kind voice. "They're up there talking about Charleston changing and stuff. That doesn't fascinate me too much."

She sat down beside me and I knew I'd have to think up some really wise things to say.

"You didn't stay very long," I said. "Didn't you have a good time, Winky?"

"Not very." Her voice was shaky and she blew her nose.

I sort of wished I'd been ninety-nine instead of thirteen. I really wanted to help her. "D'you sit on the floor and everything?"

She glanced at me. "You've been listening to Aunt Pett, I see."

"No," I said. "We didn't mention Tom or his family or you or anything after you left." (Forgive me, Lord.)

She kind of slumped her shoulders. "That jerk! He asked me to *marry* him! That fat—"

"*Tom* did?" I wanted to shout with joy. "How wonderful, Winky! You're gonna be married!"

"For Godsake," she said. "I wouldn't marry him if he were the last man on earth!"

"Oh," I said. I didn't know what to say.

"I don't know why Mother and Awnt Pett have been carrying on so. I told you and Awnt Seyruh, you know, down in Ponte

Vedra. He was just somebody to—a friend. You have to have somebody to talk to. It's so—" She shook her head.

Poor Winky. I knew what it was like to be an old maid.

"You're not going to be an old maid, Winky," I said. "Everybody likes you, and English girls never marry until later. It isn't so important to marry so young."

She looked at me again. "You really have a lot of sense for someone your age."

"I *think* an awful lot," I said. "Velvet's always telling me I put her in mind of somebody old."

She just gave this short laugh and then said, "Damn! The nerve of that weak—"

"Didn't you like him at all?"

"Yes, I *liked* him. He was a friend of this other boy I used to go with at Yale. You know the one I—" her voice started up shaking again. "Tom just showed me the clipping from the *Times* tonight. He's married, the one I used to— He just got married—"

"Oh, Winky," I said. *That* was the reason she was crying. She had been betrayed.

"Uh huh, I had a letter from him just a few weeks ago. He actually said he was coming down here. He—"

I sort of folded my hands in front of me and leaned forward. I was trying desperately to think up something to say. It was terrible.

"*Every*body's in New York," she said. "All my friends at college. And where is Winky? Charleston—good, old, conservative, quaint Charleston!"

I thought she was going to cry again. "I guess they want you to marry someone with good connections, Winky. I mean somebody from Charleston and all."

"Well, who?" she asked. "A cousin or something?"

"Don't lots of people here marry their cousins?" I thought I'd heard Mother say they did.

"Not *first* cousins, for heaven sakes!"

"Oh!"

218

"I've got to get out of here. Somehow I'm going to get out of here."

"Tom was sort of like your friends up there, wasn't he? I mean he just kind of reminded you of them."

"Something like that." She just sat there and didn't say anything for literally hours. Finally she said, "He'd bought this damn ring and everything. He showed me the clipping about Bob's marrying and then handed me the *ring!* I could have killed him! He hasn't even—" She didn't finish.

I searched my brains for something to say. "I know what you mean, Winky. Why don't you go on back to New York? I wouldn't mind going there. Arthur just hates it at home. He's all the time wishing he was back in New York." Another lie. Oh me—

"I *can't* go. I'm stuck. No money, nothing!"

"Won't they give you some? Aunt Ann and Uncle Petrie?"

"They'd rather die than see me working in New York." She shook her head again. "Everybody here's married. There's nothing. Absolutely nothing."

Nothing but old oak trees, I was thinking—and moss—long, hanging, grey moss. I really let out a sigh. It was tragic.

"Well, things aren't all that bad," she said, getting up. "But, look, Felicia, pu-leese don't say anything about all this. *You* know how it is. Awnt Pett and Mother and—"

I stood up with my hands clenched. "I *won't*, Winky! I never will *as long as I live.* I'll never tell anybody!"

"Good girl," she said. And we walked very sadly back to the house.

But poor Winky. How would you like to be some old maid in a place like Charleston where everybody else goes around all happy and married and things? It's terrible. Really. Still, to me, that was one of the most inspirational things that's ever happened to me. I mean some twenty-eight-year-old person talking to me about their troubles. Winky is one of the most inspirational people in the entire world. You've absolutely never seen anybody

219

like her. And, too, she didn't even mention my disgrace about being in the magazine. She didn't even bring it up. How like her! So kind. She knew how I was feeling.

When we started inside, I said, "Anyway, Winky, there's going to be the cocktail party tomorrow! Guess we'll have to be alert for it." I was trying to cheer her up.

"Great," she said, and sounded almost disgusted. I guess she was just trying not to cry or anything. I decided I was going to wear lipstick. I'd have to borrow some, though. Pitiful.

23

Well, Winky's *beau* came to the cocktail party! He didn't come until near the last, but all of a sudden he came barging into the room and I nearly collapsed. First, though, let me tell you what happened to *me*.

See, I decided if I was going to a cocktail party in a place like Charleston, I'd better kind of try to look like somebody from well, say, Atlanta or Savannah or somewhere. If you went in looking like somebody from a tiny town like Ashton, everybody'd think you were this pathetic hick and nobody'd speak to you. So what I did, I waited until Mother and them had already gone into the drawing room and when they were gone I started dressing. There wasn't anything I could do about my dress because the only one I had was my green linen one. It's not too bad, but it isn't what you're supposed to wear to a cocktail party. It has sleeves even. But Mother said my "little linen" was exactly what you're supposed to wear to a "little gathering" on Sunday noon. She had made me wear my two-piece, dark-blue dress to church, but since the party was in our honor she thought it was better to wear the "little linen" for that.

But it doesn't make me look fat, and also I couldn't do anything about my low-heeled shoes. I thought of breaking off one of the heels and asking Winky if she had any I could borrow, but I was afraid hers wouldn't fit and there I'd be without anything. What I did, I decided I'd do something about my face! I got out all Mother's junk—lipstick, powder, and even some rouge which she wears sometimes at night. I really packed it on and, though I hate to mention it, I looked gorgeous! I know I shouldn't say I did—I know that's very conceited and everything—but you have no idea what lipstick and rouge do to me, especially a lot of it. I look like an entirely different person. The only thing was, see, I told you, I don't have hardly any eyebrows because they're so light. But there was nothing I could do about that. So I just pulled my hair slick back from my face, and with just the bangs kind of brushed back, I looked like I was about twenty-seven years old. If only I'd had some shoes with high heels! But people don't look at your feet too much, just your face, so it was all right.

When I got through, I stared at myself for hours in the mirror. I got to thinking that maybe I wasn't going to be an old maid after all. The trouble with someone like Winky is, she doesn't wear enough lipstick. You've got to really pack it on if you don't want to be an old maid. You look at old maids—everyone of them! Not *one* wears enough lipstick and stuff.

I could hardly take myself away from the mirror, but I did, finally, and went on out into the hall. This older man was coming up the stairway and when he saw me he said "how-do-you-do." I said "how-do-you-do" back and kind of followed him on into the drawing room. Even *he* thought I was older.

There weren't too many people there yet, but the colored butler, that serves literally everybody's parties in Charleston, was already passing drinks around with his tray. I didn't much want Mother to see me, and I don't think she did because she was surrounded by all these smiling people. The butler came up to me and I could have shot him. He asked me if I wanted a Coca-*Cola!* I said, "Noooo," in that accent Arthur had when he came back sophisticated from Connecticut, "just an Old Fashioned, puleeeese."

"Oh, yes *ma'm!*" he said and had this silly kind of glad-surprised look on his face.

I was delighted! But if Mother or any of them saw me drinking it, I was going to say it was orange juice. But then I got to thinking what if I got drunk like Arthur did down in Ponte Vedra. I'd go reeling around the room, slurping at everybody, and then probably pass out on the harp or something. Mother would cave in with insanity. So I decided if I started feeling that way, even in the slightest, I wouldn't drink any more of it.

I was just standing there, tapping my fingers on this table, waiting for the butler to come back with my Old Fashioned when Aunt *Ann* came up to me!

"Felicia," she said, "would you mind passing a few—Felicia! What have you done to yourself?"

She didn't have to act like that! "Whatdoya mean, Aunt Ann?"

"Your face!" She put her fingertips to her lips. "Seyr—" She looked across the room and didn't say anything else to me. She just went over and whispered something to Mother.

Right away I turned around so Mother wouldn't see me.

"Heah you is, Miss," I heard the butler at my back.

I halfway turned and both of them were there—Mother *and* the butler.

"What is that?" Mother asked the butler.

"An Old Fashioned, Miss Seyruh. Would you like one?"

"No, no. Thank you. Felicia?"

"Huh?"

"Look here."

I turned and looked her straight in the eye. "What?" I said in this very angry voice.

She led me out into the hall. More people were coming up the stairway.

"Go in and take that off—immediately!" She kind of hissed it at me, and then because of the other people she couldn't say any more, but I think they heard her anyway. She started smiling and went up to the people. They all started carrying on with that false joy grownups have when they're trying to be nice. One of the women pointed at me and said, "Is that Felicia?"

Mother just glanced back at me. "Yes, she's doing a little errand for Ann. She'll be back in a minute."

I ran across the hall and into the bedroom. I was furious! And also I knew Aunt Ann was probably going around the room telling everybody. That's what older people do all the time. They think everything you do is absolutely hilarious and they can say anything they want to about you any time they feel like it. They don't care if you're standing right there *hearing* it half the time.

Mother came into the bedroom.

"Well, I *hope* you're sat-is-fied," I said.

"Satisfied about what?" she asked. She looked very pretty in her grey dress.

"Humiliating me in front of all those people!" I picked up this sweater on the bed and threw it across the room.

"Now, Felicia, you just control yourself!"

I *hate* that word "control." Control yourself! CONTROL YOURSELF! It makes you sound like you're foaming at the mouth or something.

"Ordering something to drink," she said. "I'm ashamed of you. And your face!"

"Go on, then," I said. "Go on. I won't even go to the cocktail party. I just won't go!"

She came over to me and put her hand on the side of my face. "Felicia," she said very softly, "of course you're coming. Now, just run in and wash your face."

I guess I was so glad she wasn't mad any more that I didn't say anything.

"Run along now in the bathroom. And I think you could fix your hair more becomingly."

"*All right,*" I said in this tone to show her I was a slave.

"Be quick," she called to me. "There're so many people who want to meet you."

The stuff was horrible to get off—especially the lipstick. I used

223

cold cream and everything and didn't ever get it all off. But, finally, I got to looking like my old, sad self again—hair hanging down on the sides, straight, and my bangs brushed all the way back. Also my face was pretty red from scrubbing it so hard. I didn't care how I looked any more, though. I made this dreadful face in the mirror and then dragged on into the drawing room again.

Without any lipstick and stuff I got to feeling tall and stupid again. Millions of people had come and I didn't know who I was going to talk to. You know, at a cocktail party you can't just stand up there grinning like an idiot. You have to talk to somebody. You've never seen such a mixed-up group of people in your life. Ancient people, as old as Aunt Pett, were there. Some were as young as Winky, but most were Mother and Aunt Ann's age. Everybody was holding glasses and talking. It sounded funny with all their Charleston accents. "Bo-ut" for boat and "ayette" for eight. All that. Finally, this older man came up to me. He was very tall and very thin and had gobs of white hair. But guess what he did? He *bowed* to me! To *me!* I shook his hand and curtsied which isn't so bad to do if the other person does what he's supposed to.

He said he was this name I didn't understand. But it sounded like Pringney. "And you're Felicia? Felicia Whitfield?" He was very serious.

"Yes," I said. "I'm my mother's daughter. Mrs. Whitfield? I'm the only girl."

"I know. I know," he said and smiled a very nice smile because he had eyes that were very blue. "But, now, don't you have a drink?"

I started blushing. "I don't drink whisky very much," I said. "I guess I'm not allowed to." I kind of rolled my eyes upward and started tapping my foot.

"Lovely," he said, "I've never enjoyed the sight of a young lady drinking whisky. But wouldn't you like a lemonade or something else?"

"Yes, I think I would. I really do." That was nice of him, telling me he didn't like to see young ladies drinking whisky. It made you feel like you were the nicest person in the whole room.

He held up his hand slightly to the butler and immediately the butler came prancing over again.

"A lemonade, please. For the young lady."

The butler kind of looked at me and I knew what he was thinking—about the Old Fashioned and all.

"Yes, *sir*," he said, and went off with the tray.

"Let's see," the man said, rubbing his chin. "Felicia Whitfield. Felicia Whitfield. I believe she is—let's see—" he glanced at me—"she is twelve years old!"

I shook my head violently. "Thir*teen!*" I said. "Thirteen! I'm in junior-high school now."

"Ohhh yes," he said.

"My brother Arthur is fifteen now. He had to go to Connecticut, you know."

"To Connecticut?"

"Yes, to this school. We thought he needed a change of atmosphere."

For some reason the man laughed, but he had a nice laugh, too. "I think we *all* need a change of atmosphere sometimes," he said.

"Uh huh, I think so, too." I was trying to think up something else to say and then it came to me. "Mr. Pringney—" I kind of slurred his name. "What do you think of Robert Browning's sanguinary period?"

"What's that?" He leaned down closer to me. I thought maybe he was a little deaf.

"Robert Browning's *sanguinary* period?" I practically shouted it.

He raised up. "Oahhh," he said in his Charleston accent, "Robert Browning, the poet."

I nearly died. "Yes, you know when he was going around with this happy outlook all the time? Instead of his downtrodden one?"

He started frowning. "Yes, of course." He looked at me with his head half cocked. "Do you read Mr. Browning?"

"All the time. I'm extremely partial to him." (Lie.)

225

"Well, I think you're a very intelligent young lady. Mr. Browning has been a favorite of mine, too."

"He *is?*"

"Yes." He smiled again, almost pitifully, and looking practically at the ceiling said:

"Oh, to be in England
Now that April's there,
And whoever wakes in England
Sees, some morning, unaware,
That the lowest boughs and the brush-wood sheaf
Round the elm-tree bole are in tiny leaf,
While the chaffinch sings on the orchard bough
In England—now!"

Sad! It gave you this feeling he really did want to be in England—even more than Charleston. "Gosh," I said.

He started to say something else but this other man with black-grey eyebrows came up to us. "Quoting poetry, Battle," he said, not even looking at me. "So that's why you're such a favorite with all the ladies."

Mr. Pringney thought that was highly amusing, but then he remembered me.

"This is Felicia Whitfield, Foster. Felicia, Mr. Foster Pereaux."

I shook his hand, but I didn't curtsy.

"Foster," Mr. Pringney said, "we have been discussing Robert Browning's sanguinary period. I'll wager you don't even know what that is."

"Robert Browning's *what?*" he asked, and lighted a cigarette.

"Sanguinary period."

"I didn't know he had one," Mr. Pereaux said and chuckled quite rudely, I thought.

Mr. Pringney thought that was highly amusing also. "Well, my young friend and I know about it. In Georgia they're very concerned with Mr. Browning."

"That so? That so?"

226

"I haven't exactly taken him up in school yet," I said. "I just kind of read it on my own. You ought to talk to my brother Arthur. He knows everything about Robert Browning. He's always writing essays."

Mr. Pringney turned to Mr. Pereaux. "Arthur is up in Connecticut getting a change of atmosphere."

"Who is Arthur?" Mr. Pereaux said. Mr. Pereaux was a very confused sort of man.

"Her *brother*. He's in school up there."

"Then I'm sure he's getting a change of atmosphere," Mr. Pereaux said.

The butler came with my lemonade. He had fixed it with a cherry in it.

"Thank you," I said to the butler and took the drink. He had to hand me the napkin. I forgot to take it. Embarrassing, and both of the men were staring, too. I'm always forgetting napkins, just like Isaiah.

To cover up my mistake, I said, "Charleston is certainly full of grace and charm."

"How's that?" Mr. Pringney said.

I said: *"Charleston certainly is full of grace and charm."*

"Good!" Mr. Pereaux said. "It's half your city, you know."

"I know it," I said. "It's not a thing like where I come from. People in Ashton don't have much intellect."

Mr. Pringney really laughed that time. "Here," he said to Mr. Pereaux, giving him his glass. And he took out a handkerchief and wiped his eyes.

Mr. Pereaux was smiling, too.

Mother came up and joined us. "What's going on over here?"

Mr. Pringney finished wiping his eyes. "Seyruh, you have *quite* a daughter! *Quite* a daughter!"

Mother looked at me, very pleased. "Felicia's going to be *all* right."

"I think she already is," Mr. Pereaux said.

I've never been so happy in all my life. Nothing has ever made me feel so like flying. I didn't even care when this friend of

Mother's came up and all four of them started talking about this friend of their's that'd fallen in love with this man that fixed lawnmowers. It was the talk of Charleston and everybody was fascinated with it. The woman had just gone down to have her lawnmower fixed, took one look at the man and had fallen madly in love. They had run away to be married and were living in some rundown place outside the city. The woman's family was in mourning.

While they were talking about that, they pretty much ignored me, but I didn't care. Things like that interest me hugely. Love and all. I can't wait until somebody falls in love with me. Probably nobody ever will, but I don't think I'd be particularly partial to somebody that fixed lawnmowers. You'd have to sit up and talk about lawnmowers for the rest of your life. He wouldn't know a thing about Robert Browning, just grease and bolts and screws, and your children would grow up saying things like "I ain't" and "he come" and stuff.

It was pretty good, though, just standing there listening to all that. I didn't have to think up anything to say, and you could kind of relax for a while. That's the thing about a cocktail party, you've always got to be thinking up fascinating things to say to people or they'll go away. It's terribly exhausting. I like just kind of standing there, listening. But then I looked toward the door and BLOOM! I saw this rather large, sandy-haired young man in a black suit walk into the room. Right away I knew who it was! Tom Gibbings! I looked about the room for Winky. She was talking to a couple about her age and had her back to the door. The young man went up to her, said something, and Winky said something to him, but she wasn't smiling or anything like she usually does at people.

I was pretty surprised at Tom. I didn't think he was so bad looking. He was sort of fat, but you knew he had muscles, too. One thing, though, his hair was too long. It was blond and kind of came swooping down at the back. Arthur would have died. He can't stand men that wear their hair too long. But really he wasn't bad looking at all. He had very nice features. His nose wasn't broken or anything, and he had very very dark-brown eyes. He looked a little like Tarzan in the movies, except he was blond and fatter.

But then out came this cigarette holder! Right away he started looking like somebody that'd half scare you to death. I got to wondering if Aunt Ann had invited him to come. But I guess Winky had and just forgot to tell him not to after he'd asked her to marry him and all.

I couldn't stand it any longer, so I spotted this bowl of cheese bits and decided I'd take up my old routine of passing things. I went straight up to them and held out the bowl to Winky. She introduced me to the other couple. The girl was very pretty with sparkling green eyes and her husband wore horn-rimmed glasses.

"And *I'm* Tom Gibbings," Tom said to me in this accent that sounded almost English. He said "Tawm" instead of Tom.

I kind of glanced at Winky, then I said: "How-do-you-do?" Up close, he was better looking than far away because you couldn't see his body and you forgot about him being kind of fat. He was the only man in the room with a black suit on.

"Felicia's from Georgia," Winky said to the other couple.

"Pi*ty*," said Tom. "That's nothing to laugh about."

I felt the blood rush to my face! But the other couple thought that was kind of funny because the husband was trying not to laugh.

"That isn't funny, Tom," Winky said. "And where are *you* from?"

"From the *world*," Tom said. "*Of* the world."

"Ohio," Winky said. "I don't think that's anything to laugh about either."

"Now angel," Tom said. He blew this great gust of smoke straight up into the air. I hated him, but I stretched the bowl of cheese bits out to him anyway.

"Th*ink* you," he said, and I noticed he had short fingers.

"How's business, Tom?" the husband asked. Isn't it funny? I don't care where you are, there's always being somebody with horn-rimmed glasses on, asking "How's business?" Men in Ashton are always asking Father that. Poor men, they really do have boring lives.

"Passable," Tom said.

"Still clipping coupons?"

"In a way."

"What he means is," Winky said, "no, he doesn't have a job."

"Why, angel," Tom said, "I *do*. I *do*."

"What?" Winky asked.

"This," he said, holding up his glass. "Peachy."

"Yes," Winky said. "Peachy."

Tom flipped his cigarette in the ash tray but some of the ashes fell off onto the table. He brushed them off with his thick hand and suddenly got this serious look on his face. "No, as a matter of fact, I'm leaving this quaint old masterpiece of a city—just about—*Wednesday!*"

Winky looked at him sharply.

"You are?" the other girl said. "Why, Tom, we'll miss you. Where're you going?"

"Back to New York. A friend at college—at least his father—offered me a job, in advertising. 'Rinso white' and all that sort of thing."

"How wonderful," the girl said.

Tom looked at Winky. "Yes," he said, "I think it's rather courageous of me, myself."

I couldn't just stand there. You can't just stand there holding a bowl of cheese bits saying nothing, so I moved on around the room, telling everybody that Father was "just fine." Everybody wanted to know. They like Father an awful lot in Charleston, but he can't ever come as much as us because he's so harassed all the time. That's what I told this one older lady and she thought that was pretty funny. Older people are always finding *something* to laugh about. It's amazing.

I didn't listen much to what most of them said though. I was thinking too much about Winky and Tom. I was thinking that if Tom did go to New York, Winky really would be all alone then. But I didn't blame Winky for not liking him. You could just tell he didn't have any good connections in Charleston. I don't know why—he just looked like somebody that wouldn't have good connections—in the South anyway. Still, he wasn't bad looking and he *did* have all that money. I'd rather marry him than a lawn-mower fixer. Maybe.

About two-thirty everybody started going home for dinner. I told you everybody has their dinner at three o'clock. That's why they like to give their cocktail parties after church. Because then everybody goes home pretty early. Aunt Ann said that some people, the new ones that've moved to Charleston, have dinner at night, but they're never invited to the old Charleston parties. It's pitiful.

Anyway, I got a new duty, helping these older ladies down the stairway. Aunt Ann suggested it, and one with a cane nearly broke my shoulder she leaned so heavily on my arm. I didn't mind too much, though, because it gives you sort of a good feeling, helping older ladies down the stairs. That's another funny thing about me, but, you know, I'm very much in favor of older ladies. They really have wonderful senses of humor and they're so much nicer than middle-aged ones. Middle-aged ones, a lot of them, are terribly snobbish. I mean *really* snobbish. Not like Aunt Pett, that is just used to her ways, but they pretty much go around hating everybody. I don't know why it is, but you just notice sometimes.

Well, anyway, there I was—going up and down, up and down, like an elevator. Mr. Pringney helped one down, too, and they laughed all the way. Older people have worlds of fun, especially in Charleston. Then, when I thought all the older ones had gone, I decided I'd better go on back up and see what had happened to Winky and Tom. But I didn't have to! Out of the blue they came racing down the stairway—together! I nearly fainted. Winky had this tan sweater thrown over her shoulders. "Felicia," she said, kind of giggling, "tell Mother I won't be here for dinner."

I didn't say a thing.

"Will you?" she asked, and gave me this huge, wide smile like she was trying to tell me something.

"Okay, Winky," I said very weakly.

"*Adieu, ma petite,*" Tom said to me.

"*Adieu,*" I said. I know a lot of French words.

But I just stood there for a while, flabbergasted, and then I hurried on outside. The gate was still open, and I went over by the tea-olive bush where I could see better. Winky and Tom were getting into Tom's car. It was a foreign car, black and sort of cream colored. Winky was brushing her hair back with her hand and she looked very gay, like she was doing everything in the world to keep from just out-and-out beaming. Then, just like that, I knew what was happening. I knew it! Winky was going to marry him. She really was. Even after last night and everything. They'd live in New York, and when they came home they'd have to stay with Tom's rich-cheap family because Aunt Pett probably wouldn't have that kind of element in her house. It made me sort of sick in my stomach.

They rode away with a great roaring of the engine and I heard Winky laugh.

"Just because she's lonesome," I thought. And then I had this vision. I kept seeing Winky, like some mist, like lonesomeness, and Tom was this shiny, brassy, new automobile. He was taking her away.

". . . And our girls marrying the-Lord-knows-who. And our girls marrying the-Lord-knows—" Aunt Pett talking. I walked on back to the house, but on the way I passed by the oak tree where the moss was hanging. It looked old and very dead, the moss, like an old, dreary Sunday afternoon when the summer's on. Charleston *was* changing, I thought. The whole South was, even Georgia. Everything was changing. The new and the old. But the new! The new! It was enough to make you want to throw yourself on the ground and die dead away—in a field of violets.

Oh, Winky, you'll miss us so!

24

But wasn't I simply a success at the cocktail party? I know that's very selfish to put in, but it really did make me feel *so* pleased. I mean so much bad had happened that it just showed I wasn't such a terrible goon after all. Now the only thing next I had to worry about was going to Connecticut. But, of course, that would be much more harassing than Charleston. Up there we wouldn't even have any relatives to tell people we were nice. Not a soul would know us and we'd be up there trying to get along all by ourselves.

I decided I'd better have a talk with Arthur about it when he came home for spring vacation. Naturally, I wouldn't tell him I was afraid to go to Connecticut, I'd just sort of ask him how he wanted us to look and stuff. Isn't life the biggest worry in the world, though? Soon as you get through with one thing, bang, you have to go flying off into something else. Always having something to worry about.

I do wish we could have stayed in Charleston longer. I would've adored to have been hanging around when Winky announced she was going to marry Tom. I could just hear Aunt Pett and them, but on the way back to Ashton Mother and I had a deep conversation about it. She said she didn't think Winky would do anything foolish like running away, but if she did she was sure Aunt Ann and Uncle Petrie would be loyal and "back her up."

"It's tragic," I said.

"What?"

"I dunno. There's nobody else for her to marry, I guess."

Mother said she hoped Winky wouldn't marry just for that reason.

"So do I," I said, "but I think she is."

We didn't talk too much else about it because Mother was too concerned about Arthur. That was the main reason we had to leave Charleston. Father had called and said *he* was all right but that we'd had a letter from Arthur. He didn't say over the phone what it was about. He tried to, but Mother didn't understand it too well. Sometimes Arthur's letter can be extremely confusing, especially over long-distance. Anyway, we had to get on back and, besides, I was dying to talk to him about Connecticut like I told you.

Well, it wouldn't've made any difference if I'd talked my head off to him. Nobody could talk to him hardly! You see, what happened was—and this is the worst thing that has *ever* happened—Arthur had grown sincere! Just since Christmas. You've never seen such a mess in all your life. The first thing we did when we got home was to read his letter. Right off the bat, he announced he was bringing the most unpopular boy in the entire school home with him. "It's Bob Leyden and he's started up again!" Somehow it had become Arthur's duty to be nice to Bob Leyden. ". . . Only last week the Head thanked me personally for my spirit in aiding the handycapped." At the end of the letter he said for Mother not to worry because "old Leyden" had these rubber sheets he took around with him all the time.

Mother was furious! She said she didn't have enough sheets to be changing them all the time and it did look as if Arthur could be a little more considerate of his own family. "Why can't Arthur help out some normal boy?" she asked.

I didn't want to say anything. Not about *that!* I could just hear everybody in Ashton talking and, besides, we'd already been exposed to the public too much already. But Father said it wouldn't hurt us to be nice to the boy. He said if necessary *he* would go down and buy some extra sheets.

Mother despises Father when he starts getting humble that way, so she went down and bought the sheets, six of them. Then she had Velvet string this rope between the two oak trees in our back lawn. "We may have some additional washing to do next week," was all she told Velvet. I guess that was why she was sort of upset when Arthur's next letter came. I mean she had gone to all that trouble and everything and Arthur wrote that Bob wasn't coming:

234

...His parents said he couldn't come because he's got to go to this doctor the Head recommended. The Head told Mr. and Mrs. Leyden that if Leyden didn't get cured for good, he believed it was a good idea for them to keep him home permanently psychologically. Poor old Leyden. You ought to see all these alarm clocks and everything he's got. I'm like the Head, though. He says he thinks it's unthinking the way all the boys tease him. And yesterday the Head told me privately that I stand a good chance of getting the Amos T. Caldwalder award because I've started showing all this character. He said all the masters had been noticing me and he hoped I don't flunk anything. I told the Head how I had always believed in the helpless and downtrodden. You have to if you want to get the Amos T. Caldwalder award. It's the highest award a boy can get. I gotta go.

Cordially,
A.

Mother became extacized over the award. "Arthur's just like my father," she said. "I don't think I ever heard Father say an unkind word about anybody." Arthur was the same way, she said. She just *hoped* Arthur would get that award and *show* everybody. "My, Allison, he really is maturing, isn't he? It makes me feel quite sad, really."

I thought about that for a while. Mother didn't mention me—she hardly ever does in conversation—but it seemed to me I was maturing, too, just about as much as Arthur. Of course I haven't had the exposure to as much intellect and travels as Arthur has, but I've even taken up reading the old boring *Sewanee Review*. It doesn't have hardly any pictures in it and I force myself to read it once a day. Articles and everything. Also, soon, I would be in Connecticut. That'll make eight states I've been in in my lifetime, I mean counting the ones you go through to get to Connecticut.

Anyway, on Thursday, down we went, back to the old train station to welcome Arthur again! The little colored children across the track had grown ten thousand inches since Christmas. I tell you, when I die, they're going to put on my tombstone: SPENT LIFE IN TRAIN STATION!

Arthur was the only passenger to get off the train this time. But immediately I noticed something different about him. At first I thought it was his glasses but I remembered he had gotten the horn-rimmed ones Christmas and I guess I hadn't got used to them yet. But, also, he wasn't running and waving toward us like he sometimes does. He was walking with his coat over his arm, very slowly, and as he got closer I noticed this peculiar look in his eyes—a kind of blue-eyed gleaming I'd never seen before. And then he came up and took Mother's hand with *both* of his, putting his left hand on the top of Mother's, not shaking it or anything, just resting it there like the minister does on top of your head when you're confirmed.

"Mother," he said as if he hadn't seen her for one million years, "are you all right, Mother?"

Mother looked down at their hands and then at Arthur. "Why, of course!" She broke into a wide smile.

Arthur ignored the smile and then looked sadly at Father. He tried to shake hands the same way with him.

"A manly shake, Arthur," Father said, dismissing Arthur's praying left and practically shaking off his right.

"How are your studies, Felicia?" he asked me.

"They're all right, I guess." I started brushing my bangs back and rolling my eyes upward. You had to do something; he looked so *old*. It was very embarrassing.

One thing, though, his socks were still all wide and stretched at the top, which showed he'd forgotten to have them washed again.

Arthur, as usual, sat up front with Father but I noticed he kept looking at everything. "The town of my youth," he said as we passed this parking lot full of broken-down cars.

Father just glanced at him and didn't say anything. Mother started talking about his character award. "That's so *fine*, Arthur! We really are proud of you."

236

"Well, I haven't gotten it yet," he said, turning all the way around to smile at her. "I really don't deserve it. It's just like Albert Schweitzer says '. . . A thoroughbred doesn't need the ear of corn.' "

"Did he say that?" Mother asked.

"Uh huh. We've taken up old Schweitzer in English." He turned back to Father. "Such a great man. If only there were more like him in the world."

Nobody said much else until we got home. I didn't say hardly anything. For one thing, I wasn't real sure who Albert Schweitzer was. Wasn't that hysterical? I know now, though, of course, and he is kind of like Arthur, in some ways.

For instance when we got home, there was Isaiah, ready to help with the luggage.

"Isaiah, how are *you?*" Arthur said very gloomily.

Isaiah said he was all right and then reached down for the luggage.

"Oh, no," Arthur said. "Let *me*. I never want to consider myself too good to carry my own baggage."

Isaiah kind of halfway raised up.

"Now, you *rest*," Arthur commanded Isaiah.

"Gosh, Arthur," I said.

"Yes, sister?"

Throw up! Arthur has *never* called me "sister" before. I *hate* that—brothers that call their sisters "sister." It's exceedingly tacky to me, but he had such a kindly tone I just said "nothing" and we went on in the house.

That night after dinner, Arthur bored us nearly all to death, talking about Knox Campbell and Albert Schweitzer. He hated Knox Campbell now because Knox didn't care a thing in this world for anything except football and all these girls he had in New York. Albert Schweitzer wasn't like that. Knox was always making people do things for him, but a man like Albert Schweitzer wouldn't let a worm work for him if he could help it. He thought we ought to fire Velvet and Isaiah.

"Whatever for?" Mother asked.

"How would *you* like to be some slave in somebody's house?" he asked Father.

Right away Mr. Hopper came popping back into my mind. I was thinking that Arthur had probably got that from Mr. Hopper instead of Albert Schweitzer.

"Pay them *anyway*," Arthur said. "We've got a lot to learn down here in Georgia. A great deal."

"What do you mean, Arthur?" Mother asked.

"We have to learn to accept *challenges* and work—even if we're jeered at. We gotta get the old molded ideas out of our *brains*."

"Where did you get all that?" Father asked.

"Get all of what?"

"Molded ideas and such."

"Just thought it up."

. "I see," Father said.

We all just kind of stared for a while. It was pretty unpleasant, so I said: "Hey, Arthur, Aunt Ann really did give a cocktail party when we were in Charleston. It was *divine!*" (I've started saying "divine" quite frequently now.)

Arthur didn't say a thing. He just sat there, staring at me and then started shaking his head.

"I enjoyed it thoroughly," I said.

He looked at Mother. "I think that's rather careless of you."

"What?" Mother asked.

"*Need* I explain." He looked back at me. "*Did you know* that alcohol *eats* up your liver? *Did you know* that it takes your *brains* away? *Did you know* that it breaks down your fatty acids until you're just this glob of—"

"That's enough, Arthur," Father said.

Arthur looked terribly distressed. "No," he said, lifting his hand, "just look at Knox Campbell. There he was—a nice guy and—"

"Don't say guy," Mother said. "It's ordinary."

"Well, this nice, clean American. Now he's practically alcoholic. *Craves* the bottle. Just sits up in his room shaking." He

238

looked back at me. "His liver is just this pathetic eaten-up—"

"I said that was enough," Father said.

Arthur certainly had gotten peculiar. He used to simply worship cocktail parties, at least last year he did.

"What are your fatty acids?" I asked.

"I think we've talked about that enough," Mother said. "Nevertheless, Arthur, I'm proud of you. I hope you never will start having drinks."

"I don't plan to. I've seen what it does to a man."

"Of course," Mother said.

Father just kind of slunk down in his chair. He just never can understand Arthur.

"But Arthur," Mother said, changing her tone of voice, "did we tell you we're planning to come to get you in June?"

I nearly died, but Arthur was very cheerful. He didn't sound like he would be ashamed of us at all. "You *are?* Gosh, then you can be there for the awards and everything!" He didn't even sound his sincere way any more.

"I think we can," Mother said. "Do you really think you might get the character award?"

"There's a good chance," he said, looking back and forth at Mother and Father like he was watching a tennis game. "I don't know of but one other boy that might get it—David Totten—but he's always secretly going around calling everybody 'sonofabitch.' The masters never—"

"Arthur!" Mother said.

"Yes," Father said. "I don't want to hear that expression in this house again—*ever!* Do you hear that, Arthur?"

"I didn't say it, I said *he* said it. Amos T. Caldwalder would turn over in his grave if he knew somebody like that got the award. Old Totten says worse than that, too."

"Felicia, I think you should go up to bed," Mother said.

"I'm not tired." Shoot, I wasn't going to miss what that boy said for anything.

"Yes, but I think it's time."

239

"Oh, all right," I said, and did my old immature thing of walking out of the room with my hip out of joint. It makes everyone *so* furious.

"And don't do that any more," Mother called. "You may *freeze* that way."

"Okay, I won't." But I did it all the way up the stairs. I can be such a child sometimes, just plain right-down silly, like Velvet says, but it irritates everyone so.

When I got to bed, though, I started thinking how very kind it was of Arthur to say he was glad we were coming up to Connecticut. Down in Ponte Vedra, you remember, even Father said he thought Arthur was ashamed of us. Frankly, I just hoped he would stay in his sincere mood until after we'd come and gone. I knew what it was going to be like up there. Arthur did too, I bet. He'd seen everybody else's parents a dozen times—people driving around in Cadillacs and giving buildings and things. And there we were, not even being able to build a new bathroom hardly. I started thinking about what that man in Charleston had said about me being "quite a girl." I think about that quite often. When things start getting kind of bad at school, like boys walking down the hall with Melissa Stewart or somebody, I think about what the man in Charleston said and it makes me feel a hundred times better.

Well, anyway, I don't know how long Arthur and them stayed downstairs. It must have been late because Arthur didn't get up until eleven o'clock the next morning. Father wanted to know if we thought Albert Schweitzer slept that late. But Mother said for Father not to be "flip" about Arthur. "He's just feeling his way, that's all. Let's not worry about him. Things could be a great deal worse."

But he kept on acting funny. Later on that week, Velvet said she thought Arthur had got "sanctified." "He acts just like somebody what's sanctified."

You don't know what sanctified is, but Velvet's got this one friend, Martha Mae Johnson, and she's sanctified. Every day at noon, she changes the sheets on her bed and lies down with

Jesus—just for twenty minutes. Velvet told me about it. She has to sit out in the living room until Martha Mae gets out of the bed. Also she says she yells so loud in church "can't nobody hear nothin' for her carryin' on like a crazy person." Velvet wouldn't be sanctified for anything.

"No, he's not that," I said. "He's just trying to get the Amos T. Caldwalder award."

"What's that?"

"It's the highest award a boy can get. We'll be up there to see him get it, too."

"Well, I wish he'd hush that racket upstairs. It gimme the sick headache."

See, Arthur had also started staying up in his room typing on the typewriter. He doesn't really know how to type. So all you could hear were these great long pauses and then an occasional click on the keys.

"Arthur don't know nothin' 'bout no typewriter," Velvet said. "He's just playin' up there."

"Mother says he's thinking."

"How come he thankin' on the typewriter then?"

"I dunno." But I told her I thought Arthur really ought to see some of his contemporaries around Ashton. They'd think he'd probably gone insane or something, never coming out of the house or anything.

Well—and this is the terrible part—Arthur just clicked too long. He went and did the worst thing almost he's ever done in his entire livelihood. It embarrassed us all out of our minds, but when it was over Mother said she thought Arthur had just fallen too much under the influence of Mr. Hopper and the Amos T. Caldwalder award. I, too, am of that opinion. You never can know all about a human being. You don't know what ever really makes them do anything.

See, it all started off one day when we were having lunch and Isaiah told Father he was wanted on the telephone. It's pretty insane but we always answer the telephone during meals. A lot of people don't, but we think it's rude not to.

Anyway, we heard Father say, "Whaaaat? What are you talking about, Charlie?"

Mother put down her fork and listened. "It must be Mr. Henry. Wonder what he wants with Allison?"

Arthur stopped eating and his eyes behind his glasses got very wide.

"It's rude to listen to other people when they're talking on the telephone," I said.

But then Father's voice got louder. "No, Henry. No, I never wrote anything for your newspaper in all my life. Yes. Yes. I know. Well, you go down there and *stop* the press then! Somebody's just trying to make a—What do'you *mean* you can't stop it?"

"Heavens," Mother said. "Allison shouldn't talk like that to such an old man."

"I guess he's gotten something wrong again," I said. Everybody in Ashton knows about Mr. Henry. He's editor of our weekly newspaper—*The Ashton Courier*—and he's always getting things wrong.

Father came back in the room and his face was redder than his tie. "Somebody wrote some damn-fool letter to the paper and signed my name!"

"What was it about?" Mother asked.

"I don't know. I didn't ask him." Father stood up. "Now I've got to go *read* what I've written for the whole town to see."

"Poor Mr. Henry," Arthur said. "I guess he does get things confused. He must be talking about *my* letter."

Father just stared at Arthur. There was a white line round his mouth and for a moment I was frightened. "*You!*" he said. "Why in the name of heaven did you sign *my* name then?"

"I didn't," Arthur said sadly. "I signed my initials and last name. I guess they are the same. Never thought of that."

Father didn't say anything. He walked out of the room, but in a few minutes he came back and he looked more harassed than I've ever seen him. "I wish we'd never heard of that Hopper fellow, Sarah. You can write your cousin Hugo *that* for me, please!

242

He's. . . ." He didn't finish and in a few minutes we heard the back door slam violently.

Even in the beginning didn't I tell you how profoundly Mr. Hopper's article had affected Arthur? That and the Amos T. Caldwalder award had practically torn our life asunder. Arthur's article was the most obscene thing you've ever read. I decided I'd never go out of the house again, not as long as I lived.

How strange and tragic life is!

25

"Felicia, your father and I have been talking and we think you're a little too concerned about the *sad* side of life. It, uh, worries us a little."

I let out this huge sigh of relief. It was after lunch and we'd already worried enough about what Arthur's letter in the newspaper would be like. Just out of the blue Mother had told me to come in the library, she wanted to "have a talk with me." I was worried out of my mind she was going to start telling me about you know what, like Melissa Stewart's mother did. But all she wanted to talk about was about me being sad, thank goodness.

"I don't think sad things all the time," I said.

"Well, for instance." She went over to her desk. "Now here's this little story you've written." She came and sat back down on the sofa.

The story she had was one I'd written about this poor old woman dying down in her basement by her booze bottle. I hadn't wanted her to read that. It was embarrassing.

"I don't think that's very nice of you to go prying around in my things," I said.

"I wasn't prying now, Felicia. I was just straightening and the story was on top of the desk. Actually, I was delighted to see you'd written a story."

"Well, did you like it?" It was just about the best thing I've ever written.

"Yes, but it's a little morbid, I think."

"I meant it to be! Life's pretty morbid, you know—for some people."

She very slowly put my story aside. "Now that's what I want to talk to you about."

"What?"

"Of course, there're sad phases in life, but there's a great deal of beauty, too."

"Like what?"

"Ohhh, the morning, I think—sunsets—marrying, having children. People can be beautiful, too, you know."

"A lot of people aren't."

"No, but a lot of them are—inside."

"Whatdoya mean, inside?"

"The way we love one another. The way we—worship—and even in the way we appreciate."

"Yes, but all that's pretty sad, too, I think. I mean pitiful people going around doing nice things for other people. That's very sad to me."

"But it's a lovely kind of sadness."

"I don't think any kind of sadness is lovely. You go around with this huge lump in your throat and feel like dying all the time."

She kept looking at me in this exceedingly curious way. I think she thought I was about to go insane.

"Well, your father and I, of course, want you to be happy, Felicia. It's the little things that make one happy."

"Like what?" I started tearing this huge fingernail off my thumb. It came off just beautifully.

"Oh, I don't know. I think you have to discover these for yourself. You will, soon. When I was your age I think I found everything sad, too."

I looked at her. "Wonder why?"

"I don't know." She was speaking very softly. "I suppose it's

244

just your age. So many new feelings seem to develop—all at once almost."

"But Melissa and Marilyn and them don't go around finding things sad, I mean, not like I do."

"Probably you're more sensitive to things than they are."

"What's that?"

"What?"

"Sensitive?"

"Oh, you feel things more keenly, more deeply."

"Is that bad?"

"No, I don't think so. But it makes life more difficult sometimes."

I sort of hung my head. "I know it," I said. "I don't think I'm going to have a very nice life." The lump was coming back into my throat again. Every time I start thinking about my pitiful life I want to cry.

"Now *there!* That's one thing I heartily dislike."

I looked up at her again. "What? That my life's gonna be terrible?"

"No, feeling sorry for yourself. That's the easiest thing in the world to do and highly selfish. I like people who have courage, the courage to be cheerful and thoughtful of others—especially now when the world's in such revolution. That's the least we can do."

"I'm pretty cheerful—on the outside."

"Yes, but I want you to be cheerful on the inside, too."

I just humped my shoulders over and folded my hands. *Now* they were getting mad because I wasn't cheerful on the *in*side. "I don't see how that's gonna help the revolution, just being cheerful—"

"Well, it will."

"Just to go chirping around all cheerful all the time. People like that bore me. Like this girl at school, she's always chirping around about something."

"Yes, well, that's not very interesting either, but it's just as uninteresting to go crying around over everything, too."

"I guess so," I said, "but I don't cry *all* the time."

245

"No, I think you're a very interesting girl. I *do* think, however, you take some things a bit too seriously. It isn't very pleasant for you."

What she said was pretty true, I guess. I do take things too serious. I mean, for instance, like going to Charleston, I worried so much about it before I got there that it hardly wasn't even worth going. And Connecticut. I'd been worrying about that for months. I can just sit down and think up all these horrible things that might happen. I wonder if anybody else is like that. I worry myself to death. But not about the revolution, I guess.

Mother came over and started brushing my bangs back with her hand. "But that's all I wanted to say to you, Felicia. Run along now. Play some tennis—*have* a good time! You're a very sweet girl, really."

I started to get up, but I flopped back down. I wasn't much in the mood to play tennis. I'd much rather have stayed on there talking about what a gloomy individual I am. That's much more fun to me than playing tennis. Not one of my friends cares a thing about talking deep. Oh, I mean they'll cry in the movies and things, but they don't know what you're talking about if you try to talk about "is there a God" or about the revolution or something. I just never even try to talk to them that way because you know they're bored anyway. Our family is the deepest family in Ashton, except for Miss Esther maybe. We never talk too much about just stupid things. Other families do. When I go to one of my friends' houses for dinner, they don't talk about President Kennedy or Cuba or Russia or anything. They just grin at you and keep asking, "Now what have you two girls been up to today?"—like they were just *forcing* conversation. And then that just leads into nothing.

The mothers of my friends aren't very cheerful either; they're always sighing and stuff. I told Mother so. I wanted her to keep on talking anyway.

"Perhaps they're just tired," she said.

"Uh uh, they're just ignorant!"

"Now, Felicia. That's not very nice."

246

"Well, they don't ever like to talk about anything important—just sewing and people that just died and things."

"Yes, well, *some* people have other interests. You must learn to appreciate everyone for their own capabilities. *I* certainly admire ladies who can cook and sew. They're lovely talents to have, I think."

"I don't think so."

"Well, you *should!*"

"But I don't." And I don't either. They're always knocking away on sewing machines with gas heaters on and pieces of string all over the floor. I can't stand that sort of thing. The gas heater puts a bad taste in your mouth. I started to say something else, but then there was this great bump at the front door.

"Oh dear, that must be the paper," Mother said. "I'd almost forgotten."

"Arthur's letter to the editor," I said.

"Yes, go get it, Felicia."

"Where's Arthur?" I asked.

"I don't know, but go get the paper. Oh dear."

Well, I went and got it and brought it back in the library. Mother quickly unfolded it and then very hurriedly and mumblingly started reading out loud. Like I said, it was the most embarrassing thing in the world and Mother kept saying "mercy" and "oh dear" all the way through it. This is what Arthur had written:

Every morning I go to my little bench beneath the spreading chinaberry tree and there I sit me down to contemplate the worms. ("Mercy, I hope they don't think Allison wrote that!") Who would make a slave of these poorly creatures—working and loving and knocking out their brains? Once of a morning I watched the worms from my little bench and I thought: "I am for you, worm." Yes, I am for them as is Albert Schweitzer. So, too, am I for the other downtrodden of the world—prostitutes and opium eaters and ("Mercy") yes, for the lowliest bum. They are my friends. They are

247

your friends. Ashton, Georgia, is full of them. They are the town's worms. ("Oh dear.")

We must fit ourselves and go toward the centril flame ("He spelled central wrong.") This means LIFE. You travel through a dark passage and then in the midst of the jungle there is this little rustling of leaves. Behold! The Centril Flame. It behooves us. Be kind, even to little worms. These are my thoughts as I sit upon my little bench. Bums and prostitutes, also, march down the aisle of LIFE. The flame burneth!

Cordially,
A. L. Whitfield
1 Woodland Road

We heard the back door slam. It was Father. "He's sick," he shouted as he came into the library. "If anybody thought I wrote that rot, they're crazier than he is."

Mother put her handkerchief to her nose. "Now, don't, Allison!" She glanced at me. "Don't let Arthur hear you. He's very proud of the letter, I know."

"Sitting on my little bench!" Father quoted Arthur. "Where is he?"

"I don't know," Mother said quietly and didn't move her handkerchief.

"Maybe he's looking at the worms," I said.

"Now don't tease him, Felicia," Mother said. "His thought is really quite fine."

"Fine my foot!" Father said, and stormed out of the room.

"Oh dear. Oh dear. Oh *dear*," Mother said.

Poor thing. She's harassed to death. All she's got is gloomy me and pitiful Arthur, exposing himself all over the place. I tried to cheer her up. I decided I was going to have a very cheerful personality. "I guess we were just meant to be public," I said. "But it looks like Arthur would've learned how indecent it is—I mean after Mr. Hopper's article and everything."

She just glanced at me. "It's just *one* thing after another.

248